BECAUSE YOU'RE MINE
(The Gallaghers, Book 3)

LAYLA HAGEN

Dear Reader,

If you want to receive news about my upcoming books and sales, you can sign up for my newsletter HERE: http://laylahagen.com/mailing-list-sign-up/

Chapter One
Ian

My brother's engagement party was in full swing, and my whole family was attending. Since we were four siblings and had *a huge* extended family, it turned out to be quite a large event. We liked to celebrate everything in style.

I couldn't believe how much had changed in my family lately. I was happy for my brother and sisters for finding their better halves, but none of this was for me. I was single and happy. Of course they gave me crap, calling me a player and all that, but I owned up to it without any shame.

"Leaving already?" my sister Isabelle asked me as I made my way toward the door. She'd offered to host our brother's engagement party at the huge house she and her fiancé bought in Tarrytown, just an hour outside of New York.

"Yeah, I promised Henry that I'd pick up Ellie from the airport." The younger sister of my best friend was moving to the city. Of course, I'd help any of my friends, but I immediately offered to help Ellie settle in. A detail no one needed to know.

"I still think he's hiding something," my other sister, Josie, noted. Damn, she was good. Being a lawyer, she naturally suspected things. She also liked to poke her nose everywhere.

"Do I smell some guilt?" Isabelle added with a questioning look.

"No, you don't. That's just your overactive imagination," I said.

My brother, Dylan, grabbed my shoulder. "I like that you're sticking to your guns."

I remained silent, but that didn't deter Isabelle. Did I mention I have a nosy family?

"I still think he has the hots for Ellie."

"She's just the younger sister of my best friend; that's it," I repeated, as much for them as for myself. Yes, Ellie was hot—but she was Henry's sister, and that was that.

"Yeah. Keep saying that. Maybe you will believe it eventually," Josie said. "Who knows, maybe by the time the next wedding rolls around, you'll show up with a date named Ellie."

I shook my head. God, they were brutal. "I already warned Isabelle's wedding planner that I'm coming alone and that she shouldn't add anyone to my table, especially not any single ladies. So if you had any matchmaking plans in mind, forget it."

Isabelle pressed her lips together, holding up her palms. "I don't have any plans whatsoever. I promise."

I laughed, leaving them to their machinations,

and moved on to bid my parents goodbye. They'd flown to New York for the engagement party. They lived in Montana and only came to the Big Apple for special events. Although, since Josie had given them a granddaughter, they'd been visiting more often. And once Isabelle announced she was pregnant too, I was sure they'd visit even more frequently.

I kissed Mom's cheek and shook Dad's hand.

"Ian, we still have to talk about you paying for the flights," he said sternly. My parents were proud and didn't like us kids pitching in where we could. But they'd taken care of us all our lives, and so my siblings and I all agreed we'd try to lighten the burden when they retired by helping out with the little things. Besides, they wouldn't even be in New York if it wasn't for us kids—so that was another reason why my brother, sisters, and I footed the bill.

"We'll talk about it later," I replied, winking. My parents were stubborn, but so was I. I was set on this.

"Don't think this conversation is over, young man," Mom said. Her stern tone took me right back to my childhood days, when I got myself (and my siblings) in trouble and Mom knew exactly who was responsible. I hadn't been able to help myself. I was known as the troublemaker of the small town we grew up in.

"Wouldn't dream of it." I winked at her too before heading out to the driveway. I got in my Tesla and drove directly to JFK. I had about an hour to get there, according to my GPS. And an hour to not think about Ellie.

My sisters were not entirely wrong with their speculations. Henry and I had been best friends since our college days in DC. Ellie was six years younger than us, and at eighteen, that seemed like a huge age difference. And the couple of times I saw her back then, she was a timid girl—and I wasn't even paying that *kind* of attention to her. She'd been just my best friend's younger sister. All that changed two years ago. Ellie was twenty-one and I was twenty-seven when we spent three weeks in Lake Tahoe with Henry and a group of friends. She was so damn gorgeous that I couldn't look away from her.

Henry made me promise not to flirt with his sister. He knew me well, since we played with the same deck of cards, so to speak—if I had a younger sister, she'd be off-limits to Henry too. I'd agreed without a second thought and had even given him shit for warning me off. The joke was on me, because I spent those three weeks fighting myself and my instincts.

That was two years ago. Then just a few weeks ago, he called to ask me to get his sister situated with her move and reminded me again that Ellie was totally off-limits. I told him I had excellent self-restraint these days.

It turned out I didn't. I saw her the first time two weeks ago when she came in for an interview. I kept myself in check. Barely.

But I was determined to be on my best behavior.

On the drive from Tarrytown to JFK, I checked her flight on my phone. She was coming in from Miami, and it looked like it was on time.

When I arrived at the airport, I parked in short-term parking and checked the flight app again; the plane had landed two minutes ago. Hopping out of my car, I dashed to the main entrance and patrolled the waiting area, glancing at the arrival doors every time they opened.

About forty minutes later, Ellie walked out. She was pushing a cart filled with five huge bags. I could barely see her behind them, but as soon as she saw me, she was smiling from ear to ear. Damn, damn, damn. *Keep eye contact, Ian. Don't look at that long brown hair that reaches to her waist.* Or her huge round eyes almost as dark as her hair. *Eyes up, Ian.*

Way to go, asshole. Ten seconds in, and I was checking her out. Ellie Cavanaugh was testing my self-control already.

"Only five bags, huh?" I teased her.

"Hey, I love clothes," she said with a shrug. "Most of the time, I'm in my kitchen uniform. So when I'm not working, I like to dress up."

She looked gorgeous in her jeans shorts that showed off her perfect ass and a simple yellow top that molded to her curves. She was no taller than five foot two, tiny compared to my six feet. I could scoop her up with one arm, she was just that petite. I shook my head. What was I thinking? I nudged her aside and began pushing the cart and reminded myself—

No touching. No thoughts about touching or anything else either. She is off-limits.

"So gallant. Thank you for pushing my baggage cart," she said.

"How was your flight?"

"Uneventful. I just read a book. Thanks for picking me up. You know it's not necessary, right?"

"Of course it is. How else are you going to carry all your five bags?"

She grinned, and I barely restrained from leaning in closer. I was in deep shit for sure. "That's true."

"Besides, I promised Henry I'd help you settle in." That's right. Talking about her brother should make me stop this nonsense.

"Oh, my brother… always so overprotective, but he means well. I think he hopes you're just going to slip into his shoes and play the big brother role."

"Yes, he does," I agreed. "And I promised him I'd do just that."

The corners of Ellie's mouth twitched. She nudged my arm with her shoulder. "A word of warning: he's going to ask for a report from time to time."

I frowned. "No, he won't. He's not like that." What, she was trying to press my buttons?

"He is when it comes to me."

"Well yeah, but I *know* Henry."

"True, and he *knows* you." She burst out laughing, averting her gaze as we walked to the parking lot.

"What's that supposed to mean?"

"I'll tell you on the condition that you don't indulge his overprotective urges and tell him to mind his own business when he asks about me."

I considered this for a few moments and put myself in Henry's shoes. Dylan and I had lived in DC for a long time. But before moving here in New York, I constantly checked on my sisters. I didn't exactly want a report, but I understood where he was coming from. I knew that Ellie had lived in other states too, where Henry didn't have friends, but in New York, he might want me to be his eyes and ears.

"Okay, I take back the deal," she quipped, twirling a strand of hair between her fingers.

"Why?"

"You took too long to think. So that means you *agree* with Henry."

"Sort of."

"Ha! I knew it."

She was a spitfire, and I liked it a little too much. She wasn't the shy kid I remembered. I leaned in closer to her ear and whispered, "That doesn't mean we can't make a deal."

She swallowed hard, turning to look at me. She looked at my mouth only for a split second, but I caught her.

"I'll think about it," she said slowly as I pointed to my car. I loaded three of her bags in the trunk and stuffed the other two on the back seat. She was putting her address in the GPS when I sat behind the wheel. Her apartment was in the

Columbus Circle area, a good hour away from the airport if traffic was good. On the drive, she shared some more information about the restaurant where she was starting on Monday.

"Are you excited?" I asked her, glancing over her way, noticing how happy she looked.

"Oh yeah. Working in a Michelin-starred restaurant was my dream ever since I went to culinary school. I'm so lucky this job popped up. Honestly, I've been applying to New York restaurants since I finished school and never even managed to get past the first interview. But this time, everything just fell into place." I liked her energy and the way she used her hands when she spoke, like she was personalizing everything she said. She glanced around with a huge smile. I knew the feeling. I'd only moved to New York recently too. It was an exciting place to be. My brother and I ran a software company, Gallagher Solutions, and we'd been in DC for years before deciding to expand and move to New York. It was the best decision we ever made. The business was booming. I still had to go to DC once in a while when one of our customers needed help, but my home base was here in New York.

"I was also super, super lucky to find this apartment. I really wanted to live in Manhattan so I wouldn't be so far away from work, and you know, all the excitement of those touristy places. It took some research on Craigslist to find it."

I eyed her carefully. "You found your apartment on Craigslist?"

"Yes. My new roommate posted it. Her old one moved out, so she needed someone else to share the rent."

"Please tell me you know this person."

"Well, I know her from Craigslist."

"And you've never met her in person?" No matter what city one moved to, I thought this was a bad idea.

"No, but we did Skype before I signed the lease. I wanted to put a face to the name and see if we have chemistry. And we do."

"You're moving in with a stranger?" I asked, realizing my voice sounded a lot like a growl.

Ellie laughed. "Oh, you sound like my brother—all overprotective. I've moved around a lot in my life. I'm used to living with strangers. It's not the first time."

I didn't say anything, but she laughed even harder. I might have growled again.

Ellie chuckled. "You're going to be just as overprotective as you were in Lake Tahoe, huh? You were like my own personal bodyguard. I just hoped it was because Henry was around, making you keep an eye on me."

"That's because trouble was following you around. Actually, now that I think about it, you seemed to go looking for trouble," I reminded her.

"I'd just turned twenty-one. I wanted to take advantage of it."

Yes, that included going to bars and staying up late. Henry and I took turns going with her to make sure she wasn't taken advantage of.

"Looking for trouble," I repeated.

"You sound more and more like my brother," she teased. "Finding a place in Manhattan for a short period of time wasn't easy. I'm subletting the room just for six months."

I looked at her in surprise. Henry didn't mention this. "You're here for only half a year?"

"Yes. The restaurant I'll be working at has three locations: New York, New Orleans, and San Francisco. I'll be spending six months in each city. It's a trainee program."

When we reached Columbus Circle, she looked around with even more curiosity. The hustle and bustle of the city could be overwhelming. Ellie's street was five blocks away from where we were. A few minutes later, she pointed to a barber shop next to a ninety-nine cents a slice pizza store.

"That's me. I live on the second floor." It was a prewar building with black windows and gray bricks. From the outside, it was not the least bit impressive, but the area seemed safe.

Who was I kidding? I *was* worried Ellie was living on her own in the city—you had to be on your game here, be aware of your surroundings. I got out of the car with her, taking out all five bags. I bet each one was over the fifty-pound limit.

"I'll come up with you," I offered. I wasn't letting her get into an unsafe situation. I had to check this out.

"You don't have to," she said. Then she eyed

my arms. "I'm going to make some good use of your muscles. I don't think I can carry the bags all by myself."

"Happy to know I can be of use," I said jokingly. The building did have an elevator, but carrying the bags up the first three steps was no easy feat.

"What do you have in here?" I asked.

"Shoes, lots and lots of shoes, and some clothes too. Don't judge."

"I'm not. I have two sisters. They also like shoes and clothes."

"Oh great, maybe you can introduce me to them sometime."

"I was planning to do that," I said. "I think you'll click with them."

"Thanks." Her eyes widened in genuine surprise. Why was she so taken aback? "I'm really looking forward to meeting people."

The elevator looked ancient, but it was a nice surprise that it worked. I lived in a completely different building that was five years old, so every modern amenity imaginable was available.

Ellie rang the doorbell, and a tiny blonde opened the door.

"Hey, Harper," Ellie said.

"Ellie, welcome. I've been cleaning up, waiting for you." She glanced at me.

Ellie looked at me over her shoulder. "This is my brother's friend, Ian. He lives in New York and wanted to help me today at the airport and make sure that you're not a serial killer."

Harper nodded. "As he should. I have to say, it's still nerve-racking to move in with someone you don't know." She opened the door, and we both went inside.

Ellie's room was so small that there was no space to move after bringing in the bags.

"Well, this room is even tinier than it looked on camera," Ellie said. Harper was right behind us.

"I know. I tried to take a pic from a good angle for you, but I wasn't able to."

"That's fine, Harper. It'll do." Ellie's warm smile and dismissal of this turn in her living situation put everyone at ease. I liked that about her—that she didn't snap at Harper for not taking a better picture. Some of the women I'd dated in the past would have pitched a fit and made demands. Big reasons why they were "in the past."

"Okay," Harper said. "I'll just be in the kitchen if you need anything."

I was pleased to see Harper seemed like a nice person. She appeared genuine, and I was much less concerned about Ellie living here.

Ellie glanced at her bags and around the room, then at me. The corners of her mouth twitched. I just burst out laughing.

"There's no way I'm going to have space for all my clothes," she said. "I'll find a solution. I wanted to live in Manhattan but not spend all my money on rent, and this seemed like a good compromise. Not sure what to do with my bags."

"Honestly, Ellie, I was impressed that you didn't go nuts over the tight accommodations. I can keep the bags at my place until you need them; that should free up some space."

"Really? That would be great. I won't need it until I move again; so, if you could store everything until then that would be awesome."

"When is your first day of work?" I asked as Ellie started to move things around, preparing to unpack and get settled.

"Monday. I'm on probation for two weeks, but that's normal. Anyway, I just have today and tomorrow to explore the city a bit."

"I can explore it with you," I said. "My sister Isabelle was a tour guide when she first moved to New York. When Dylan and I moved here, she offered to show us the city. My brother wasn't in the mood, but I went on a few of her tours, and they were interesting."

"So you want to be my guide?" she asked with a smile. "Was that the job description my brother had for you?"

Fuck no. Her brother had just told me to look out for her, and right now, all I could think about was how damn perky her ass was in those jeans. Henry would punch me if he knew my thoughts.

"Well, today I'll probably just unpack and settle in. But we can text tomorrow and see how it works out."

"Sure," I said, realizing I was already anticipating her text.

"Thank you so much, Ian. I really appreciate you picking me up and touching base."

"My pleasure, Ellie." I kissed her cheek, inhaling the sweet perfume of vanilla and some sort of flower. I barely kept myself from moving my lips and nose down her neck, just to bury my head in her scent and get more of her. "Text me tomorrow. And we can talk more about that deal too."

Chapter Two
Ellie

I unpacked until past midnight, so I woke up at ten on Sunday, grinning as I looked around. I had far too many clothes for this room. I had a small double bed that had drawers under it, and at the side was a closet and some shelves. But I still ordered a clothes rack from Amazon that I could squeeze in somewhere. It would make moving through the room a bit awkward, but I'd get used to it. After showering and dressing, I poked my head in the living room. Harper was there, working on a craft project of sorts. She was using the dining room table as a desk, and it was full of paper in various colors. I found out on our second Skype call that she was an elementary school teacher.

"Hey, Harper," I asked, poking my head in the living room. "Do you want to go out for a bit and explore the city with me?"

I was super happy that I'd arrived when I did. I had one full day to relax and look around.

"Sorry, I promised the kids I'd have this paper robot ready for tomorrow. But I do have lots of recs for you." Grinning, she rubbed her palms together. "You're going to love Columbus Center. There's a great ice cream shop just around the corner. And also a coffee shop that has amazing hot chocolate."

"I'll keep them in mind. Do you want me to pick up anything while I'm out?"

"I shopped before you arrived, so I'm good, but I saved you space in the fridge."

We'd agreed that each of us would buy our own groceries, and we'd split things like milk, oil, salt, and other essentials.

"Thanks a lot. By the way, I love what you've done with the living room."

"Thank you, Ellie. I love personalizing my living space, and my first roomie didn't mind. If you want me to take down anything or you want to bring in your stuff, just let me know. I'm flexible."

I liked Harper a lot.

"I wouldn't change one thing about the living room. And I'm just here for six months anyway, so it wouldn't make sense."

Harper was an excellent decorator. The living room had a brick wall with a huge TV. Next to it was a piano and a chair. She had a few guitars hanging on the wall. She was also a music teacher in her spare time. The wall around the window had a huge bookshelf that went right up to the ceiling. She even had a ladder for it. The green metal coffee table contrasted with everything, but it somehow worked.

My small bedroom was all white. The last roomie left it in great condition, though it was repainted and the orange fluffy rug was professionally cleaned. The wood floors could use some polishing, but the rug was large enough to cover most of the area. I needed some decorations to make it feel homier though.

I went back to my room, checking my phone. On a whim, I texted Ian.

Ellie: Does your offer still stand? I want to explore the city a bit.

He answered almost immediately.

Ian: Yes. I'm in Central Park with my sisters and my niece. Join us.

Ellie: That's great. Can you share your location? That way I can come to the entrance nearest to where you are.

A few seconds later, he sent me a message along with the link to a map.

Ian: Sure. I can't wait.

Ellie: Me either.

I wondered if this was the best idea. The man was so sinfully hot that I had a hard time not fanning myself when I was around him. When I first saw Ian, I'd been twelve years old, but even then, I thought he was cute. I was too shy to even speak around him though. Henry had brought him to Mom's house. I'd woken up one morning, striding into the kitchen wearing pink, fluffy pajamas, and there he was. I'd blushed all the way to the tip of my ears, spilled tea on myself, and disappeared into my room.

I saw him a couple more times over the years, but it wasn't until I was seventeen and I stayed with Henry for a full week that I realized Ian wasn't just cute—he was sinfully hot. I'd loved his humor and daredevil attitude. He didn't even look my way, though. I didn't think I registered as anything more than Henry's little sister.

The summer I turned twenty-one, Henry asked if I wanted to spend a few weeks with him, Ian, and a couple of friends in Lake Tahoe. I said *yes* before he even finished the sentence. It had been hands down the best vacation of my life: lying around in the sun for hours, enjoying cocktails and a good book. And Ian… well, I wasn't going to lie. I'd had a bit of a crush on him. But who could blame me? He was six feet of pure muscle. He was different than anyone I'd dated in college. They'd all been boys, but Ian was a man… who'd seemed intent on keeping me from sneaking into shady clubs, but nothing else.

I hadn't touched base in the two years since, but seeing him when I came to interview for this job was like a shock to my system. I'd hoped that I had grown immune to him by the time I met him again, but that hadn't happened. Maybe I'd get luckier next time. I was sure that my body wouldn't react the same way again.

I called my brother before leaving. He'd left me a few messages already.

"Hey. I was waiting for your call yesterday," he said. "Figured you had a lot to do to get situated."

"I was up to my elbows trying to unpack."

"So how do you like the city? How did Ian treat you?"

"Well, I didn't see anything of the city, and

Ian was very friendly. He helped me carry all my suitcases, even offered to show me around the city. I'm meeting him right now."

"Okay. I'm glad he's available to give you a tour, but a word of caution. Ian is an excellent friend. Very loyal and sticks around; he's always been there throughout the years. But that said, he wouldn't make a good boyfriend. Not at all. He's a player, just like me."

Oh, Henry, could you be any more obvious? "Thanks for the warning, brother. You've only mentioned that like a million times already."

"I mean it. He's my best friend, remember? I know him very well, and he's just not the right guy for you."

"I'll keep that in mind. I promise. If it makes you feel any better, I'm also meeting his sisters."

"I don't think you need a chaperone, Ellie. That's not what I meant."

Really? Because I felt that I might need a chaperone. If he looked at me again with those sinful blue eyes, I was going to combust spontaneously. *Oh, Ian, Ian.* He *had* made an impression on me. He was so gallant, helping me with my bags and everything. I loved his humor too. It gave him an edge that enticed me.

"You have nothing to worry about, Henry." I tried to reassure him. "I'll check in with you later today. Okay? I want to open the map he sent me on my phone so I know where I'm going."

"Have fun. I'm very proud of you." Henry

and I have always had a good sibling relationship, supportive of one another, so him saying that to me made me happy.

"Thanks." After hanging up, I put on my sneakers and glanced in the mirror. I was wearing jeans and a thin white T-shirt with short sleeves. It was still warm outside even though it was September.

Henry and I were very close despite the age gap. Our parents divorced when I was in middle school. They both remarried, each bringing more kids into their marriage. We had a stepbrother from my mom's side and a stepsister from my dad's side. Henry and I lived with our mom, but neither of us fit in either of the new families very well. We always joked as kids that we were lucky because we had twice as many presents on Christmas, birthdays, and every other occasion. But it was quite lonely. It was perhaps one reason Henry and I were so close, even though he moved away for college while Mom and I remained in Ohio.

My brother was always looking out for me.

Not that I made it easy for him. In culinary school, I lived in Los Angeles. After graduation, I worked at a seafood restaurant in Portland and then Miami until I got this opportunity. But Henry knew how happy I was—and was always so supportive.

Once I stepped out on the street, I put on sunglasses. It was a warm autumn day, and I looked around with a smile.

The apartment building might be old, but it

had a lot of character. I liked the high ceilings and absolutely loved the hand-finished plaster walls.

I liked Columbus Circle. It was pretty, with a mix of modern and historical buildings up and down the street. The storefronts were quaint, restaurants offering outdoor seating kept warm by portable heat lamps. The area had a big-city feel with a hometown vibe.

The pizza shop displays looked pretty delicious, and I was certain that I'd become a regular. It was perhaps a bit unusual for someone who finished culinary school to eat cheap takeout. But the last thing I wanted after coming home from work was to cook. Most times I didn't even care what I was eating, I was usually so beat from the long day.

I followed the route to the location that Ian had shared with me. It was just a fifteen-minute walk to Central Park, which was perfect and gave me enough time to soak in the city. All the tour guides I'd read recommended visiting New York in the fall. I felt particularly lucky that my job started in September, since it was still warm and the tree foliage was just beginning to turn a mix of green and red. In a few more weeks, it would look completely different.

Usually, I listened to music while I walked, but not this time. I just wanted to soak in the sounds of the city, and there were plenty—lots of hustle and bustle from the congested traffic. Central Park was the favorite meeting point of New Yorkers, primarily because it was one of the few places in Manhattan that wasn't concrete. There were so many people on the sidewalk that I had to pay extra attention or risk slamming into someone. When I was closer to the park, Ian shared his location with me again, and I found him without a problem.

Damn. The man just appeared hotter every time I saw him. He was wearing a black T-shirt that made his biceps appear even more defined. His ass was round and begged to be squeezed. And those blue eyes were mesmerizing. How could he be this hot?

Riiiight… I made a mental note not to reach out to Ian every time I wanted to explore the city. He winked at me when he saw me, and I joined the group. Up close, I noticed that his shirt was tight enough that I could spot some serious abs. He cocked a brow, and I quickly averted my gaze. My pulse quickened as I focused on the two women next to him. One of them was pushing a stroller. I had never met his sisters. They didn't go to college in DC with Ian, so I never ran into them. Come to think of it, I'd only met his brother Dylan a couple of times, though I didn't remember where. He wasn't with us in Lake Tahoe.

"Hey, Ellie. These are my sisters, Josie and Isabelle. This is my niece, Sophie."

Josie was the one pushing the stroller. The siblings looked nothing alike. Isabelle had a wild mane of red hair, and Josie had dark brown hair that brushed her shoulders. None of them had Ian's dark blond hair or angular cheekbones.

"Hi, nice to meet all of you. I hope I'm not intruding on family time. I was just dying to go out and about with someone who knows the city."

"No worries. You're not interrupting anything at all, and it's lovely to meet you," Isabelle commented right away and added, "And I understand your excitement. I moved to New York about a year before my brothers did, and I'm still excited about the city. I was a tour guide for a while, so if you need any tips on where to go or not go, ask me."

"Thanks so much," I said. They all seemed so kind. And even though I was there for a short time, I wasn't going to hesitate to reach out to Isabelle for some suggestions.

"I've been living here for over fifteen years," Josie said. "So I know my way around the Big Apple. If there's anything you need, just let us know. I'll give you my phone number."

"I'll give you mine too," Isabelle added.

As I typed in their numbers, I couldn't help but feel a bit overwhelmed. Why were they welcoming me with open arms? I was a perfect stranger. Yes, I was Ian's friend's sister, but they didn't know me from Adam.

Since I moved around after graduation, I didn't maintain any close friendships. Josie and Isabelle would be easy to befriend. I liked them instantly.

"Do you want to see something specific in the

park?" Isabelle asked.

"Not really. I'm open to anything."

"We were going to suggest the North Woods trail," she replied, and we all nodded in agreement.

"Sounds great to me."

After a few short minutes of walking, I realized the deeper we went into the woods, the more I felt like I was in a forest and not in New York. Tall, thick trees surrounded us, and we even walked by a small waterfall. A multitude of birds chirped around us; it truly was a magnificent place to see.

"When do you start the new job?" Isabelle asked as we were crossing a rustic bridge. Josie was carrying Sophie in her arms, and Ian had the folded stroller over his shoulder. He kept looking around us, shooing everyone to one side if large groups passed us. His protective streak was strong! He and Henry were definitely two peas in a pod. I couldn't stop checking out Ian's biceps. And that ass. His presence was overwhelming my senses. *Oh wow.*

"I start tomorrow. I'm very excited. I've wanted to come here for a couple of years, and now it's finally happening." Almost tripping on a vine, I gathered my balance and my thoughts and continued. "I want to learn *everything*. Hopefully, in a couple of years, I'll have enough knowledge to open my own restaurant."

"In New York?" Josie asked.

"I could never afford to open it in New York, but honestly, I'm used to moving around the country. So I will just follow the dream and see where I find a place I can afford. Anyway, that's still a few years away. So I'm not making any specific plans yet." I was twenty-three. I was hoping to open my own place in my early thirties. Until then, I was going to save as much money as possible and soak up all the culinary knowledge I could. I couldn't wait to move to New Orleans and learn the ins and outs of Southern cuisine. The mix of Creole and Deep South foods intrigued me.

"But it's good to have a goal in mind," Josie said.

I nodded in agreement. We talked a bit about the city as we walked, but we mostly just took in our beautiful surroundings. The air was cool and crisp, and the smells of the forest were intoxicating. I was already planning my next hike; maybe Harper would go with me… or maybe Ian.

"By the way, Brayden and I are going to postpone the wedding," Isabelle said out of the blue. I assumed he was her fiancé.

"Why?" Ian said. "What did he do?"

He transformed right in front of my eyes from laid-back to overprotective brother, and I liked it a little too much. How was that even possible? I wasn't a fan of Henry when he got like this.

Isabelle burst out laughing. "Nothing, but I'm three months along now. I'd be five months pregnant for the party and the reception, and I just don't think I can deal with the wedding and the paparazzi while also worrying if all the stress is affecting the baby." Turning to me, she explained, "My fiancé is Brayden

Clarke."

My jaw dropped, and my voice sounded high-pitched as I exclaimed, "The lead singer of GreenFire?"

They were my favorite band. I was stunned that I didn't know this, that Ian didn't mention it earlier. Not that he had an opportunity, but still.

Isabelle nodded. Ian appeared more relaxed and said, "Okay, that sounds reasonable. So when are you going to have the wedding?"

"Not sure, but we'll keep everyone posted. Okay, where do we go from here?"

We reached a crossroad. There was a huge map in the center, but I was terrible at reading these kinds of maps.

"Right, looks like we hang a right," Josie said. The trail was 3.7 miles, and we finished it an hour and a half later. Sophie fussed for twenty minutes before she got downright upset, crying in her mom's arms.

"I think that's my cue to go," Josie said. To my astonishment, Ian leaned over, smiling at Sophie and tickling her under her chin. Sophie calmed down a little and eventually smiled big at Ian. I had no clue that a grown man making faces at a baby could be considered hot, but *damn.*

"Wow. Since when are you a baby whisperer?" Josie asked. I liked the cute banter between the three of them and that they were a team, obviously supportive and caring of one another.

Isabelle clapped her hands. "Excellent. Pretty

please, practice that skill more until my little one comes along."

Sophie started wailing again, more uncontrollably, and Josie grimaced.

"I have to go. It was great meeting you, Ellie."

"Likewise."

Isabelle left with Josie and Sophie, leaving me alone with Ian. I instantly became hyperaware of him. Something about him just demanded my attention. I was certain that he turned heads in any room he walked into. His presence was magnetic. I felt the heat of his body and *knew* he was watching me. I carefully looked up out of the corner of my eye. My stomach cartwheeled when our gazes crossed.

"What do you want to do now?" I asked.

"Actually, I have to go too. I have an appointment with a client."

"On Sunday?" Disappointment rolled through me, making me realize just how much I enjoyed being with him this afternoon.

"Yep. The perils of running your own business."

"Thanks for today. I like your sisters."

"And they like you too."

"So they meant it when they said I could touch base and we could go out whenever I want to?" I asked as we walked lazily to the coffee cart. The park looked less like a forest here and more like a smattering of trees against the urban landscape of glass and steel towers I remembered from photos.

"Yes. My sisters never say anything they don't

mean."

I ordered a cappuccino, and Ian a black coffee. I felt his gaze on me the entire time the barista prepared our drinks. After we took our cups, we sat on a wooden bench with chipped brown paint just a few feet away. I could hear the traffic in the distance.

"This is very tasty," I said, still feeling this unexplainable tension between us.

"It's my favorite coffee cart in the park."

"Cool! Do you have other recs?"

"Yes. Between the two of us… I'm a much better tour guide than Isabelle."

"Is that so?" I said, acutely aware of how close to each other we were sitting.

"Oh yeah."

"And why is that?"

"You'll see." He pinned me with that molten gaze of his. My breath caught. My heart rate sped up. How could my body react like this to him? I searched my brain for a topic of conversation before I risked turning into a tongue-tied twelve-year-old again.

"I can see why you and Henry are friends, by the way. Your protective streak is just as strong as his."

"Talking about Henry… now that we're alone, how about we negotiate that deal?" he asked, making me laugh.

"Henry didn't bad-mouth you, Ian. He just said that you're a great friend… but warned me off dating you. Said you've never had a serious girlfriend."

Ian flashed me a half smile. "He's right. And he's warned me off too."

I turned toward him so fast that I nearly spilled my cappuccino. "What? My own brother bad-mouthed *me*?"

"Fuck, you're cute. No. He said that given *my* reputation, I shouldn't even dare cross a line, flirt, check you out, nothing."

"And what did you tell him?"

"I promised to keep myself in check. I thought it was going to be easy, just as I did when we went to Tahoe."

"What about Tahoe?" Was that my voice? It sounded strangled. My breath caught.

"It was the first time I realized how damn gorgeous you are. And you're even sexier now. Might have checked you out a couple of times." He wiggled his eyebrows. I felt my face heat up. Clearing my throat, I licked my lips and straightened my shoulders.

"It'll be our secret," I said, hoping he couldn't tell how much his compliment pleased me. My brother's warning rang in my ears, but somehow, the image of *Ian, the player,* didn't match the one of *Ian, the baby whisperer.*

I mentally shook myself. None of this mattered. He was my brother's best friend, and I wasn't going to come between them just because Ian was hot as hell.

"Now that I've confessed, I don't feel guilty

anymore." He wiggled his eyebrows again. "How about we start with a clean slate?"

"Let's drink to that." I clinked my cup of coffee to his. Our fingers brushed, sending a jolt of heat through me. Holy shit! Was I on edge just from a brief touch?

This was a bad omen for our clean slate if there ever was one.

Chapter Three
Ellie

There was a cardinal rule in the kitchen: Always follow the chain of command. The chef was the most important person in the restaurant. On Point was on the Upper East Side, on the fourth floor, looking straight at some of the grand buildings from the Gilded Age. I planned to enjoy the view as often as possible outside of my shift. The kitchen had no windows, but even if it had, the pace we kept left no time for admiring the view.

My job was pantry chef. I made cold dishes like salads and starters. I'd been a pastry chef in my last job, which honestly was easier because there wasn't a ton of room for experimenting when it came to making pastries. The recipes had to be followed to the letter every single time. But starters were more creative. I already liked my new job.

I started my day at ten and finished at six, then the shift changed. The other pantry chef worked from six until two o'clock in the morning. I loved the general madness of the kitchen: voices shouting orders, knives on chopping boards, the sound of oven doors opening and closing, and so on. For me, it was like a piece of exciting background music.

It was invigorating, but as much as I loved my job, I couldn't deny that being on my feet all day was exhausting. I was even wearing ugly compression socks because they helped keep my feet from becoming too sore. At lunch, I practically inhaled a sandwich so I could get back to work. It wasn't until the afternoon that I had my first real break.

I went to the staff break room, a plain, small room at the back of the kitchen with a few chairs. I put my feet up, glancing at my phone. My stomach somersaulted when I noticed the text from Ian.

Ian: How was your first day of work?

He was checking in on me. That was so thoughtful.

I replied instantly.

Ellie: Tiring, but super exciting.

Ian: What are you doing after?

Ellie: I'm going to crash and watch Netflix.

Ian: Do you want to grab dinner together?

I bit my lip, considering this. I tapped my fingers on the phone, wondering what to reply. I was ridiculous. Ian was an attractive man, of course, but it wasn't like I didn't see handsome men regularly. I wanted to be friends with him and his sisters, not push him away just because he was hot. That was unfair to him. But I wasn't going to be fun at all tonight feeling as tired as I was right now.

Ellie: I think I'll be too exhausted. Let's

meet later this week once I've had time to adjust a bit.

Ian: Okay. If you need anything, let me know.

I grinned, feeling giddy after I finished my break.

As I'd predicted, I was bone-tired when I arrived at the apartment in the evening.

"You've got a few packages," Harper informed me. "I already took them to your room."

"Thanks. You didn't have to do that, but I appreciate it," I said excitedly. I'd ordered a curtain rod, a drill, and curtains from Amazon on Saturday evening, and they'd already delivered it all. Yes! I could start decorating my room.

I felt full of energy as I unpacked the rod and the drill. Since I moved around a lot, I was used to assembling all sorts of furniture, though I'd only put up shelves before, not curtain rods. How difficult could it be?

Half an hour later, my room looked like a battlefield.

I'd bought the wrong type of drill. It was too strong for brick walls and made a giant hole. The window area was full of dust and debris, and I'd made a big mess.

Harper laughed, looking around at the shambles. "I searched for a handyman once on Craigslist, but they're pricey."

"You don't know anyone, then?" I asked,

hoping she'd found someone to do whatever it was she was looking to accomplish.

"Nope."

Damn. I was in trouble and owed Harper for the damage if I didn't get this fixed.

I sighed, putting my hands on my hips. "Okay, I'll think of something."

"Why don't you ask the hottie who came with you the first day if he knows someone?" she suggested.

I laughed. "Hottie?"

"Oh, please, girl. I have a boyfriend, but I can still admire a fine specimen when I see one. And Ian is *more* than fine."

"I agree," I replied with a blush.

"Are you two friends with benefits or something? It's none of my business, but I feel like we need some sort of code. I'm over at my boyfriend's place a lot, but I don't want to accidentally come home when you two are all over each other."

"No, no. We're just friends." *Yes, Ellie, and don't you forget it,* my inner voice screamed at me. I sighed, quickly changing the topic. "I'll just clean up the mess I made and think about a solution."

I felt myself blush even more as the image of a naked Ian wreaked havoc on my senses. How would it feel to have that hot, hard body moving against mine?

I had nothing to compare it with because I was a virgin. Yep! At twenty-three, I still had my V-card. I honestly had no idea how that happened. I'd dated in college, but I'd never wanted to have sex unless I knew the guy for some time, and none of my relationships lasted long enough. And after graduation, dating became even more difficult. One guy even broke up with me when I told him I was a virgin, claiming it was too much work. I'd felt *so* small.

I wasn't a prude, though. I had a battery-operated friend that I used on my clit (I didn't want to lose my V-card to a rubber penis), and I was very proficient with my fingers.

Shaking my head, I looked at my room, thinking about how to clean this place up. No more sexy thoughts about Ian. Henry said he was a player, and my brother wasn't a liar. The last thing Ian would want would be to get involved with a virgin.

I vacuumed the floor first before wiping the windowsill with a wet cloth. Then I lay down on the bed and scrolled through Craigslist myself, hoping my roomie overlooked someone. Harper was right. The prices were astronomical. Just as I was getting discouraged, I wondered if Ian knew a handyman who had better rates. I called him quickly, before I could talk myself out of it.

"This is a pleasant surprise," he said instead of hello. My whole body lit up at his husky, rich voice.

"Hey!"

"Did you change your mind about dinner?"

"No, I'm spent, especially after trying to

mount a curtain rod and failing. Harper looked on Craigslist, but a handyman is expensive. Do you know one that can maybe give me a friendship price?" I asked hopefully.

Ian replied quickly, "I'll do it."

I blinked. "Really? You want to spend an evening drilling?"

"I want to spend the evening with you."

I brought a hand to my belly, grinning. Was this flirty tone his idea of starting over with a clean slate?

"Thanks, Ian. When do you have time this week?"

"I'm always free in the evening."

"I'm impressed. When you went to a meeting on Sunday, I thought you might be a workaholic."

"Nah, some meetings are unavoidable. I accommodate clients if they only have time in the evening or the weekends, but it's the exception, not the rule. I don't want to let work take over my life, and I'm in a position where I can make my schedule."

"That's a very cool philosophy."

"I just like making the most of my free time. I usually hang out with Dylan or my sisters. I'm a third wheel lately, but they pretend I'm not."

I liked how close the Gallaghers were. It made me miss my brother even more.

"I'm yours whenever you want me."

I laughed nervously. Did he purposefully work an innuendo into every other sentence, or was this just the way he spoke?

"Let's do Wednesday. I finish my shift at 6:00 p.m. and can be home in half an hour."

"Or I can stop by your restaurant, and we can walk together."

Ah, more time to spend with this sexy man who proposed we start with a clean slate but somehow set me on edge with every word he spoke. What could go wrong? Possibly everything, but I just couldn't say no.

"Okay. I love walking. Besides, it will give you a chance to prove just how good your guiding skills are, handsome."

Wow, what was I doing? Was that me flirting?

"Handsome?" he asked with a laugh.

I sighed, licking my lips. "I'm super tired. I can't be held responsible for anything I say. Please ignore me and forget it."

He laughed again, this time deeper and for several seconds. "I'll ignore it for now, but I won't forget it."

Oh, Ian, Ian.

"So I'll see you in two days?"

"Yes. And Ellie? On Wednesday, I *will* hold you responsible for whatever you say. Or do."

On Wednesday, I was full of energy the whole day.

Was it because the chef called me by name? No.

Was it because a customer was so happy about the salad dressing that he asked for the recipe? Also no.

Was it because I was meeting Ian later? Hell, yes.

At the end of the day, I showered, thankful for the amenities the restaurant had for the staff because I was sweaty and smelly after a full day of work.

I changed into a white dress that had short sleeves and reached my knees. I paired it with a light coat and black high heels and glanced at myself in the mirror. Yes, I was aware that it was a bit ridiculous to doll myself up too much, but I didn't like the clothes I wore all day in the kitchen, and I needed to feel sexy and beautiful when I was off the clock.

I ran a hand through my hair, pouting. I washed my hair every evening, but it was already just a little bit greasy and flat from wearing my chef hat. I didn’t like washing my hair at the restaurant because I always needed a ton of hair products to tame it. I applied a bit of dry shampoo and then ran my hand through it for volume. Even though my feet were hurting, I liked that I was wearing high heels. Besides, I'd probably get to wear them for about two months before the cold weather set in, and then I'd only wear UGG boots until March.

When I walked outside the building, Ian was already pacing around, looking every inch as delicious as I remembered. He was even more delectable in his t-shirt and tight jeans. He was even carrying a toolbox. I smiled, walking up to him, fixing my gaze on his eyes. "You're sure you still want to be my handyman tonight?" I asked.

Ian flashed me a half smile, pointing to his toolbox. "Friend, handyman. I'll be whatever you need me to be."

I swallowed, licking my lips. Did he say that in a dirty way, or was I reading into everything?

"Are you trying to get in my brother's good graces?" I asked.

"No. I'm trying to get into yours."

Wow. I was already close to combusting, and we'd only been together for a few minutes. This evening was off to a good start.

Chapter Four
Ian

I was an easygoing guy. I played things by ear and didn't take anything too seriously, but even *I* had a few rules. The most important one was—don't mess with your best friend's sister. And I wouldn't cross that line.

Especially after *both* Ellie and I agreed on starting over.

I couldn't tell why the impulse to flirt with her won over logic. Maybe because she blushed deliciously when I talked dirty. Or maybe because she seemed to light up each time we toed that line.

"How're you liking work so far?" I asked as we strolled toward Columbus Circle.

"It's honestly amazing. I'm learning so much, and the pace is insane. It's faster than any place I've ever worked. I'm half expecting to chop my fingers off every time I'm preparing a salad. I haven't even finished the one I'm working on when the next order pops up—it's crazy." We laughed, and she added, "But the vibe in the kitchen is just incredible, and there are so many amazing chefs."

I loved the passion in her voice.

"My parents always tease me about my choice of career." I was sort of surprised to hear this, since Henry had the utmost respect for his little sister's occupation.

"Why?" I asked.

"Because neither of them likes to cook. We lived on takeout when we were kids."

"You lived with your mom after the divorce, right?" Somehow, I barely remembered hearing this story from Henry early on in our college years.

She nodded. Her shoulders slumped a bit. "Yes. I was spending summers with Dad but lived with Mom the rest of the year. Henry went to college not too long after the divorce, but I had six years of living in both households."

She looked so damn vulnerable. It made me want to cheer her up.

"Are you on good terms with your parents? I know from Henry they both remarried."

"Yes, I am. And after so many years, they are almost on good terms with each other too, but it's not always easy to keep everyone happy. I also like my stepparents a lot."

Making her family happy was important to her. It was something we had in common. The Gallaghers were always a tight group; it was how my parents raised us. No matter how mad my sisters would get at us or vice versa, we supported one another through thick or thin. The way I saw it, the unconditional support I got from family was one of the best things in my life.

"We're not—"

She yelped as I pushed her sideways in the nick of time.

"Watch where the fuck you're going," I yelled after the maniac biker who had nearly run her over.

Focusing on Ellie, I looked her up and down just to make sure she was okay. Her eyes were wide, her cheeks flushed.

"Are you hurt? Did he brush into you or something?"

"I'm good. Just shocked; it happened so fast. I didn't hear him."

She was leaning with her back against a wall full of neon yellow graffiti, drawing in heavy breaths. I cupped her cheek, looking at her intently.

"It's okay. It was just a scare," I said, trying to reassure her. My protective side kicked in like a reflex.

She nodded, but her body was still stiff.

"I'll shake it off. I just need a minute."

I absentmindedly stroked her cheek, touching the corner of her mouth involuntarily. Ellie exhaled sharply. Her pupils dilated. Fuck, what was I doing?

On the other hand… it seemed to distract her from the incident.

I took a step back, pointing for her to lead the way.

I kept my hands to myself for the rest of the walk. Ellie chirped on about her neighborhood. She ended up being the tour guide. I didn't know anything about Columbus Circle, and I liked watching her so animated about everything. I'd never met anyone so expressive. She gesticulated with her hands, even twirling a couple of times when she pointed to several buildings she'd read about.

She got lost in her surroundings—no wonder she hadn't heard the bike coming up on us before. I kept a close eye out again, just in case we happened upon any other out of control objects.

When we entered her apartment, Harper greeted us from the living room. "Hey, guys. I'm going to just stay here in the living room to work on a craft project. I hope that's okay. I feel like I don't get enough air in my bedroom."

"Sure," Ellie said. "Ian's fixing the rod and the wall in my bedroom, so we might bother you just a little drilling two holes."

"That's fine. I have noise-canceling headphones on," Harper said, pointing to her ears.

"Great," Ellie commented with a wave as we walked the short hallway to her room.

When Ellie opened the door, the space felt even smaller than before—maybe because it looked as if she'd crammed the entire inventory of a department store inside it.

I glanced up at the wall and barely held back a laugh.

"What's that?" she teased, pointing at my mouth. "You look like you want to laugh."

"I made a bet with myself that you'd

demolished half the wall."

"Hey, I didn't *demolish* it. A piece of it just fell, but that's fine. I figured we could just drill the new holes higher up, and then the curtain will cover it, and I won't even see it. And I'll fix it another time."

"I have everything I need to fill that up."

"Wow. Really?"

"Yes." God, she was too cute.

"You're thorough."

I looked straight at her. "Always."

She blushed, brushing a strand of her hair behind her ear and licking her lip. I wanted to capture her mouth and explore it until her legs shook.

"Um, okay, so do you need my help?" she asked. "Otherwise, I can just go buy us some dinner."

"I don't need any help. I'll probably need about twenty minutes though."

"Great. I'll buy something from downstairs." It was cute, the way she tried so hard to keep her eyes on my face when I could tell she was dying to check me out.

I went to the window, setting the toolbox on the windowsill. I smiled, feeling her watch me, and glanced over my shoulder. "Ellie?"

"Hmm?"

"Do you need anything, or are you just looking your fill?"

She blushed. "I'm not going to answer that."

I grinned. "That's an answer all in itself." She laughed nervously, turning on her heels.

It took me fifteen minutes to finish everything. By the time she came back, I'd even packed my toolbox.

"I'm back. Oh, wow. Are you already done? It always takes me forever."

"I'm handy like that," I said, winking. "Honestly, it's all about the tools. This drill piece is special for brick walls." Feeling a bit hungry after smelling the aroma from whatever she was holding, I asked, "What did you buy?"

"Some empanadas at the shop in the next building. The lady running it, Maria, is from Buenos Aires, and I am trying to convince her that she has to charge more for them, because they are delicious. I hope she takes my advice. Until then, I'm just going to tip her generously."

I was fascinated by how quickly she befriended someone she'd just met. I grew up in a small town in Montana, and I'd always missed the deep bonds of a small community. Connections were different in DC and New York—somehow, they only tapped the surface. I knew none of the neighbors in my building. New Yorkers in general were a cautious bunch, as they should be, but it made it difficult to make their acquaintance.

"I'll bring a plate with empanadas, and we can eat in here. I don't want to disturb Harper in the living room."

"That's fine by me."

I sat on the windowsill, looking outside. There was no view to speak of; it looked directly into another building. Everyone had curtains so that you couldn't see inside the other apartments, because they were just that close. I assumed it was the same reason Ellie wanted some, to ensure her privacy as well. She came back, sitting on the other ed of the windowsill, the plate between us.

"Thanks for helping me out," she said.

"No problem. Next time you need something done, just call me."

She grinned. "I definitely will before I do more damage. I want to personalize the room a bit without investing too much time and money, since I'll be moving to New Orleans in six months."

"Why do you have to go again?" She'd briefly alluded to this, but I never really understood it all.

"The job takes me to three restaurants. Same brand, different cities with cuisine tailored depending on the location."

"And at the end of it, they'll give you a permanent job?"

"It's a possibility, but nothing is for sure. It will look great on my résumé anyway, to have worked at these diverse locations, so I'm sure I'll be able to find a good job after that, or even another rotation. And then hopefully, in a few years, I'll have enough knowledge and capital to open my own restaurant."

"I like that you know exactly what you want." I really did. Lately, I'd felt like I'd been missing something.

"I read once that it's good to keep your end goal in mind, especially when things get tough."

"True. Dylan and I wanted to create software for an insurance model for people with businesses in weather-dependent industries. Our parents operated a ski resort, and we had a few years without enough snow. So little, we couldn't even make enough of it with our snow machines. It nearly ruined them financially, because insurance doesn't cover that. Anyway, the plan was to submit the software in a competition. The winner would have access to a wide network of partnerships to roll it out nationally. We messed up the submission, so we were disqualified. We were discouraged initially, but then I realized we could do it on our own—the goal wasn't to win the competition but to create a product that would make people's livelihoods like my parents less of a roller coaster. We have the product, so that's a win. Now we're working on finding partners. It's moving more slowly than if we'd won the competition, but we're making progress."

"Are your parents still operating the resort? Did you go skiing a lot as kids?" she asked. I got the impression that she wanted to hear everyone's life story from the moment she met them, and I liked that about her. So many women I'd dated were only into themselves.

"We did. As kids, we were on the slopes a lot after school. And my parents are retired now."

"How are they taking retirement? My mom's is coming up, and she's a bit grumpy."

"Honestly, they're enjoying it. They're happy that they have a granddaughter to spoil and over the moon that Isabelle's pregnant too. That will be their second grandchild, and they're ecstatic. Which makes me happy, as I'm now off their radar."

I took a second empanada. The first one had been with shrimp. This was with chicken.

"You were right about the empanadas. They're great," I said. I wolfed the second one down, and when I reached for the third one, my hand brushed Ellie's. She drew in a sharp breath. I looked up quickly, just in time to see her glance away. The air between us instantly filled with tension, and we were just *talking*. This was insane.

"I know, right?" she murmured. "I think I'm going to ask her for the recipe."

"How did you get into cooking if your parents didn't like it?"

"Oh, well, after the divorce, my mom got a full-time job, and she worked odd shifts. She wasn't home a lot in the evenings, so I started downloading recipes. I liked following them to a T initially—it just gave me a sense of pride that I achieved something. Cooking made sense, and let me tell you, not many things did make sense to me back then. I couldn't understand at all why my parents got divorced."

"How old were you?"

"Eleven."

"You cooked your own dinners at eleven?" I didn't mean to sound harsh, but what the hell. All my protective instincts were on high alert. This girl was doing strange things to me.

"Yes," she said a bit defensively. "Henry

always had soccer practice in the evening, so I was on my own after I came from school. Had to fill those long hours with something."

There was more to her statement, but I didn't want to push her, even though I had a million questions. Didn't she have any friends? Why did she spend all that time alone? Clearly, it wasn't because she wasn't a sociable person.

I knew right then and there that heeding Henry's warning was going to be even more difficult than I thought, physical attraction aside. Something about Ellie drew me in. Maybe it was her warmth or her resilience, I had no idea, but I'd never had this impulse before to get closer to someone. It was more than an impulse. It was a primal need.

"I was just surprised, Ellie, that's all. Do you want the last empanada?"

She grinned. "Yes, I do. Will you fight me on it?"

"We can just split it." She really was adorable.

"Nah, splitting the last bite is a form of torture. I can't enjoy it properly. It doesn't give me enough to taste the flavor." She sat back a bit against the window frame, her eyes narrowed in concentration. "I like feeling the explosion of flavors on my lips and tongue for as long as possible."

I groaned, zeroing in on her lips. All that talk about her mouth was making me hungry for her. She dangled one leg along the windowsill, brushing mine. She jolted slightly, as if the contact was too much for her.

Ellie licked her lower lip before sharply exhaling. I couldn't look away. Blindly, I pushed the plate toward her. She could have the empanada.

I wanted something different.

I wanted her.

I watched her closely as she ate the last empanada, washing it down with water. She carefully set the plate on the shelf next to the window and got up from the windowsill at the same time I did.

She glanced up at me, then quickly looked away, biting her lower lip. I couldn't hold back anymore. Hooking an arm around her waist, I brought her up against me. I sealed my mouth over hers, exploring her deeply. She wrapped both hands around my neck, pushing herself up on her toes. I buckled because she was so tiny, but then I lifted her. Putting my palms under her ass, I propped her against the windowsill, kissing and kissing and not getting enough. I wanted to explore her all night long. She pressed her upper body against me, digging her heels in my thighs. Feeling her breasts on my chest turned me rock-hard. She tasted delicious, and her skin was so damn soft everywhere I touched her—neck, arms, hands. If exploring her mouth was this exquisite, how would it feel to explore her entire body? Her moans drew me out of my thoughts, and I pulled back.

"Fuck. All I want is to taste you again," I said, skimming two fingers over her lips. She blinked slowly.

"Then do it… oh, wait." She blinked more

rapidly, smiling, but her eyes were serious. "I lost my head. Ian… I don't want to come between you and my brother."

"No, I don't want that either." I also didn't want to jeopardize the relationship with *her*. I could be a good friend to her, but anything else was a stretch of the imagination.

"I might need a few minutes to cool down," she said with a teasing smile. "Or days. Or weeks."

"Kiss that good?"

She laughed. "You know it was."

I tried not to zero in on her mouth. I instantly knew that it wouldn't matter if days or weeks passed until I saw her next. I'd still want her with every fiber in my body.

Chapter Five
Ian

"Earth to Ian. Ian, come on. Why do you keep checking your phone?" Dylan asked. I looked up from my cell phone to my brother. We were in my office, going over some lines of code, and I'd just blanked out reading a text.

"Just checking what Ellie sent me."

Dylan cocked a brow. "You're checking private messages during coding time? That's not like you."

True. I wasn't big on rules, but I had a golden one: never check messages, emails, or answer calls during coding time. It just pulled me out of the zone, and it took longer to get the job done.

I usually had no problem keeping to the rule, but over the past few days, I'd broken it more than once. I just couldn't stop myself.

"I keep hearing Ellie this, Ellie that. I just want to point out that you haven't mentioned once how hot she is. I'm suspicious."

I grinned. "She's fucking hot. Too hot, but off-limits."

Dylan's eyes bulged. "What are you talking about? Nothing is off-limits for you."

"Ellie is," I said. I didn't believe myself any more than Dylan believed me. But if I kept repeating it often enough, maybe I'd start believing myself.

"Because of Henry?"

"Yes, partly. But also because I don't know how to be anything other than a friend."

Dylan's eyes bulged again. What the hell? What did I say?

"Are you sick or something?"

"Fuck off," I replied.

"This is the first time you even hinted you would like to be something other than a friend."

"That's not what I said."

"Yeah, it kind of is."

"No, I said I don't know how to be one." Dylan was a good brother, and I loved working with him, but sometimes I wasn't in the mood to put up with his shit.

"Whatever, Ian. I'm not good at dissecting this crap. Call Isabelle."

"I will. She always has good ideas."

"A word of warning: she's going to read stuff into it."

"That's Isabelle, man," I said. "She'll read into it anyway. I'm not afraid of our sisters the way you are."

"Hey, I'm not afraid either. I just like to keep to myself," he exclaimed before adding, "Ian, I need your head in the game."

"I know." Besides the rollout of Project Z, which took considerably more time than I'd thought, we also had clients to tend to. We offered comprehensive software solutions for small and midsize companies, and some of those clients were a pain in the ass. Their continued trust and business made us rich, though, so I wasn't complaining too much.

"Good. Anyway, whatever you do, get this out of your system; otherwise, I give you one month before you get stir-crazy and decide to throw caution to the wind."

I flipped him the bird. I heard his laughter all the way out in the corridor.

I focused on the code after he left. It was more difficult than usual. I loved my work at Gallagher Solutions, and I was proud of everything my brother and I had achieved, but sometimes I felt a restlessness I couldn't shake away or explain. When we'd first decided to open Gallagher Solutions, many people warned Dylan that doing business with family wasn't smart. Especially when said family was me. Apparently liking to play hard and having a sense of humor made me a bad candidate. But Dylan trusted me, and I wasn't going to make him regret that. My usual restlessness wasn't why I had troubles with the code though.

I leaned back in my chair, laughing at myself. Dylan was wrong. I wasn't even going to last a month.

***

Ellie

A week later, I was still feeling his kiss on my lips. Ian was getting under my skin, and I wasn't sure how to stop it or even if I wanted to. But I had to. I was only here for a few months, and anyway, this couldn't work out. I shuddered at the mere thought of telling Ian that I was still a virgin. Guys didn’t understand stuff like that, and how would I tell him of all people anyway? I had no choice. I just had to keep us strictly in the friend zone, but he sure wasn't making it easy for me. He checked in on me every day, and I was looking forward to every single message.

Typically he texted when my shift was over and I was already home in bed. But tonight, precisely eight days (yes, I was counting) after our kiss, he hadn’t texted anything yet. It was eleven o’clock in the evening, and I was lying in bed, staring at my screen before opening the Netflix app on my phone and playing my favorite fantasy show. I got lost in it, right until Ian texted me, and then not even the sexy hunks on screen could keep my attention. My heart was in my throat.

Ian: Hey! How was your day?

I sat bolt upright in bed.

Ellie: I was watching a show. Now I’m dancing with joy in my bed.

Ian: How does someone dance in bed?

I sucked in a breath, wondering what to reply to that, then I saw that he was still typing, so I decided to wait.

Ian: Never mind. I don't want to know.

I grinned, but instead of leaving it at that, I started to type back. The angel on my shoulder told me to behave, but the devil on my other shoulder was full of sass.

Ellie: Why? Afraid you can't handle it?

Ian: Pot, kettle. You're the one who said you need time to cool off.

Ellie: True

Ian: By the way, how is the cooling-off situation? It's been eight days.

Was he counting too? Grinning, I face planted in my pillow.

Turning around on my back, I held the phone in front of my face.

Ellie: Still not entirely cooled off.

Ian: Ellie…

I could hear his voice in my mind, that delicious low baritone. Goose bumps formed on my skin. Wow! I was in deep trouble if just imagining how he'd sound saying my name elicited this reaction.

Ellie: I don't know how to do this.

Ian: What do you mean?

I bit my lip, wondering if I should tell him everything, but I couldn't exactly text my conundrum.

Hey, I still have my V-card. On a scale from one to ten, how much does that scare you?

I couldn't do that, but I wanted to be as

honest with him as possible.

Ellie: I'm not good with relationships. I'd blame it on my moving around all the time, but I think I'm the problem.

I sent it and expected silence, but he replied almost instantly.

Ian: No, you're not.

Ellie: How would you know?

Ian: I just do.

I laughed, shimmying against the mattress, yawning.

Ellie: I think I'm going to fall asleep.

Ian: Am I boring you? 😊

Ellie: Not at all. I'm just exhausted from work. Still getting used to the insane pace.

Ian: Sounds like you could use a break. I can help with that.

Oh my God! Why did he have to sound so swoonworthy? I couldn't help wanting to know more.

Ellie: What do you have in mind?

Ian: What are you doing tomorrow evening?

Ellie: I'm going out with Isabelle and Josie to dinner. I was so surprised when Isabelle texted me.

Ian: I told you they like you. We can make plans for another evening. I'll tell my sisters not to monopolize all your free time.

Ellie: Why not?

Ian: Because I want you for me.

Wow. I pushed off the blanket from my body as a wave of heat coursed through me.

I typed a few words, then deleted them, then typed another sentence, and was about to delete that too before finally pressing send.

Ellie: Care to elaborate?

Ian: Yes, I will. When I see you. In A LOT of detail. But I'll let you go to sleep now. Good night.

Ellie: Good night.

I was grinning from ear to ear, clutching a pillow to my chest. I was dying to know what those details entailed, but… I wanted them face-to-face.

The next evening, I met Josie and Isabelle at the Italian restaurant *La Bella Vita* along the Hudson River. They were sitting at a table outside. It was getting chilly for that, in my opinion, but restaurants all over New York were very creative. They had heaters everywhere and also blankets to keep their patrons warm. It was a habit of mine to memorize the setup of restaurants and notice small details. All this experience was going to help me when I opened my own place.

"Hey, girls. Thanks for texting me."

"Sure. We wanted to check on you and see how you like your first weeks in New York," Josie said.

"I'll bring you up to date," I promised, sitting down. "But first, let's order, because I'm starving."

"You don't eat lunch at the restaurant?" Isabelle asked.

"Well, we do have lunch and all sorts of afternoon snacks, but honestly, I've skipped them. It's incredibly busy in the afternoon." I ordered spaghetti with seafood. The girls each wanted pizza. Josie and I asked for white wine too.

"When I first moved to New York, I was a bit overwhelmed by everything. Luckily I had Josie here to lean on," Isabelle said, lightly patting her sister's arm.

Josie smiled at her sister. "Well, she adapted quickly. Then she made me aware of a completely different part of the city. I think I could live my whole life in New York, and there would still be things that surprise me."

"True. It's the most interesting city I've lived in."

"How do you like the job?" Josie asked.

I told them a bit about the restaurant. Our wine came pretty fast, and I took a few sips before the food arrived. The pasta was cooked just how I liked it—not too long so it was mushy, but also not too little that it was hard. Some chefs completely misinterpreted the meaning of *al dente.*

"The food scene is incredible," I said through mouthfuls. "You find hidden gems everywhere. For example, there is a *panaderia* in the building next to mine. It's so cheap that I was afraid even to try it in the beginning, but they are extraordinary. My roommate loves them. Ian liked them too."

Isabelle and Josie exchanged a glance. Taking another sip of wine, I said, "He helped me set up a curtain rod. I tried it myself and ruined the wall. Then when I asked him if he knew a handyman, he offered to do it himself. He came over and was all chivalrous and handsome and took care of everything."

Josie laughed. I looked at my glass of wine. Was I tipsy already? I pressed my lips together, determined not to say anything else.

"You were about to add something?" Isabelle asked, a twinkle of amusement dancing in her eyes.

"I think I'm talking too much," I said, fiddling with my glass of wine. Josie set an elbow on the table and propped her head in her palm.

"But we're here to listen."

I shook my head. "If I say it out loud, I won't be able to stop thinking about it."

Isabelle shook her head. "Trying to suppress thoughts doesn't work. As a therapist, I advise my clients to get things off their chest by talking about them. Otherwise, things might… explode."

"I think they already did. We kissed that night," I went on. The cat was out of the bag. I might as well tell them the whole story. They didn't say anything right away, just exchanged another glance.

Isabelle narrowed her eyes. "I hope it's okay that he's joining us for dessert. I bugged him about it."

Holy shit. I sat ramrod straight, looking from one to the other. Why didn't I know this? Then again, he was their brother. They could meet whenever they wanted to. Okay, this wasn't such a big deal. I had some time to sober up, and I was hoping that once I finished my meal, I'd feel better.

My head cleared as I ate my spaghetti, and I felt good as we were about to order dessert. I wasn't a tipsy Chatty Cathy any longer.

The second Ian arrived, I realized it didn't matter. He trained his molten blue eyes on me, and I fidgeted in my seat. Goodness, just his presence made my body light up.

"Ladies, good evening. What's looking good?" He sat between Isabelle and me, glancing at the menu.

"Since we're four, I think we should order their Dessert-Palooza. It has eight mini desserts," Isabelle said.

We all agreed and placed the order immediately. I fidgeted in my seat some more. Heat just radiated off him—or maybe it was the wine in my body making me shudder.

"Okay, why are you two looking at me like this?" Ian asked, glancing between his sisters.

"No reason. Ellie shed some light about how you helped her with her curtain rod," Isabelle exclaimed.

I felt myself blush. Holy shit, I thought Henry and I were close, but the Gallaghers were in a league of their own.

Ian cocked his head toward me. A smile played on his lips. My face was so hot that I was barely restraining from fanning myself.

"There are two things you need to know about my family. One: no one minds their own business. Two: once they're on your case, they won't back off."

"I'm gathering that." Grabbing my water, I took a quick swig, still feeling as if my cheeks were on fire.

"I did text to ask you if it's okay if I join you," he said in a serious tone. "You didn't answer, so I assumed you didn't mind."

"My phone died, so I didn't see them. But of course I don't mind." I was touched that he'd wanted to make sure I was okay with this. But how couldn't I be? It was his family; I was the outsider.

Besides, I was starting to think there was no cooling off when it came to Ian.

"Awww," Isabelle said. "You two are cute. In my defense, I didn't know something was going on. I just wanted to cheer Ian up."

"What happened?" I asked him.

He just waved his hand. "Work is stressful. I'd love to let some clients loose. They're so damn demanding."

"So why don't you?" I asked. "You're your own boss."

"Some clients are a pain in the ass, but cutting them loose would make us look bad."

Josie raised her glass. "I admire your work ethic. If a client gives me too many headaches, I just politely point them to someone else. It's different, though. I take them on case by case, whereas yours are long-term. But you could set boundaries."

"Or just pass them on to Dylan. You take on all the difficult clients," Isabelle added.

Ian laughed. "That's because they annoy Dylan more than me. Let's not talk about work anymore."

"Okay," Josie said.

I watched them in awe, liking how they gave each other advice and shared everything from sorrows to work stress. … joys.

Ian moved his leg under the table, and when it accidentally brushed mine, I sucked in a breath, and my belly, as energy zipped through me from the point of contact. How was this even possible? We were both wearing jeans. I hoped he didn't notice my reaction. As discreetly as possible, I glanced at him, only to realize his gaze was trained on me and his nostrils flaring. *Oh, my.*

I studiously looked at my empty glass of wine, trying to gather my wits.

"By the way, we should go out with my husband's cousins, Tess and Skye Winchester," Josie said. "We're all very close, and I think you'll like them."

"I'd love that," I said. Could they tell that I'd love to have a group of girlfriends? I couldn't believe they were so accepting of me.

Our dessert was served quickly. I liked this restaurant a lot—they were attentive, the food was great, and the menu was eclectic. They seated around fifty, and the servers moved swiftly. The kitchen must operate at the same level of efficiency.

"Oh, I like these," I said, looking at the platter with the eight desserts: strawberry cheesecake, Tiramisu, a giant, burger-sized macaron, cronut, chocolate cake, and three types of cupcakes. We split each in four, so everyone could taste everything. They were all delicious. My favorite was the chocolate cake.

"We have to do this again," Josie said, placing her napkin on the table and gathering her things. "But I'm going to leave now. I promised Hunter I'd be home so we can both put Sophie to bed. I'll pick up the bill."

"No, you won't," Ian said sternly.

"Ian—"

"I mean it. It's on me."

"Thanks," Josie said.

I started to protest too, but when he trained his gorgeous eyes on me, I closed my mouth right back. As if to prove his point, he actually paid while Josie got ready to leave.

She put on her jacket, sending everyone air kisses before ordering an Uber.

Isabelle yawned. "I probably won't stay long either. The little one is making me so tired. I've been falling asleep at nine every day this week."

Ian cocked a brow at her, and his sister grinned. They were having one of those silent conversations I sometimes had with Henry. I was dying to know what they were saying. On second thought, maybe I was better off not knowing. I had an inkling it might be about me.

"Well, if we're staying, then I'm having another glass of wine," I said.

"I'll order one too," Ian said. Even though he'd only eaten dessert, he reached over and grabbed the wine menu, and a whiff of his cologne reached me. It was exquisite: a mix of vetiver and bergamot that made me want to lean in closer.

My body was like a live wire since he sat down. I was operating on another frequency, aware of even the smallest detail. We ordered wine for the two of us, and the waiter immediately returned with the drinks.

Isabelle only stayed for another fifteen minutes, during which she and Ian kept exchanging more eye messages, as I liked to call them. I was bursting with curiosity, and after Isabelle left, I finally gave in. Ian and I had nearly finished our wine.

"Okay, so what was all that about? The eye thingy and gestures."

Ian laughed. "That obvious, huh?"

"Yeah. I do it with Henry too, but you three are on a different level."

"She was very transparent in her attempt to leave us alone. I gave her nonverbal shit."

I blushed again. "I thought it might be that."

He looked at me with a wry smile. "They like you."

"Oh, that was part of the nonverbal communication too?"

"No, just my observation."

"I'm so happy you introduced me to them. It's lonely at first when I move to a new city." I played with the stem of my nearly empty glass, breathing in deeply. I loved New York. I'd only been here for a short time, but the energy of the city was amazing.

"Come on, I'll walk you home," he said.

I grinned. "Want to protect me from some more cyclists?"

He grinned back, and I tried hard not to swoon at the sight of his dimples. "Or whatever else crosses your way."

"You know, I'm usually very good at taking care of myself. Had lots of practice. Something about you messes with my focus."

I thought he'd laugh at my not-so-subtle hint, but his gaze turned hard.

"Why did you have lots of practice, Ellie?"

Oh, crap.

I played some more with the stem of the glass, shrugging. "When I was a kid, I was a bit of a misfit at school. And after the divorce, I shrunk into myself even more, and other kids started making fun of me. It was harmless in the beginning, but then they got mean. And then they started fighting me for real."

"Fuck."

"So I looked up self-defense classes on YouTube and learned a lot."

"Why didn't you attend one?"

"I needed an adult to sign me up, and I didn't want Mom to worry. She had enough on her plate. Henry caught me exercising once, going through the moves, and he enrolled me in a class. We told Mom I was taking dance lessons."

It was one of the reasons Henry was so protective of me. The vibe between Ian and me had gotten a bit too serious for my liking, so I rolled back my shoulders and said, "So I am perfectly equipped in case someone tries to rob me. For speeding cyclists, on the other hand, I think your special skills are required, handsome."

His eyes lit up immediately, and we rose from the table. "In that case, let's go. Before you change your mind."

My apartment was forty minutes away on foot, and we decided to walk. Even though my feet hurt from standing in the kitchen all day, walking actually helped me feel better.

The evening was chilly, but we walked at a brisk pace that kept me warm. Ian's arm around my shoulders was contributing to my rising body heat. He even offered to walk me up the stairs to my apartment, making tonight feel like a test. Could we be just friends… who were a bit touchy-feely? And who sometimes flirted?

"So thoughtful," I teased him, but he just watched me intently as I went up the stairs. When we reached the door, I looked over my shoulder, and my knees buckled at the intensity in his gaze.

"Want to come in?" I asked.

A deep growl reverberated from his throat. "No way. I've been thinking about kissing you so often since the last time I was in there."

I licked my lips. "How often?"

"You don't want to know."

"I do."

"All the fucking time," he said. Coming closer, he skimmed his thumb just under my lower lip. I shuddered, realizing I wanted more of him too.

"Ellie, I know I shouldn't touch you. Want you. But I do. I want to *know* you. It's new to me and not something I'm used to."

Wow. I licked my lips again. My heart hammered against my ribcage.

"Say something," he prodded.

"I can't think straight when you're this close, handsome," I teased, but it was the truth. Instantly, he stepped back, putting a bit of distance between us, and I immediately missed his nearness.

He tilted his head playfully. "I see that. You only call me handsome when you're…" He made a gesture with his hand as if the right word escaped him.

"Under your spell? I agree. And I—"

The door opening interrupted us. Harper stood in the doorway.

"Hey! What are you—oh, hi, Ian. Is the door stuck or something? I heard you come up a while ago."

"Umm, no. Ian and I just got to talking. I didn't even try to unlock it."

"Come in, Ian," Harper said, but he shook his head.

"No, that's fine. I'll leave you two. Ellie and I had a great evening, and she has a lot to think about," he said with a playful smile.

"Like what?" I challenged, wiggling my eyebrows. I was playing with fire.

"Like how she defines crossing lines *exactly*… or if she's using that as an excuse for something else." Wow! I was shocked that he'd seen right through me. He kept my gaze, and I didn't even blink despite feeling my whole body heat up. "And being under spells. In general."

Harper laughed. I just chuckled. If tonight was a test, we'd failed it with flying colors.

Chapter Six
Ian

"So, how are we on that bet?" Dylan asked the next afternoon after we came out of a strategy meeting for Project Z. We'd just convinced a big partner to work with our software to develop an insurance product, so I was in a celebratory mood.

"What bet?" I asked.

"The one where you won't last a month before deciding off-limits wasn't in your vocabulary."

I shrugged as I made myself a coffee at the machine we kept in the reception area. Our office was in a high-rise near Battery Park. From the window, I had a direct view over the Hudson River.

"I never made that bet."

"Because you knew you'd lose?"

"Exactly."

He clapped my shoulder. "I always appreciate your honesty."

There was no getting whatever this was out of my system. I was talking myself into asking Ellie out with every passing hour. Dylan made himself a coffee, too, checking his phone.

"Mom and Dad are coming to the city again," he exclaimed. "Next month. They want to celebrate their wedding anniversary with us."

"Cool. It's nice they're coming out more often. Are we buying the tickets?"

Dylan nodded. "Yes. I spoke with them after you left the engagement party, when they mentioned the possibility of celebrating it here. They sort of agreed for us to pay for the tickets."

"Sort of?" I asked with a laugh. "I don't want to know details."

"Let's buy them before they change their mind."

"Yes. I'll do it this time."

Even though Dylan, Josie, Isabelle, and I were financially well off, my parents flat-out refused monetary help. It was exasperating. I understood they had their pride, but if we could help them, why not? I wanted them to live comfortably. So we all took turns funding their flights.

"What are you doing this afternoon?" he asked.

"I'm planning a coding session but won't stay too long." I liked leaving early on Fridays. It was past lunchtime, so I didn't have much of the afternoon left, but I still could get in a few hours. Many business partners were surprised that Dylan and I still wrote our own code, but I enjoyed it. Sometimes it didn't even feel like work.

I went straight to my office, sitting in my chair, lifting the armrests to a comfortable height for typing hours on end. It was a chair that gamers usually used, but it did the job.

I'd barely opened my laptop when the screen of my phone lit up with an incoming call. It was from my sister. She rarely called during working hours because she knew I frequently turned the phone off, and reaching my voicemail exasperated her. I assumed she wanted to talk about our parents' upcoming visit.

"Hey, Isabelle," I said.

"Ian, are you busy?" Her frantic voice set me on edge. I sat up straighter in the chair.

"What's wrong?"

"Ellie just texted me that she had an accident at work and she's at the hospital. The doctor advised her to call someone to take her home, but I have a client coming in, and I can't just leave."

"Fuck. Tell me the address, and I'll get her."

I rose to my feet, jotting down the address on a Post-it. Why hadn't she come to me first?

"I've got it. I'm going there now. Do you know what happened?"

"No. I don't think it was anything too serious. She called herself, and she seemed fine."

Then why would Ellie need someone to take her home?

As soon as I hung up, I left my office, ordering an Uber before I got in an elevator. When I stepped out of the building, I groaned. It was stuck in traffic, so the trip was canceled. I ordered a new one.

Dylan had a driver during the day, and it always seemed pointless to me, but I was starting to change my mind.

Ten minutes later, I was in my Uber, heading to the hospital. Isabelle was right. If Ellie had called her and not some hospital staff, it couldn't be too bad. But I wouldn't calm down until I saw her with my own eyes.

When I arrived, I just followed the instructions Isabelle texted me. It looked as if she'd forwarded me the message she got from Ellie. I found her in a small room by herself on the eleventh floor. She was lying down on the bed, looking up at the ceiling. I scanned her body. She was in her chef uniform—long white pants and a white coat buttoned up in the middle. Nothing seemed wrong at first glance, but my nerves were still on edge.

"Ellie, hey," I said, walking up next to the bed. She looked at me with a bright smile.

"Hey. Thanks for coming."

"What happened to you?" I asked.

"Kitchen accident. It happens all the time. I slipped and hit my head. They sent me here to get checked. The doctor says I have a minor concussion. I'm just a bit dizzy. Otherwise, I feel fine."

"Shouldn't they keep you here for observation?" My tone was harsh, but Ellie just chuckled.

"I've already been here a couple of hours. I just called Isabelle once they gave me the all clear to go home."

I sat at the edge of the bed, taking one of her hands in mine. They were cold.

"Wait, how long have you been here?"

"Umm, I slipped right after I started my shift, so five hours, I think."

"Why didn't you call me when they brought you in?"

"What for?" she asked as if this was the most ridiculous thing she'd heard.

"To wait with you."

Ellie laughed, waving her hand. "If I had a penny every time I got an injury in the kitchen, I'd be a millionaire right now. I'm used to this."

"What, being in the hospital on your own?"

"Yeah."

"Well, while you're in New York, get used to me waiting with you. Next time something like this happens, call me right away."

She opened her mouth in protest. I silenced her, putting a finger against her lips.

"Don't fight me on this, or I'll kiss you right here."

Her breath caught. A doctor joined us just then.

"Ah, Ms. Cavanaugh, how are you? I just signed your discharge, but I want to ask how you are before you leave."

"I'm good."

He looked at me. "I want a few moments alone with the patient."

"Sure."

I stepped outside, looking for something to cheer up Ellie. There were just a few vending machines with food and drinks. No, wait, there was also a small gift cart by the elevators. It was meant for children, but I was sure Ellie was going to laugh her ass off, which was the whole point.

I chose a green teddy bear and paid quickly by card. I kept an eye on Ellie's room and saw the doctor leave. As soon as I grabbed the green toy, I headed back to her room, holding it behind my back.

"What are you hiding?" she asked.

I took the teddy bear out in a somewhat theatrical move, and Ellie's face exploded in a grin.

"That's for me?"

"Yes."

Walking up to her, I handed her the toy. She squeezed it against her chest like it was some prized possession.

"Thank you. I love it. I can't believe it."

To my surprise, there was genuine emotion in her eyes. I mean, it was just a green kids' toy meant to cheer her up, but it seemed to mean more to her. She attempted to push herself up from the bed, and I immediately splayed my palm on her back, helping her into a seated position, then putting the jacket that lay at the foot of the bed on her shoulders.

"Ian, what are you doing?" she asked.

"Helping you."

The corners of her mouth twitched. "I don't think I can injure myself by getting up. But thanks for having my back. Literally."

"Is this amusing to you? You scared years off my life." Although I said this a little lightheartedly, the meaning was still the same.

"Oh!" Her smile faded as if only realizing what I was saying. Wasn't she used to anyone caring? I knew Henry did, but then again, they'd always lived in different cities, so maybe that made things different.

"Do you need to fill any prescriptions?" I asked.

"No, I'm just supposed to take Tylenol if I need it, and I have some at home."

"Then let's go."

When she rose to her feet, I put an arm around her waist, guiding her down the hall to the elevator. I ordered an Uber just before we went into the elevator, which was crammed, and I kept her tightly against me. The ride down to the main floor seemed like it took forever.

By the time we stepped out of the hospital building, the car was already there. I helped Ellie in and then went on the other side, climbing in.

"I'm fine. Don't fuss about me. I feel so silly," she whispered as the car lunged forward.

"You're not silly. Ellie, tell me if you need anything, okay? It doesn't matter if it's during the day or in the middle of the night. I. Want. To. Know."

She exhaled sharply, nodding.

We were silent for the rest of the drive, but I kept looking at her from time to time. She rested her forehead against the window, smiling whenever she caught me looking at her. She was carefully holding the teddy bear in her lap like it was something special.

I touched the back of her hand with my fingers until I heard her breath quicken. I wasn't used to getting so uptight about anyone I wasn't related to. I could pretend I cared because Ellie was Henry's sister, but it went beyond that. Whenever I saw, texted, or spoke to her, my whole demeanor changed. Even if I was stressed because of a client, I felt better just by being around her.

Her apartment was empty when we went inside.

"Tell me you're not working tomorrow," I said.

She shrugged off her jacket, grinning. "I'm tempted to tell you I am just to see what you'll do."

"Ellie!"

"I'm not. I never work weekends, okay? And anyway, the manager forbids me to come back until I'm in top shape. She said I could take off next week if I want to, but I won't do that."

"Why not?"

"Because I want to make a good impression. I'm not going to miss work unless it's necessary."

"Ellie! You have a concussion."

"A *mild* one. Barely even that, really." She put her hands on her hips, looking me straight in the eyes. "What are you going to do? Show up on my doorstep Monday morning to police me?"

I stepped closer, tilting my head, looking her straight in the eyes. "Not even close to what I'm thinking. You don't want to know what's on my mind."

Ellie blushed and didn't press the issue. I was so close that I could smell her perfume again. It was driving me crazy. I wanted to taste her so bad.

She slipped past me, walking to her bedroom. I followed her, leaning against the doorway, watching as she sat on her bed and placed the teddy bear on the shelf just above the headboard.

"When is Harper coming home?" I asked. She pulled her brown hair behind her back, running her hand through it. It was thick and silky, and I wanted to thread my fingers through it before wrapping my hand around the strands, pulling her to me, claiming her lips.

"Harper is gone for the weekend. She's visiting her parents."

I didn't like that for one minute. She was going to be alone the whole weekend, and that was not good.

"Didn't the doctor say you shouldn't be alone?"

She waved her hand. *This woman!* "Doctors like to overreact. Besides, he said I shouldn't go home alone, not that I needed someone to watch me."

I walked inside the bedroom, crouching in front of her.

"Ellie, I want to be the first person you call, no matter what. Do you understand? Not Isabelle, not Josie. Me."

She smiled faintly. "I know. I wanted to call

you, but then I thought maybe… you know."

I leaned in with a growl. "The first person you call, you understand?"

"Why?" she whispered.

"Because you're mine."

Chapter Seven
Ian

Her eyes widened. I cupped her cheek, running my thumb up and down her soft skin. I had no idea where the words came from, but they were true. *They were so fucking true.* I claimed her mouth, needing to kiss her. She tasted like mints and responded to my kiss with so much fervor that I instantly turned hard. She moaned against me when I deepened the kiss. Fuck, I was losing control already. I was desperate for more. She tugged at my shirt, sliding her hands underneath it and tracing my abs with the pads of her fingers.

I skimmed my hand from her neck down to the side of her breasts and put it on her hip. Then I remembered what brought me here in the first place, and I pulled back.

"Ellie, you're not feeling well."

"Yes, I am," she whispered, but she sounded uncertain. She closed her eyes, drawing in a deep breath before opening them. "There's something you need to know. I… I've never done this before."

"What?"

She bit her lower lip, looking uncomfortable. A moment of silence sat between us before she said,

"Sex. I'm a virgin."

My brain froze. Several seconds passed until her words sank in. I pulled back a bit so I could look at her better. Her eyes were wary. She was biting her lower lip, obviously worried about what I was going to say next.

"It's not a big deal," she said quickly, interrupting my thoughts as I considered how to respond. "It just never happened when I was younger, and then as I got older, it became a bit weird whenever I brought it up…."

She sounded apologetic. Why the fuck would she think she needed to apologize?

"Ellie, you don't have to explain yourself." I ran my fingers through her dark hair. It felt even smoother than I imagined.

"I just thought you should know… before you get in there." The corners of her mouth tilted up in a taunting smile, but her eyes were *still* wary. Some asshole made her feel bad about this, I was sure of it. I wanted to punch the nameless, faceless bastard. I cupped her cheek with one hand, resting the other one on her hip.

"Ellie, let's get a few things straight. First: you don't have to feel ashamed about anything. Second: you're not going to lose your virginity after you've had a concussion and the doctor told you to take it easy. I just got… carried away."

Her smile faded. "You don't want this anymore." Her hand motioned between us, then stopped. "Me?"

She tried to crawl back further on the bed, but I caught her ankles. "Ellie, I want you so much that I can barely think straight. But your first time... it's not gonna be like this. I'm going to take my time with you, and it's going to be special. I'll make it special."

"I wasn't expecting this," she murmured.

I frowned. "What did you expect?"

"Not sure. Doesn't matter. I'm not a prude or anything. I have a vibrator, and—"

I groaned, pulling her closer to me, until her mouth was almost level with mine. Grabbing her hand, I pressed it against my erection. She gasped.

"Ellie, I'm hard as fuck. Talking about a vibrator will not make things better."

She giggled. "I'm sorry. I didn't think about it."

I kissed her hard. My cock pressed painfully against the zipper of the jeans. I needed to explore her body, feel her skin beneath my fingers. But I couldn't do any of that tonight and not lose complete control. I'd meant what I told her. I wasn't going to rush this. But I couldn't help myself and kissed down the side of her neck. It was the only bit of skin not covered by her chef jacket. A light quiver took over her body as she dug her fingers in the mattress.

I straightened up, looking her straight in the eyes. "I need to take a cold shower."

She smiled, shimmying against the mattress. "That bad, huh?"

"Woman, stop teasing me."

She schooled her face in what she probably thought was a serious expression, but by the firm way she pressed her lips together, it was obvious she was holding back laughter.

"It's outside on the left," she said.

The bathroom was as tiny as the one in my dorm room when I was in college. You could practically sit on the toilet and wash your hands and hair at the same time. When I got inside the stall, I could barely move without hitting my elbows against tiles. Fucking hell. Ellie was a virgin. I didn't see this coming at all. Grabbing my cock, I moved my fist up and down, imagining it was her hand and groaned. I immediately dropped my hand. No. If I rubbed one out, it wouldn't calm me down. It would have the opposite effect. I turned the water as cold as possible, just standing under the spray.

Afterward, I dried off and put my jeans back on, but I didn't bother with the T-shirt since it was just the two of us.

I found her in the kitchen, taking food out of the fridge. She was wearing black shorts and a pink tank top, looking so damn delicious that I just wanted to bend her over the kitchen counter. Damn it, no. I knew that I had to think about something else.

"What are you doing?" I asked.

"Emptying all the containers of takeout from this past week so that we can have dinner."

"Ellie, get on the couch. I'll bring the food to you."

She looked at me over her shoulder. "Why?"

"You were in the hospital because of a concussion."

"But I'm feeling better," she said.

"Go. Sit." My tone was stern and brooked no argument. She sighed, strolling to the couch, stretching out on it.

She wasn't kidding when she said that she was emptying take-out containers. I put a sandwich and a slice of pizza on the platter and brought it to the couch. Fuck me! She was lying down on one side. Her breasts were squished together. Her upper thigh was slightly bent in front of the leg beneath. She looked like a goddess.

"Oh, you're distracted already," she said. "I like where this is going."

I shook my head, looking her straight in the eyes. I sat down at her feet, holding the plate between us.

She sat up. "I like this. Want to bring me breakfast tomorrow too?"

"Yes. I want to stay here the whole weekend and take care of you."

She looked up at me in surprise. I was shocked too, if I was honest. It wasn't my usual MO. But the instinct to make sure she was all right was stronger than anything else.

A smiled inched on her face. "Oh, please do. I'm enjoying this immensely." We ate the pizza and the sandwiches—they didn't taste like much, but it was enough to stave off the hunger. After she pushed the empty plate to the coffee table, she lay back down. I took her feet in my lap, massaging her soles and her calves. She hummed, stretching into full relaxation.

"Oh, I like this. My feet are always killing me."

I laughed but then looked her straight in the eyes. "You scared me today, Ellie. Don't do it again."

"Yes, sir."

I growled. She looked at me intently, opening her mouth, then closing it again. Did she want to talk about earlier?

"Ian… about earlier… do you want to talk about it?"

"Only if you do. A word of warning. No mentioning vibrators."

She grinned. Good. I wanted her to feel at ease.

"I didn't mean to spring it on you. I just didn't know how to bring it up before. Being a virgin at twenty-three is not something I intended. But when I dated in college, it never got that far, though I did other… things."

My mind went blank. No. Fucking. Way. I couldn't picture Ellie doing anything with someone else or I'd go stir crazy. When did I become so damn possessive? It wasn't like me.

"And the older I got, the weirder it became when I brought it up on dates. It seemed to scare off guys, making them think that I was waiting for someone special. Maybe I was. I mean, I wasn't going to sleep with just any guy off the street."

"Good to know I rank above that," I said in a teasing tone.

"You definitely do. I mean, you bought me a teddy bear and want to stay the weekend, even though you'll probably have blue balls."

I growled again. "Another rule: I don't want to hear the word 'balls' from you." She smiled, mimicking a zipping gesture over her lips. "Now, I want to talk to you about something else. Tell me when you're sick or have an accident. Don't just stay in the hospital by yourself."

"Okay." She bit her lip, wiggling her toes. "Ian, about… you know… crossing boundaries."

I groaned, pulling her legs to me until her ass was nudging my thigh. "It's no use pretending we can respect them."

"True," she said.

"Fuck boundaries, Ellie."

"I agree."

She looked down, shaking her head. "How did I end up inches away from your cock again?"

"You want to drive me crazy?"

"I was just asking a question," she said with sass.

"And I was answering it. That's another word I can't hear out of that pretty mouth tonight."

"What? Cock?" she asked with fake innocence.

"Yes, Ellie. Damn it. Have some mercy."

I fondled her ass, kissing her shoulder, then up the side of her neck. She shimmied in my lap.

I loved her reaction and the way she responded to the slightest touch. But despite what she said, her doctor's order had been for her to rest. I wanted her to fully recover, and concussions were nothing to play with. She pouted when I set her back on the couch, but then she lay down, looking around on the floor.

"What are you searching for?" I asked.

"For my phone. I just realized my stepdad's birthday is next week, and I forgot to order his present. I always send them directly to their place. I hope I don't forget to do it later."

"I'll remind you," I said. "So you get along with both sets of stepparents?" I asked while I resumed massaging her legs. She seemed to like it, and I wanted to please her.

"Yes, I try to. As a teenager, I resented them, but then I grew to appreciate them. My parents couldn't make each other happy, but they found happiness with others."

"I can't even imagine what that's like. My parents were always happy together. I rarely remember them fighting."

"You're lucky. I honestly think watching their relationship fall apart gave me some issues. Even though they did find happiness with the stepparents, Henry and I were caught in the middle for so many years. I played peacemaker every time one parent complained about the other. After the divorce, Mom was devastated in the beginning, before meeting my stepdad. She was too proud to go to a therapist, so she mostly spoke to me. I couldn't give advice, but I listened, and that helped her." She looked vulnerable, and I wanted to erase those unhappy memories. She was so strong and fucking incredible. Even though she'd been a kid and suffering, she'd still wanted others to be happy.

She yawned, holding her palm in front of her mouth and then rubbing her eyes.

"You should go to sleep," I told her. "I'll take the couch."

She jerked her head back. "No, you won't. My bed is big. We can share it."

I stared at her. "Bad idea."

"Why? Am I so hard to resist?"

"Yes," I said honestly.

"Well, I have full confidence in you. Besides, this couch is horrible. I fell asleep here one time after work and woke up with a sore neck and back two hours later. Can't imagine how bad it is after spending one night on it." She rose from the couch, pointing with her head toward the door.

"I'm going to shower."

I wiggled my eyebrows. "I'll wait in bed."

She blushed, giving me enormous satisfaction. This was a bad idea. I knew it even before I got into her bed, but I did it anyway. When it came to Ellie, I clearly couldn't heed my own advice.

I yanked off my jeans, getting in her bed in my boxers. When she came back from the bathroom, with her hair piled up on top of her head, I nearly swallowed my tongue. She was a sinful sight with her pink top clinging to her skin. It was damp in places—like her navel and breasts. I instantly turned hard at the sight of her puckered nipples.

She turned off the light, but I caught her shy smile just before the room went dark. My heart was pounding against my ribcage. I'd never slept next to a woman without having sex first. I'd also never taken anyone's virginity. There were many firsts with Ellie.

"Are you comfortable?" she whispered, cramming in next to me.

I grunted noncommittally. The bed was all right, but my raging erection was painful. I turned on one side, reaching for her in the dark and pulling her close. She smelled amazing, like fresh flowers or fruit, or a combination. I parted her lips with my thumb before claiming her mouth. Being so close to her and not making her mine was torture. I needed this at least. She tasted delicious, and I couldn't get enough. Deepening the kiss, I moved one hand down the side of her body, cupping her ass. She lifted one leg on top of me. On instinct, I moved my hips forward. My cock nudged her clit. She moaned against my mouth, tugging at my hair. Goose bumps broke out on her arm. The leg she had around me shook.

Fuck. Fuck. No.

I pulled back, trying to regain some semblance of control. Moving my fingers down her thigh, I felt the raised flesh there and on her calf too.

"Right. Kissing is off-limits tonight too," I said.

"Ian," she whispered. "We can kiss."

I touched her lips with my fingers, feeling how swollen they were. I couldn't stop imagining them around my cock. *Mind out of the gutter, Gallagher.*

I smiled, bringing my mouth to her ear. "I know we can. It's just not a good idea. Not right now. Good night, Ellie."

"Good night."

She curled up inches away from me. Heat came off her in waves. Her smell was intoxicating. I wanted to know exactly what it was. Only a few minutes later, her breath slowed, and I realized she was already asleep. I was awake for what felt like hours, thinking about everything she'd shared with me. Even though she'd downplayed everything, a sentence stuck in my mind: *I wasn't just going to sleep with any guy off the street.*

Sex was important to her. Waiting wasn't my strong suit, but I was going to wait for her. Even though being so close and not making her mine was pure fucking torture.

Chapter Eight
Ellie

The next morning, the bed was empty when I woke up. My first thought was that Ian had left after all. My stomach bottomed out. I grabbed the teddy bear from the shelf above my head and stayed in bed, clutching my covers, remembering last evening, until I heard a sound in the kitchen. I sprang to my feet so fast that I lost my balance. Holy shit, he was still here. Happiness took root in my body, filling me from the tips of my fingers to my toes. *He's still here. He wants to stay the weekend and take care of me.* I couldn't believe it.

I went to the bathroom first, brushing my teeth with minty toothpaste and combing my hair before grabbing a Tylenol. Fortunately, my head wasn't aching and I didn't feel woozy like I did after the fall, but I took the medicine anyway to prevent anything from coming on.

I also washed my face and applied face cream to look fresh. Fresh didn't equal attractive, though, since I was still half-asleep and my eyes were slightly puffy, but it made no sense to apply makeup. I was wearing my fluffy pink pajama shorts and a tee, so I was feeling a little bit presentable.

I tiptoed to the kitchen, smiling when I saw him at the counter. He was wearing jeans and no shirt. His back muscles were gorgeous and sexy. I had plenty of stuff for breakfast, like tomatoes, feta cheese, and hearty bread with herbs in it, and it looked like he'd found it all.

"This is hands down the best breakfast ever," I said, announcing myself. He turned around to me. "Oh, and it's getting even better. I thought your back was gorgeous, but that chest, damn. It should come with a warning sign or ten."

He grinned. "How are you feeling?"

"Great." I tiptoed closer to him, running my finger between his pecs. I quickly found his six-pack and traced each of them. "Someone pampered me like a princess."

"And this someone… do you like having him around?"

I tapped my finger against my chin, then stroked it theatrically as if this required a lot of thought. "Let me think. Oh yeah, especially when he wanders around without a shirt." I reached for a slice of cheese and noticed a bottle of champagne on the counter. "Okay, I'm pretty sure I don't own a bottle this expensive. What's it doing here?"

"I ordered it from Dumond Foods this morning. Thought we'd celebrate."

"What? That I went to the hospital?" I asked.

"No. That you've made it past your two-week probation period."

I was stunned that he remembered. "Okay.

I've never thought about celebrating that, but yeah, I'm excited."

"I checked with the hospital, and you're not allowed to drink alcohol, so I bought nonalcoholic champagne."

My eyes bulged. Had he called the hospital? I couldn't believe he was so thoughtful. I was silent as we ate, munching on the feta cheese and tomatoes and bread. Ian kept surprising me. Henry made him sound like some kind of super player, maybe even a jerk. Well, actually, no, he'd never made him sound like a jerk, just that he'd be a guy that wouldn't stick around. My brother always did say Ian was a loyal friend… but that he doubted his boyfriend qualities. As we ate next to each other, standing at the counter, I couldn't help but ask myself… could he be a loyal boyfriend? Was there any universe in which he'd even want that?

I started mentally chastising myself. Why was I even thinking like that? It wasn't like I was moving to New York for good. In six months, I was going to New Orleans to learn all about Creole cuisine. The thought didn't excite me as much as it did when I first got this job, but I was sure it was just a phase. Everything I'd learn in this rotation program would be invaluable when I opened my own restaurant.

"What are you thinking about?" he asked.

"That I'm only here for a few months." I pressed my lips together, unsure what else to say. I didn't want to make it sound like I was asking where this was going. We'd just slept together, the platonic kind of sleeping together, for God's sake.

His gaze turned hard. "Let's not talk about that. In fact, I've already pushed it to the back of my mind."

I looked straight at him, catching my breath. I wasn't sure what that meant. Did he mean what he'd said about wanting to be my first? I knew I wanted him to be, but I wasn't going to focus on that right now. I had a crazy-sexy man in my kitchen. He was mine for the weekend, and I was going to take full advantage of this.

He popped the bottle of champagne open after we finished breakfast. While he poured it in clean coffee cups, since I had no idea where the wine or champagne glasses were, I massaged his shoulders.

"What are you doing?" he asked with a laugh.

"I want you to relax. These shoulders have been working hard."

"Doing what? Pouring champagne? You're just looking for an excuse to touch me."

"True. These muscles are so irresistible. They beg to be stroked." He turned around, handing me a cup. We clinked them, and then I took a sip. It was exquisite.

"To making it past your probation period," he said, then added, "Cheers."

"You're right. I shouldn't forget about this important milestone."

"It's good from time to time to take stock of what you've accomplished so far and enjoy it. I see so many people just set their eyes on the next goal, forgetting what they've just achieved and instantly taking it for granted."

"You don't, do you?" I asked.

"No. Never. I feel very grateful for all my brother and I built. We come from a humble background."

"You said your parents used to run a ski resort, right?"

"Yeah. They did," he said, taking my hand and moving me to the beanbag that I call an armchair. He sat down on it, pulling me into his lap. I shimmied for good measure, smiling when he groaned. I liked sitting on him. "I mean, we did have a good childhood. They gave us everything we wanted. We just had a few very hard winters when there was no snow and barely made ends meet. I remember overhearing my parents. They worried about paying the mortgage and so on."

"But this insurance model you're working on is going to change that, right?" I asked, remembering the conversation.

"Yes. That's what we are aiming for. It's going to be rolled out nationally, so it's going to take longer than we hoped. It's a one-of-a-kind thing, and it's a lot of work, but it's worth it. We're licensing the software to insurance companies, but we have to tweak it for most of them to work in their operating systems."

I loved hearing about what drove him and what motivated him. Yet again, the image I had of Ian Gallagher was changing. He was a guy who liked taking care of his family and me.

"I can't believe you're staying here to keep an eye on me."

"Why?"

I shrugged. "I don't know. I never made a fuss when I was sick, unless I was super sick. I just didn't want anyone worrying, like you are now."

"I'm not worrying. Everything will be fine. As long as I'm here to look after you."

Was he even aware of how adorable he was?

"Did you tell your family what happened?" he asked.

"Ian! Seriously. I don't want to make a fuss. But speaking about family, do you see my phone? I really don't want to forget about ordering the present. I researched a lot to find something he'd really like."

"What are you buying?" he asked.

"My stepdad likes fishing, so I bought him a fishing set. I spent a lot of time on forums, trying to learn which one was the best. And I asked my mom to send me pics of all the sets he already owns so I don't buy the same things."

"You're so fucking cute. I suck at getting presents. When we were kids, Dylan and I got our parents the worst presents. Our sisters always had something that was just perfect that Mom and Dad loved. They were so damned smug about it too."

I laughed, loving to hear him talk about his family. "That sounds like fun."

"Next time I need a present, I'll ask you for

help."

"Sure, anytime. I don't know my way around New York, but I can shop online like a pro."

I only took a few sips of champagne. I couldn't even tell it was nonalcoholic.

Looking up at Ian, I was surprised to find that he was looking at me intently.

"What?" I asked.

"I just like looking at you."

My cheeks heated up. "Henry never mentioned you were so good with words."

"You don't know a lot of things about me." He leaned in, cupping my cheek, running his thumb over my lower lip. The touch electrified me. "And the reverse is true as well. I'll enjoy exploring you."

He pressed his thumb on the bow of my upper lip, setting me on edge completely, but then he took a step back.

"So, what are we doing today?" I asked. "I wanted to explore Broadway and Soho this weekend. Josie said her husband's cousins have lingerie shops there."

"Ellie. The doctor's instructions were to rest."

"But strolling *is* resting."

He tilted his head, determination flashing in his eyes. It sent a wave of heat through me. "It's not. I checked that this morning also. It's relaxing indoors."

I melted at his concern and that deep baritone of his voice.

"Okay, then I guess I'll visit the lingerie shop

another time. What are we going to do? Watch movies?"

"Whatever relaxes you." Leaning in, he wiggled his eyebrows. "I'm even offering up my body."

I burst out laughing. "What a sacrifice, right?"

"Hey, don't mock it. Who knows what you'll want to do with it?"

"Terrible things," I teased. "Terrible."

"Sounds about right."

"So wait, kissing is allowed today? And can I say words like balls or cock?" I had no idea why I was so sassy around him!

He groaned, stepping closer. "Ellie! I told you I don't want to rush this. I won't lie, this is new for me."

"What?"

"Waiting. But it's worth it. You're worth it."

Oh my God. I totally melted.

"I want you to get to know me," he went on, as if he didn't just turn my insides to mush. "To trust me. So that when we're finally together, it's going to be amazing for you."

He hooked an arm around my waist, lifting me off the floor a few inches until we were face-to-face. Then he captured my mouth, stroking my tongue with his until I forgot what I was thinking and where we were. Everything faded except him.

Kissing Ian was all-consuming. Just being in his arms made my stomach swoop. His strong arms held me tightly against him. I clasped my legs around him. I was still swooning, remembering the exact moment he said he wanted to stay over last evening. *Oh, Ellie, you're already way too deep in this.* A doubt wiggled in my mind. He wasn't used to waiting. He'd told me as much himself. What if he was going to tire of waiting? I pushed the thoughts to the back of my mind. I was just happy that he was here, and I didn't want to dampen that happiness.

Chapter Nine
Ian

The next week was insane. The Project Z rollout was going so well that we needed to schedule strategic meetings daily. And I still had my usual client meetings on top of that. I'd stayed at Ellie's until Sunday evening but hadn't seen her since. I felt restless, so when Dylan suggested we go to the gym on Wednesday before lunch, I didn't even hesitate. It was a great way to blow off steam.

Isabelle was coming too, so it also doubled as a sibling get-together. Since she'd moved to Tarrytown with Brayden, she only came into the city two or three times a week.

I spent about an hour and a half doing my cardio and weight training routine and then headed with Dylan to the break room. Pouring myself a glass of orange juice, I realized how tense I still felt despite the workout. The empty break room with their buffet and Feng Shui, or whatever Isabelle called it, wasn't working either.

"What did you do last weekend?" Dylan asked, pouring himself sparkling water. His fiancée, Mel, was also with us. She was a trainer at the gym. This was how they met.

I just grunted noncommittally. He cocked a brow.

"Hey, don't pester Ian," Mel said.

"Thank you, Mel. Finally someone who understands."

"I'm going to try and talk some sense into him at home. But I have to go now. I have a client waiting." She sent an air kiss to me and Dylan as she headed out of the break room.

"You're seriously not going to tell me why you were AWOL all weekend?" Dylan asked just as Isabelle joined us.

"Why do you look so perplexed, Dylan?" she asked.

My brother shrugged. "I'm just trying to figure out what Ian was up to on Friday."

Isabelle batted her eyelashes. "Oh, I know that."

Dylan jerked his head back, nearly spilling sparkling water out of his glass.

"Without doing any detective work. How? You can read minds now?"

Isabelle wiggled her eyebrows, looking at me.

"Let me guess. You went to the hospital, went all knight in shining armor, and took Ellie home."

I nodded.

"That still doesn't explain what he did the whole weekend. He ignored my seven calls."

I rolled my eyes. "That's because it's the *weekend*. Some of us don't work all the time."

My sister perked up. "Wait a second. All

weekend?"

Dylan confirmed with a nod.

"Holy shit, you spent the whole weekend with Ellie?" she asked.

"Yeah," I said. "She had a concussion, and her roommate was out of town. I didn't want her to be on her own."

Isabelle stared at me for a couple of seconds, and I knew without a doubt that my explanation wouldn't cut it. When she tilted her head, smiling coyly, I had my confirmation.

"Right. So that means you somehow fell into her bed and didn't get back up?"

"Nothing happened," I insisted.

Isabelle cocked a brow.

I flashed a grin to Dylan. "See, that's how you can question someone and actually get answers."

"Hey, she had insider info. That's not fair."

"True," I admitted.

"So, what does this mean?" Isabelle asked.

I ran a hand through my hair, shrugging. "That Henry is going to kick my ass when he finds out."

Isabelle and Dylan exchanged a glance.

"Am I imagining things, or does our brother here seriously have the hots for Ellie?" Isabelle asked.

"I'm withholding my opinion until I have more info," Dylan replied.

I looked from one to the other. Were they pulling my leg?

"Do any of you have actionable advice?" I

asked.

My brother clapped a hand on my shoulder. "You have the hots for your best friend’s sister, who’s in town for half a year. Do I have this right?"

"Yeah."

"Then you're screwed."

"Thanks, man, that's really helpful."

"I'm going to the showers," Dylan said. "I'll leave you two to gossip."

After he left, I looked at Isabelle. "Okay, you always have good ideas and always talk my ear off. Why are you silent now?"

"I'm just trying to tailor my approach."

"Okay. You make it sound like a science."

"It can be," she said.

My sister was a talented counselor, and I wasn't too proud to admit that I was in murky territory here.

"What do you want, Ian?"

"Ellie," I said without hesitation.

"So then just take her out. Do couple stuff."

I frowned. "Can you elaborate? *Couple stuff* is not really my thing."

"Yes, but first, let me point out that you didn't flinch at the word couple. That's progress."

I shrugged, scratching my chin. I never understood what my siblings and friends liked about couplehood before, but I’d experienced a side of life I hadn't had before spending the weekend with Ellie. I enjoyed relaxing with her all day long, listening to whatever she wanted to share, giving me an insight into who she was.

"I can't see Henry getting upset because you spend time together," she said.

I cocked a brow. "He was my wingman in college, Isabelle."

My sister winced. "Okay then, he might have concerns. Just don't overthink it, Ian. Follow your instincts."

That was good advice. I thought about Isabelle's words as I returned to the office. I had a call with one of my least favorite clients, Bill. It lasted forty-five minutes, and I wasn't in a good mood after it ended.

Taking out my phone, I tapped Ellie's number and instantly felt the tension leave my shoulders.

***

Ellie

I loved being back on my feet and in the kitchen, hustling and bustling. We had a staff member in charge of chopping all the vegetables for me now, but I still had plenty to chop before I could put my salads together.

No one was paying attention to me, which was good because I'd felt a little silly and guilty on Friday as everyone fussed around me. I'd slipped on a piece of lettuce I'd dropped, and it took me by surprise—lesson learned. I'd be more conscious to keep the floor clean. However, I did like having Ian dote on me the whole weekend. He made me feel so special and important, and I wasn't used to it.

I was mostly on my own my entire life, and I had vague memories of being sick as a kid. My parents used to pamper me, but then after the divorce, Mom was so overwhelmed with the full-time job that I tried not to take up too much of her time. I didn't want to add to Mom's plate. So when I had a cold or something, I didn't make a big deal of it. If I had something nasty and needed to see a doctor, then I'd bring it to her attention. Mom was good about taking care of me when I asked, but I didn't tell her often. I didn't want to be a burden on top of everything else she was dealing with. But the weekend with Ian had been like a slice out of someone else's life.

My phone beeped as I finished plating three salads, and I took a cursory glance at it. My stepdad sent me a thank you message. I'd shipped his gift with speedy delivery on Sunday, and it arrived early. I smiled, sending back a heart emoji.

I grinned, remembering Ian's surprise when we spoke about gifts. Oh man, I *had* to stop fantasizing about the weekend. We hadn't made any more plans, and I didn't want to think too much about what that meant. Maybe Ian thought we should go back to being friends. My heart felt heavier at the thought. I really had to stop thinking about our weekend, because I just found more reasons to swoon every time I did.

"Ellie, five salads needed, no walnuts. Allergic."

"Okay, I'm on it," I acknowledged, paying special attention to the specific order. Whenever someone with allergens ordered something, I changed my gloves and my cutting knife and chopping board—basically everything. It wasn't just a matter of not putting nuts on it; everything could have remnants of nuts and had to be changed.

My phone pinged again while I was focusing on the salads. It pinged twice in a row, so I assumed that my stepdad wanted to chat some more. After I finished the salads and Raul took them to the lunch crowd, I checked my phone. Holy shit, it wasn't a message from my stepdad. It was from Ian.

Ian: When do you get a break? I want to talk to you.

Okay. *Breathe in, breathe out, Ellie. Breathe in, breathe out.* Yeah, that wasn't helping. Just like that, I was thinking about the weekend, swooning again. I glanced at the clock and typed back.

Ellie: I have a break in 20 minutes.

Ian replied immediately.

Ian: Call me when you're alone.

Ellie: What kind of call is this going to be that needs me to be alone?

Ian: The kind that makes you blush.

Oh, my God. I was blushing already. I could feel my cheeks heat up.

Luckily, since I was in the kitchen, most people were flushed because of the insane pace at which we moved and the heat of the ovens.

Ellie: Duly noted. I'll make sure I'm

alone. But you'd better keep to your word. I don't want to go to all that trouble of finding a private space for nothing.

Ian: Game on.

Guess what was all I could think about for the next twenty minutes? That's right, my call with Ian. I tried to imagine how it would go. Maybe he wanted to talk about us being friends again, but he'd said he would make me blush, so that seemed off the table.

Nineteen minutes later, I ran to the pantry. That's right; I *ran*, didn't walk. I only had a five-minute break, and I didn't want to lose even one second.

I could go to the staff break room, but I'd more than likely bump into a coworker, and the man did say he was going to make me blush. I didn't want to risk anyone overhearing us. It was pleasantly cool in the pantry because it was air-conditioned, and I knew that my colleagues rarely came in here. Typically, we took what we needed out in the morning to have it on hand.

I called him right away, leaning against the wall.

"Ellie," he answered in a deep baritone voice that made my toes curl.

"Hey," I said. My voice was ridiculously high-pitched. I put a hand to my stomach, trying to draw in a deep breath so that I wouldn't make a complete fool of myself.

"How are you feeling?" he asked. That was his first question? He wanted to make me swoon already? This wasn't fair. How was I supposed to compartmentalize?

"I'm fine. I feel good as new."

"How long are you working today?"

"Until six o'clock, like usual."

"On your first week back?"

I swear I could hear a growl. The protective streak in his voice was not helping with the swooning.

"Yep. As I said, I feel perfect. I even went for a checkup, and all is well. I didn't see any reason not to come back full-time."

"I'd like to see you this evening. Go out somewhere."

"Oh." I wasn't sure what to say. "Okay."

"You don't sound too convinced." There was an edge to his voice that wasn't there before.

"No, I am. I mean, I do want to go out. I'm just wondering if you want to go out as friends or…."

"Ellie, I told you I'm going to make you blush. In what world do you think we're going to be just friends?"

I laughed nervously, shrugging even though he couldn't see me. "I don't know what your definition of friendship is. Or blushing."

"First thing I'll do when I see you is kiss you until you're wet for me."

Holy shit! I clenched my thighs together, already hyperventilating.

"That's a promise right there," I whispered.

"And I'll make good on it."

Instead of thinking about the weekend for the rest of the day, I thought about our upcoming evening. Was this progress? I couldn't even tell.

Chapter Ten
Ellie

I practically jogged home after work, eager to get as much primp time as possible. Harper was in the living room, as usual. For once, she was watching Netflix and not grading papers or doing a craft project.

"Hey, roommate," I said.

"Hey, do you want to grab dinner?"

"No, I'm going out with Ian, and I'm not sure, but I think it's a date."

She straightened up. "Finally. You need to jump his bones. He's too hot to be just a friend."

I grinned. "He really is hot. I'm not sure what to wear," I said honestly.

"When in doubt, dress for a date," Harper said with conviction.

I laughed. "I was thinking the same thing."

I chose to put on a red cashmere dress. It was warm and cozy—one of my favorite outfits. It was a steal I bought in a thrift store this summer. It was simple, but it molded to my curves in a way that sweaters never did. I paired it with high-heeled ankle boots, and I also had tights underneath. They were nude, so they weren't super noticeable unless you were close. But I needed them because October had rolled in with a bang—namely, a freezing wind. I also put on a white coat. It wasn't water repellent, so I hoped we would get lucky with the weather or that we wouldn't have to walk much.

"You look stunning. I love your style," Harper said. "You look like a million bucks."

"Thanks. I buy everything on sale, and I go to thrift stores regularly."

"Really? I can never find anything there."

"I have lots of practice, and you can find so many gems. Sometimes I don't understand the people who gave them away, because they are so beautiful. But hey, their loss is my gain."

The doorbell rang at seven o'clock on the dot.

"Just pretend I'm not here," Harper said before disappearing into her room. I buttoned up my coat, opening the door. Ian took a huge step back, looking me up and down. I swear I felt as if he could see through my coat. I'd arranged my hair in fluffy curls and put on long earrings. They were sexy—just like my ankle boots.

I closed the front door, and he kissed me the next second, pressing me against it. Oh my God, thank heavens I didn't have lipstick on. He explored my mouth until I felt his kiss in every cell of my body, as if he was kissing me everywhere. I pressed my thighs together and sucked in my tummy. When he pulled back, I said, "That's the best way to say hello."

"And make you wet." He parted my legs with

his knee, trapping my gaze with his.

"I will neither deny nor confirm that." I infused my voice with as much sass as possible.

"I'll check later. And I'll be very thorough."

"What are we doing?" I asked, needing to change the subject before I melted. "Where are you taking me?"

"Where do you want to go?"

"Hmm… why don't you surprise me? Take me somewhere *you* like."

He looked at me intently as if he was trying to figure something out.

"I know just the place."

Half an hour later, we were sitting on one of the wooden benches in the Battery Park Overlook, watching the New York harbor. The air was humid, and seagulls circled above. I enjoyed the view immensely.

"I love this place," I said.

"It grounds me."

"I can understand that." Ian bringing me to this special place of his made my heart happy.

He immediately pulled me into his lap, making me laugh.

"What?" he asked.

"It took you no time at all to do this."

"It's the best way to keep you warm," he said seriously.

"I see. Very gallant of you."

He rubbed his hands up and down my arms

before undoing two buttons of my coat.

"You're undressing me to keep me warm?" I challenged, fighting laughter.

"I'm not undressing you. Just undoing these two buttons so I can do this." He rested his palms on my waist. I felt my body temperature rise the second he touched me, so maybe there was something to his theory.

"Ian… what are we doing exactly?" I asked.

His gaze turned serious. "I enjoy you, Ellie. When I'm not with you, I think about you. I'll be honest. I have no clue what I'm doing. I'm not good at relationships. I haven't even tried before. And I know you're going to New Orleans soon, but until then… you're all mine."

I touched his lips, considering his words. I liked that he was so open. I didn't want to think about further down the road any more than he did. Usually, I was excited about my next placement and would research the city thoroughly, but not this time.

"I like the sound of that."

"What did you feel this weekend?"

"I was happy," I said honestly. "The way you took care of me, I'm not used to it..." His eyes clouded, and I wondered if I said too much and if I was scaring him away.

"What are we telling Henry?"

I considered this for a few seconds. "Not sure. I wouldn't even know what to tell him."

Ian nodded. "He's my best friend, though. He might be able to read between the lines."

I shimmied in his lap, putting his hands back on my waist. "Well, if he does, we'll deal with it. I'm just not in the mood to hear a speech about how I'll end up hurt and—"

"Ellie!"

I startled at the urgency in his voice. He took one hand out of my coat, putting it on my cheek.

"I can't promise you much, but know this. I won't hurt you, okay? I won't."

"I believe you," I said playfully, even as my chest filled with warmth. "But Henry might not."

He groaned. "Yeah. He might not. But he's a good brother. He's just looking after you and wants the best for his sister—a guy who checks off all the boxes."

I didn't like him talking about another man in my life. I didn't want to think too much about what was coming after New York. After Ian.

"How often do you come here?" I asked, looking to change the subject.

"Probably once or twice a month—whenever I have a stressful day and want to decompress. It reminds me of home a bit."

"Montana?"

"Yes."

"How come? It's not green or anything."

"It's not too crowded. I love New York, but I like quiet and space too, and those aren't easy to come by in the city."

"You could move to Tarrytown, like Isabelle. I googled it after you told me about it. The pictures look amazing."

"I might one day," he said vaguely. "But right now, I like being in Manhattan."

"I love it too. It's an exciting place to be. And the gastronomy scene is hands down the best in the country."

"Then why enroll in a program with a rotation? Why not just apply for a permanent job here?"

"Several reasons. It's incredibly hard to get a job in New York even though it has a ton of Michelin-starred restaurants."

"And the other reason?" he asked.

"Oh, yeah. Well, a rotation helps me get more experience. Typically, if you work with one chef for many years, you sort of learn their style. I want to develop my own, so that's why I looked for a rotational program."

Ian looked at me intently but didn't say anything else for a few seconds.

"So after you finish the rotation, you're going to search for another one?"

"I haven't thought that far yet. I'll see. I have seen a few programs that are on different continents—one even had a one-year placement in Tokyo."

"Tokyo?" He frowned as if he wasn't sure he understood me.

"Yes. Did you know that it has the highest density of Michelin restaurants in the world?"

"No, I didn't know."

"It's everyone's dream, but I'm not sure if I want to travel that far. I'll see. The downside to all these rotational programs is the pay, to be honest. It's a fraction of a normal salary, and I'm not sure how long I'll want to have roommates and be super frugal."

He was silent for a few beats. I wondered what he was thinking about.

"I've never been passionate about what I do the way you are," he said after a while.

"Really?" That was surprising. "I assumed you went into software because you liked it."

"I do like it—mostly because I'm very skilled at it. I'm just not passionate about it. But a few years ago, Dylan wanted to start a business, and I didn't want him to shoulder all that risk by himself. We came up with Gallagher Solutions."

Oh, wow. This man was incredible.

"What's with that look?" he asked.

I tried to school my features. "I don't know what you're talking about."

"Yes, you do."

Shrugging one shoulder, I brought my mouth to his ear. "You can't know all my secrets."

He pulled back a few inches, looking me straight in the eyes. He cupped my jaw, touching my lips with his fingers. "I'll learn them. One by one. I'm patient."

His voice was so deliciously sensual that I wasn't even sure what to do with myself. I needed a distraction. I curled up in a position that made it easier to look around us.

"It's so peaceful here," I murmured. "I've always liked being outdoors. Back home, I spent hours in the backyard, reading. When Dad was still at home, that's where I went when they started fighting. Henry was lucky. Being older, he spent a lot of time at his friends' houses, but I didn't." I'd felt lonely without my brother, especially once he left for college.

"Did it get better once they divorced?"

"Sort of. There wasn't much fighting anymore, but Mom was very sad. I'm not sure if it was actual depression or not, but she wasn't herself. Sometimes we'd even drive to where the *other* woman lived so that we could check if Dad's car was there."

My stomach clenched at the memories. I remembered clutching the seat, and my heart beating so fast that I could hear it in my ears.

Ian frowned. "And you never told her it bothered you?"

"No, I didn't want to hurt her feelings, and she had no one else to talk to. I think she felt ashamed—like other people might judge her or something. I'm not sure."

"And your dad?"

"I didn't see him much. Mostly weekends or vacations. I used to wait in front of the house for him to pick me up so Mom didn't see him. She got in a frenzy every time. I think she was also a bit mad that I still wanted to spend time with him despite the stuff she told me. Part of her was hoping I'd be too angry to want to see him again."

Thinking back on those rough years always made me sad, but sharing it with Ian somehow made me feel lighter.

"That's harsh."

"It was a very difficult time for her. I don't blame her. She did the best she could, and she's changed a lot since then."

"Did your dad marry the woman he was with after the divorce?"

"No, they broke up. He met his current wife shortly after that. Everyone found their balance eventually. But let's not talk about them anymore. We're here in this amazing place. Let's enjoy it."

A buzzing sound caught my attention. Ian took the phone out of his pocket. I didn't mean to look, but the screen was right there next to me.

Up for some drinks and fun in bed?

I froze. Ian groaned. He looked from the screen to me. I was trying to put on a poker face, but I felt a knot in my throat.

"You saw that?"

I nodded, unsure what to say. My heart was pounding in my ribcage.

"She's someone I hooked up with months ago a couple of times, nothing more."

"Okay." My heart rate intensified yet again. It felt like it was about to jump out of my chest. "So, what are you going to tell her?"

"No, obviously."

Relief rushed through me. My whole body felt

lighter. Ian must have noticed the change in me, because he turned to me, bringing both hands on my face. "Ellie, you thought I'd sleep with someone else?"

"No, I mean… I don't have experience with this, and we never talked about it." I spoke quickly. My voice was a bit uneven.

"Let me make this clear: I'm not even thinking about anyone else. Only you. Do you understand that?"

I nodded again. A smile popped up on my face of its own accord, and it just kept spreading until my face was literally hurting.

"I like the sound of that," I confessed, feeling a bit silly. "Let's talk about something else. Does Dylan also like to come here?"

"I always come here by myself," he said.

"Thank you for sharing this place with me."

"It's our secret."

I made a zipping gesture over my lips. "I'm not telling anyone."

Butterflies roamed in my belly. I couldn't believe I was the first one he brought here. Still, unease gnawed at me because of that text. With the way he looked, I imagined he got lots of them. What if he tired of waiting for me? I bit my lip, snapping myself out of that train of thought. He'd shared this place—and a part of himself with me. That meant something, and it filled me with immense joy.

I was usually always on the lookout for the next phase of my life, but for once, I was happy right where I was.

Chapter Eleven
Ian

"Did you ever think about doing something other than software?" I asked Dylan two weeks later while we went through a frustrating report about repeated crashes in the software solution we provided for a big client.

He looked up from his report, cocking a brow. "No. You?"

"Not seriously. I'm just wondering if there's anything out there I'd enjoy doing more. I sometimes get restless."

Spending time with Ellie was rubbing off on me. I couldn't get enough of the passion in her voice when she spoke about the restaurant she wanted to open one day. I'd never had a passion to follow. I went into software programming only because I was very good at it, but I couldn't say it was my dream career. I didn't have one. Spending time with her was making me consider new things, ask myself questions I never did before. Watching her go after what she wanted at full speed was making me question things.

"Where is this coming from?" he asked, pushing the report to one side. I did the same. We'd spent the whole morning on it, and we'd likely spend the rest of the day troubleshooting. We could afford a short break.

"Whenever Ellie talks about the restaurant she'll open one day, I realize I've never been passionate about anything. Not like that."

Dylan shrugged. "It's the same with Isabelle. Her counseling practice is more than a job. I can't say I've ever wanted to do anything else, but if you do, I'm sure we can work something out."

I knew my brother would always have my back, and I wasn't going to let him down.

"It's all talk," I said. "Want to go back to the report?"

Dylan flashed me a shit-eating grin. I pointed at it, saying, "Judging by that, the answer is no."

He laced his fingers on top of his head. "So what other life-changing questions is your best friend's off-limits younger sister making you ask yourself?"

I burst out laughing, tapping my fingers against the desk. Okay, I deserved it. I made so much fun of Dylan when he first started dating Mel that this was more than warranted.

"Wouldn't you like to know?"

"I do. It's fascinating to watch you going through this change."

"What change?" I asked blankly.

Dylan started counting on the fingers of his right hand. "Let's see. One: you are going out with the same woman for more than a week. That's a record, right there. Two: you're spending time with her, not just sleeping with her."

I wondered what he'd say if I told him I took her to the Overlook but decided not to tell him. He didn't have to know everything. Some things were private, even in my family.

"And now you're questioning your life choices, and it's only been a few weeks. I'm trying to figure out what's going to happen months down the road."

"Nothing," I assured him. "She'll be in another city, completing the next stage of her placement."

The words were bitter in my mouth. Dylan narrowed his eyes.

"Why are you looking at me like this?" I challenged.

"I'm trying to figure something out. But I'm in over my head. I'll just let Isabelle do all the heavy lifting."

I was utterly confused. "What are you talking about?"

"I don't know how to explain it. But, speaking of Isabelle, she and Josie are already looking for a present."

"Fuck me. We're still competing?"

"There was never any competition. Our sisters win by default."

"Not this time."

"Why not?"

"Because Ellie's gonna help us."

Dylan's eyes bulged. He opened his mouth but closed it again without saying anything. That was a first.

After he left the office, I messaged Ellie.

Ian: Dylan and I have no clue what to buy my parents for their anniversary. We need help. Are you in?

Ellie: YES.

I grinned just imagining her huge smile right now.

Ian: Want to stay in my condo?

Ellie: Mr. Gallagher, you like to live dangerously. We can barely keep our hands off each other with Harper as a buffer. How are we going to fare alone?

Ian: I have faith in us.

Ellie: I don't.

I laughed, even though I kind of agreed with her. Being completely alone with Ellie *was* dangerous. Even though my condo only had one bedroom, it was more spacious than their apartment. I liked Harper, but I wanted time alone with Ellie. I wanted her all to myself. I chuckled, imagining what Dylan would say if he knew that Ellie and I didn't even sleep together. He'd probably say he didn't even know who I was anymore. I almost didn't recognize myself. But I wanted Ellie to be ready. *She* was the important one here.

***

"Why are we making a list?" I asked Ellie that evening, perplexed.

"Because I need to get a feeling for what your parents like."

Ellie was lying on her belly on my couch; legs bent at the knees, feet up in the air. She'd piled her hair on top of her head and stuck a pencil in it. She was holding another pencil in her hand, scribbling furiously everything I told her, which wasn't much. So far, I'd come up with *their home, Montana, barbecue, Christmas*.

I wasn't what you'd call observant. Certain details didn't register.

"You make lists for everything?" I asked.

"I make vision boards usually." She smiled sheepishly. "I'm a visual person, so I think better in images."

"That sounds… the opposite of how my brain operates. I think in lines of code and numbers. It explains the atrocious gifts I give. So what do you have vision boards for?"

"Ha! Everything, honestly. How my dream restaurant should look—from architecture down to the menu. My favorite design for a home. Outfits."

Ellie was fascinating to me. She was so vibrant and full of life and a dreamer through and through. And it made me consider things I'd never thought about before, things I'd dismissed all my life, such as spending a quiet night in my condo with Ellie. Dylan's words rang in my mind. *It's fascinating to watch you going through this change.*

Change was a good thing, right? Even though it was temporary. After she left New York, my life would go back to the same old same old. I didn't like the thought of it.

"Can we call Dylan?" she asked with a grin.

"Sure." Taking out my phone, I put it on speaker, calling my brother's number.

"Hey! You're on the speaker, and Ellie's here too," I said as soon as he answered.

"Hi, Ellie!" Dylan said. "Nice to meet you."

"Likewise. I think I saw you once when I came to DC, but it was years ago," Ellie said.

"Oh? I don't remember you at all, but I can't wait to meet you in person. What's with the phone call?"

"Ian and I are brainstorming what to get for your parents. I'm making a list of things they like, and it's not too long."

"You're making a list? You're thorough." He sounded stunned.

"Help us out. What do your parents like?"

"Montana. Barbecue," Dylan said immediately. I barely held back laughter.

Ellie groaned. "I already have that. As well as their home and Christmas. Anything else?"

Dylan didn't reply. If we were in the same room, I was sure he'd look at me desperately for help. It was why I called him.

"Honestly, no clue," he said eventually.

Ellie kept chewing at the pencil. "Okay, I'll work with what I have."

"So... what are you guys doing? Brainstorming over dinner in the city?" Dylan asked.

"You're so obvious, brother," I countered. Ellie glanced at me in surprise. My brother chuckled.

"We're in my condo. And since you're not helping...."

"I'll back off. I'll back off," he said quickly. "Great meeting you, Ellie. Even through the phone."

"You too," Ellie said.

After the line disconnected, she trained her eyes on me. "What was that about?"

"My brother was fishing for information," I explained. "I recently told Dylan I wasn't sure software was something I was passionate about. He was intrigued. Especially when I told him that spending time with you is making me consider all sorts of things."

Her eyes widened in surprise, but I could tell she was pleased.

"What else would you like to do?"

"That's it. I don't even know. But I do like the company I've built with my brother, so I wouldn't do anything drastic like pulling out and disappointing him."

"Why would you think that?" she asked, looking revolted. Talking to her was surprisingly easy.

"During college, he was always the serious one. I didn't take too much seriously. Even all these years later, some of our business partners aren't happy that I'm so laid-back."

"Is there a rule that you can't be laid-back *and*

good at your job?"

"In some circles, it is. But Dylan and I never cared about what other people said."

"I like the dynamic between you two." Her face lit up before she went back to the list, staring at the words as if she could get the information to multiply just by looking at it.

"Do you want wine?" I asked.

"Oooh, yes." She wiggled her toes, looking up from the sheet of paper. I had a wine fridge in the kitchen, and Ellie looked at it intently. "I want a sauvignon blanc."

"Yes, ma'am." Uncorking a bottle, I poured us both a glass and handed one to her.

"That's the sexiest thing you've done all evening," she said, wiggling her eyebrows. On instinct, I leaned into her, kissing the side of her neck. First, I only gave her my lips and then my tongue. I felt her shiver and brought my mouth to her ear.

"I'm going to do a lot more than this, Ellie. That's a promise."

She drew in a sharp breath. Mission accomplished. Straightening up, I went back to the dining table where I was sitting before. I liked watching her from a distance. I liked that she was here in my condo, spread out on my white leather couch.

Our conversations usually revolved around work or our families. If something special happened during the day, Ellie would text me about it, and we'd talk about it on the phone or whenever we got together. I'd never had anything remotely resembling this before, and I liked it.

"I need more," she said thoughtfully, munching on the end of the pencil. Fuck, she was adorable, concentrating on this like she was writing a thesis.

"I'll think about it."

"Can we get Isabelle and Josie on the phone?"

"Isabelle and Josie are the competition, remember?"

Ellie laughed, tapping the pencil against the sheet of paper. "I love your competitive streak. Why didn't you ever just join forces and buy one huge gift?"

"We thought about it, but it seemed lame to just get them one present from four kids. Besides, it became some sort of tradition. I don't even remember a time when Dylan and I weren't competing against our sisters."

"That's not very helpful, but it's funny. I'll give you that."

"We have enough time to buy them something," I said. "They're coming in two weeks."

Ellie turned on one side, propping her head in one hand. "Not as much time as you think. Not all online shops have fast delivery, and I don't know my way around the city. Obviously, if it's something we can find in a department store, that's okay. But if it's anything more specific…."

I moved from the chair at the dining room

table to the end of the couch, taking her feet in my lap.

"Okay, enough research for one evening," I said.

"But I've only begun."

"Then let's take a break."

She grinned at me. "I can do that. Can I get a foot massage?"

"You can get whatever you want."

"Are you serious?"

"Very."

"Is it because I'm helping with the gifts?"

"Yes, but not just because of that."

"Hmmm… what else could it be? Oh, I know. Is it foreplay because you have dirty things in mind for later?"

I leaned closer to her, speaking directly against her lips. "Ellie, foreplay makes you wet. This is just a foot massage. You're on your feet all day."

She cleared her throat. "Glad we clarified it."

I moved further away, pressing my thumbs along her ankles. Her breath caught. I trained my eyes on her, feeling her body hum under my touch.

Licking her lips, she glanced at the bar. "Can I inspect that? It's so fancy."

"Sure."

She rose from the couch, and I followed her closely.

I went behind her as she looked at my bar, paying close attention to the selection. I skimmed my fingers on her arms. She shuddered as I pushed her hair to one side. I kissed down the back of her neck. The shudder in her body intensified. She smelled like apples and flowers, and it was an intoxicating combination. Her skin was so soft that I couldn't stop imagining how it would feel to touch the rest of her. To taste every inch of her skin. Her breath caught, shifting something inside me. I turned her around, stroking her cheek with the back of my fingers, tilting closer.

I licked her lower lip with the tip of my tongue before kissing her. I moved my mouth over hers at a slow pace, savoring her, taking my time with her lips and her tongue. But I needed more. I wrapped my fingers in her hair, tilting her head to a perfect angle so I could explore her even deeper. She wrapped an arm around my neck and tugged at my hair.

Her taste was intoxicating. I scooped her up in my arms, keeping my hands firmly under her ass. She wrapped her legs around me. I intended to bring her to the couch, but instead, I ended up pinning her against the wall, only pausing the kiss to make sure she was okay.

Leaning in, she nipped my Adam's apple. I groaned, rocking my hips forward. My cock was painfully hard now. She gasped, rolling her hips.

“Ian!” The urgency in her voice nearly snapped my control. "I want you. All of you. I'm ready." She tugged at my shirt as if she couldn't wait one more second.

Her words unleashed something inside me. I

kissed her ferociously, for once not holding back anymore. I only needed enough self-restraint to bring us to a bed. I was going to have her against the wall too, against every damn wall in this condo, but not tonight. Tonight, I wanted her to be comfortable on a mattress. It was her first time, and it needed to be special, the best experience of her lifetime.

Lifting her up again, I brought her to the bedroom, putting her on the bed. She drew in a sharp breath, looking up at me from under her eyelashes. Her chest was rising and falling fast. I undid the buttons of her shirt, kissing her neck, then lower between the cups of her black lace bra.

"You're so beautiful," I whispered, feeling her relax under my touch. "Are you sure, Ellie? I need to know that you're sure."

"I'm sure," she whispered. I took off her jeans slowly, feeling her smooth skin under my fingers. I took my time, touching her thighs and then her ankles until I yanked them away. Then I traced the same path back up with my mouth, alternating between just pressing my lips against her skin or also giving her my tongue. She gasped every time I did the latter.

I looked up at her when I reached the apex of her thighs. Her pupils were dilated. I turned her over on her stomach, spreading her thighs wide. She looked over her shoulder, biting her lower lip with a devilish grin. I kissed the back of her right knee, moving upward on her thigh. I wanted her to be ready for me and all the pleasure I wanted to give her.

I moved my lips up on one ass cheek, inching my hand up her inner thigh, right until my thumb reached her pussy over the fabric. I took my time, skimming my finger up and down until the fabric was wet. She fisted the sheet, pressing her forehead against the mattress, moaning. I moved to the other ass cheek, continuing to touch her pussy, feeling her ass muscles contracting. Her legs went rigid. I had her exactly where I wanted her. Ready for everything I wanted to give her. She turned around, facing me, and tugged at my shirt, sliding her hands underneath it and tracing my abs with the pads of her fingers. I couldn't focus on anything except how much I wanted her. I unclasped her bra, throwing it to one side. She was so damn beautiful.

I pushed her further on the bed, kissing her nipple, worshiping her breasts.

"Ian," she whispered, shimmying her hips against the mattress. I moved from one breast to the other and then down to her navel in a trail of slow and lazy kisses. I knew they were driving her crazy. They were driving me crazy too.

I was so hard that the zipper of my jeans against my cock was painful. I wanted her desperately. I pressed two fingers between her legs, groaning at how drenched the fabric was. She shuddered. I couldn't wait to see how she'd react when I put my fingers directly on her skin and then my tongue.

I was so hard, and I could barely think, but

one thought stood out: I wanted everything to be perfect for her. I got down from the bed, taking off my shirt and pants.

I took a condom from the box beside the bed, sliding it on. The touch of the rubber against my cock was already insane. I was on edge. Putting a knee on the bed, I lowered myself over her. I wanted her so desperately that I hadn't made up my mind where to touch her next.

"Please don't stop."

I looked straight at her. "Ellie, if you change your mind, tell me. Okay?"

"I won't. *Please.*" She nodded vigorously, her brown hair spilling around her shoulders and her breasts.

I skimmed both hands to her panties, taking them off. She was smoothly waxed and damn gorgeous. I put my mouth on her pubic bone, teasing a bit before descending to her clit. She opened her legs even wider. I was going to lose my mind.

"I want to feel you come like this while I have my mouth on you. I want your orgasm on my tongue," I told her. I worked her clit with my mouth, drawing small circles with my tongue and sucking it between my lips.

I stroked her curvy body with my hands, touching her breasts and her hips. When her breath started to hitch and her chest rose and fell faster, I clasped her ass with both hands, keeping her in place, giving her so much pleasure that her legs started to shake. She came apart spectacularly, crying out my name. I felt as if I was going to explode.

I straightened up to my feet, pulling both her legs with me so she was at the edge of the mattress. The bed was high enough that her pussy was at the same level as my cock.

She bent her legs at the knees, nestling her ankles above my hips.

I pushed inside her very slowly, watching her face intently, reining in desire. I needed to go at her pace. She gasped, tugging at the sheets.

Bending at the waist, I kissed up her shoulder, bringing my mouth to her ear.

"Are you hurting?"

"Just a little. But it also feels good. More. Please."

I slid in another inch, feeling her inner muscles clamp down around me, and I stilled.

She rolled her hips back and forth, taking me in at her own pace, until I was inside her to the hilt.

"It doesn't hurt at all anymore," she whispered.

I liked seeing her like this, open and exposed. Her breasts were spilling out to her sides. The way she looked at me made my chest clench tight. This was an entirely new sensation for me.

I pushed in and out slowly, watching us, feeling everything intensely. The pleasure magnified by the second, coiling through my whole body, radiating from where we were connected. My senses were heightened. I tilted slightly forward, touching her thighs and breasts, occasionally circling her clit, but not too often. I wanted to build up a second orgasm slowly. Every time I dragged my thumb around her clit, tremors coursed through her body and she tightened around me.

I wanted to see her surrender to the pleasure, bit by bit—give herself to me completely in a way she never had before. I wanted to own every part of Ellie. I pushed in and out as the orgasm started to form deep inside me. I came so hard that my thighs shook. My knees weakened for a few seconds, but I pushed through it, still moving slowly, thrusting until she came a second time. She cried out even louder than before.

I fell on the bed next to her, barely drawing in a breath. She was completely silent and still. I turned my head to look at her. There was sweat on her forehead and her chest.

"How are you feeling? Are you sore?"

She spoke with a lazy, sated smile. "No. I feel good. Better than good."

"Are you sure?"

"Yes."

I moved closer to her, touching her cheek. A dangerous thought was circling in my mind. I didn't just want to be her first. I wanted to be her last. "What are you thinking about?" I asked after a while.

"All the things I want. You did just say I could have everything before. That opens up so many possibilities. I'm wondering what to bring up first."

"Take your time. I'm here to please you."

"See? You just make me swoon when you say that."

"It's true."

She closed one eye theatrically, looking at me intently with the other one.

"Why do I feel scrutinized?"

"Because that's exactly what I'm doing. Wondering if you're real or I'm just making up this amazing evening in my mind."

I bit her lower lip lightly. She giggled.

"Okay, that felt real. Maybe I should touch you too, just to make sure."

"Feel free to."

She poked my right arm. I caught her wrist in one hand, pressing my thumb on her pulse point. The rhythmic thrum intensified. She licked her lower lip as her breath caught.

"Why are you so awesome?" she murmured. "It's so…." She stopped abruptly, as if catching herself saying something she shouldn't.

"So what?"

"I don't know. This is so new to me. I've never been this close to anyone."

"I haven't been either."

"Before, it was always easy to move on wherever a job took me. This time—" She pressed her lips together, shaking her head. "Never mind. Just ignore what I said."

"Ellie…"

Her expression softened. Her eyes were vulnerable. I didn't want to ignore anything, but I also didn't want to put her on the spot.

"Want to go take a shower?" I asked, deciding to switch topics.

"Yes, please."

I took her hand, kissing the back of it before we rose from the bed. With my other hand, I smacked her ass lightly on the way to the bathroom. She chuckled, wiggling her eyebrows before looking at herself in the round mirror hanging above the sink.

I threw away the condom quickly, kissing her shoulder.

"I'm so happy," she whispered.

"Music for my ears." I stood behind her, circling her waist with my arms, looking at her in the mirror. "I'm happy you came here tonight."

She giggled. "You had a good excuse too. Helping you not get a crappy gift."

"It was not an excuse. Dylan and I are just bad at it. We have a lot to make up for."

"I think it's so cool that they fly out to be with all of you for their anniversary."

"They're coming to the city more and more often. How often do you see your family?"

"Not as much as I'd like to. It's one of the downsides of being all over the place all the time."

"How is it any different to just living in one place? Unless it's the same city they're in, one of you still has to fly out."

"True. But flights are expensive, and on a trainee salary, I try to save wherever possible. And it's even more expensive for them to come to visit me because they have to pay for two tickets. Besides, they have lots to do, so they don't have much free time." Sadness flickered in her eyes, twisting my insides.

I knew from Henry that their Mom and Dad weren't very close. They were on good terms and cared about each other, and it was enough for Henry. But Ellie was more sensitive. She had a lot of warmth and affection to give, and she needed the same in return.

I had this incessant need to make all her wishes come true. Maybe that would keep her here. I shook my head, dispelling these thoughts. She wanted to chase her dreams, and I wouldn't get in the way. I knew what it meant to have a goal in mind and focus everything on achieving it. I'd done it for years to build Gallagher Solutions to be a successful business. It was one of the reasons why I hadn't paid attention to my personal life. The other reason was that I simply never wanted more than hookups and casual dating. But this ease and closeness with Ellie was something I never had and never even craved. Until now.

Chapter Twelve
Ellie

I was loving New York more than any other city I'd worked in. There was something about the Big Apple that just awed me. I went out exploring almost every morning before work, nose buried in a guidebook or just looking around. I'd already gone through the main museums, but honestly, I liked being outdoors more than inside, so I just wandered around Manhattan.

I went to NoLita, shopping for Ian's parents. I liked the area a lot. It was a trendy and hip neighborhood with lots of shops, mostly focusing on fashion, jewelry, and furniture. After a lot of consideration, we decided on a pro set of grilling tools as a gift. Neither Ian nor Dylan was sure if their parents already owned something like this, but we were buying them a professional collection that restaurants used. Hopefully the high-end, quality grill set would outshine anything they already had.

I didn't find anything with quick delivery times online, so I checked out a shop in NoLita that catered to restaurants but also sold to the public. It was small but well-stocked, and the set of grill tools was just what I hoped it would be. And an added bonus, because I was a chef, I got a discount.

I immediately texted Ian.

Ellie: The set is great. I think they'll like it.

Ian: If the chef approves, I'm game.

Ellie: Chef approves. I'm buying them.

Ian: Thanks so much for doing this. I'm going to be extra rewarding tonight.

Ellie: Ooohh, I want details.

Ian: Not telling you anything. I'll show you everything.

His parents were flying in, and we were to meet them that evening, so I wondered when exactly he planned to do it all, but I had faith in Ian. He was very creative. The past two weeks, ever since we'd had sex the first time, we'd met almost daily after work. I still couldn't believe how amazing that night had felt. Every detail was branded in my memory. He'd made me feel like I was a goddess. Before Ian, I'd been almost ashamed that I was a virgin at twenty-three. But maybe I was meant to wait for him. *Don't be ridiculously romantic, Ellie.*

But I couldn't help myself. I shimmied my hips, smiling from ear to ear. I was ridiculously giddy as I paid for the gift. Ian had given me his credit card, and I was extra careful when I put it back in my wallet. I'd lost more cards and wallets than anyone I knew—no clue how I managed that.

I loved buying presents, and I also loved giving them to people, and lately, I wasn't able to do the latter because I was always away. But this time,

I'd be right there when Ian and Dylan gave their parents the present.

After I left the store, another little shop caught my eye. It sold fabrics. Most of Mom's clothes were made by a seamstress; she loved to stroll through a fabric store choosing her favorite patterns. As a kid we'd always stop and shop in the most random stores until she found exactly what she wanted.

My fashion sense didn't apply to fabrics 100 percent, especially since I wasn't sure what Mom would want to have it sewn into, but I couldn't resist the temptation of going inside.

I perused the shelves and was a bit overwhelmed at the sheer number of choices: floral patterns, solid colors, plaids, and more; every type of fabric imaginable. I could text Mom pics and ask what she'd want, but I'd ruin the surprise.

Ultimately, I chose a burgundy cotton because I knew Mom liked both the color and the fabric and bought enough to make a dress out of it if she wanted to.

I walked out with a grin so huge that my face was hurting. Then I realized I started my shift in fifteen minutes and went into panic mode.

I Ubered to the restaurant, and during my shift, I kept imagining how Mom would react when she received the fabric and how Ian's parents would respond to their present.

I liked his loyalty to his siblings, especially to Dylan and the company they'd built together. And I couldn't believe how seriously he'd taken our conversation about being passionate about what you do. Dylan said I was a good influence on Ian. Ha! Me! I was bursting with pride.

After my shift, I went straight home and changed into a bright red dress with a golden belt and black tights. My hair was all over the place, and I didn't have time to wash it, so I just combed it in a way that gave it lots of volume. It resembled a lion's mane a bit too much for my taste, but I could make it work.

"Roar. You look like a rockstar," Harper said, leaning against the doorway of the bathroom. I wasn't seeing as much of her lately because I was spending quite a few evenings a week at Ian's place, and Harper had practically moved in with her boyfriend.

"It was the only hairstyle I could pull off."

"Girl, you're rocking it. What's with the gift bag next to the front door?"

"The gift is for Ian's parents."

Harper looked at me intently. "And you two are still not serious?"

I shrugged. "We're enjoying each other a lot, but given everything, there's no room for serious."

"Define everything."

"You know. My rotation is over in a few months, and I don't think this will last longer."

"Are you sure?"

My stomach flipped. I didn't want to analyze this too closely, because the truth was, lately, I wasn't sure about anything.

Ian picked me up at six forty-five. He was waiting for me in front of my building, leaning against a black car.

"Hello, gorgeous," he said. He relieved me of the bag, putting it on the back seat before pulling me toward him. He feathered his lips against mine, and just the bare touch was enough to light me up. When he captured my mouth, kissing me hot and heavy, I just melted in his arms. I forgot everything… including the fact that we were out on the street.

Heat coiled through me. I rose on my toes, lacing my arms around his neck, needing to be even closer. I only came to my senses when he groaned. I pulled back, looking to my right and left, giggling.

"Oops… I forgot we were in public," I said. "You, sir, have a dangerous effect on me."

"I'm counting on that."

"Should we get in the car?"

"Nah. I want to kiss you some more." The intensity in his gaze made it clear he wanted to do much more than that.

"Bad idea," I whispered.

"I don't think so." He looked at my mouth until I squirmed against him. With a dimpled smile, he stepped to one side, opening the door for me.

We were to meet at a restaurant on the city's outskirts, which I'd thought was an odd choice until I researched the place and saw how beautiful it was. It was in a greenhouse of sorts. It was completely made of glass, and there were so many plants inside that you felt like you were outdoors, smack dab in the middle of nature.

"Thanks for buying the gift," he said once the car was in motion. I gave him back his credit card before I forgot about it.

"You're welcome. I love buying presents. Even found a store selling fabrics, and I bought some for Mom. I'm going to FedEx it tomorrow."

He looked at me with warm eyes. My heart skipped a beat.

"How come we're not meeting at Isabelle's house? You said she offered," I asked.

"Because my parents are stubborn. We paid for their trip, so they decided to invite us to a restaurant, which is more expensive than if they'd paid for the tickets themselves. I don't know why they're resisting us taking care of them so much."

He sounded exasperated. I just wanted to lean over and give him a hot and wet smooch, but I kept myself in check. Did he know how swoonworthy he sounded when he spoke about taking care of his family?

"Tell me about your parents and everyone else who will be here tonight."

"It's a small group. Us, Dylan and Mel, Josie and Hunter, and Isabelle. Brayden couldn't make it."

He gave me insights into everyone. That Isabelle was a foodie. That Josie loved to have lunch in the park when it was sunny outside. Dylan was addicted to workouts—though Ian wasn't sure if it wasn't just an excuse to spend time with his girlfriend, who was a trainer at the gym. And he thought he didn't notice details? My sexy guy was underselling himself.

When we arrived at the restaurant, I was awed once again by its beauty. It looked even more majestic in real life than in pictures.

I knew Isabelle and Josie, but this was the first time I'd met Dylan. Ian introduced me to Hunter and his parents, Jim and Dora, next. Ian and Dylan both resembled their dad—they had the same tall and strong build, as well as intense eyes.

Isabelle and Josie didn't look too much like their mother, but I was one of those people who didn't see the resemblance in family members unless it was very obvious.

Dora was ecstatic. "Goodness, I couldn't believe it when Dylan told me you were coming with Ellie."

I blushed, looking at Ian. He'd mentioned this dinner so casually that I didn't think it would be a big deal. Dora seemed to think the opposite.

Ian put an arm around my shoulders, glancing at Dylan. "Didn't you say Isabelle was the family informant?"

Dylan grinned, holding his hands up in defense. Isabelle elbowed him playfully.

"Hey! You're bad-mouthing me now?" she asked.

"Me? Never."

I grinned at their banter. Gah! I missed Henry

even more when I was with them. He texted me daily, and we chatted twice a week, but it wasn't the same. In fact, I missed my whole family. I so wished we could all be just a bit closer. I was grateful that my parents weren't warring with each other anymore, but I'd love for us to get together more often.

"When are we giving the presents?" Dylan asked, clearly trying to shift the focus.

Jim and Dora smiled at the group. "Whenever you want. We can do it after the toast, or we can open them right now."

"Let's do it now," Isabelle said. She looked a bit smugly at Dylan and Ian. Right! Sibling rivalry on.

We can win this!

Ian put our present on the table, which didn't only consist of the set I bought. There was also a voucher for a cooking class specializing in barbecuing back in Montana.

They opened the other package first. Everyone was on pins and needles, me included.

Dora took out what looked like a neoprene suit, like one used in Scuba diving, along with a voucher too.

"Mom, you were so happy when I sent you pictures from skydiving on my honeymoon that I knew you had to try it one day. Dad, you'll love it too."

"Oh, this will be wonderful," Dora said.

Jim nodded. "I think so too." He glanced at his sons. "Are you competing again?"

Dylan grimaced. "You knew we were

competing all along?"

"Of course," Dora replied, already opening our package. "We get the best gifts this way."

Ian took my hand, kissing the back of it. Warmth traveled through me. I was so excited!

They opened it together, and Jim clapped his hands, whistling.

"A professional grill set?" He looked straight at me. "The chef is responsible for this, right?"

"Your sons told me about how both of you love barbecuing, and I just gave them my professional opinion."

Ian pulled me closer to him, kissing the side of my head. "Don't downplay your role. She made lists with the stuff you like and then did thorough research."

Dora yelped when she saw the voucher. "We even have a voucher for a class."

They were thrilled. I loved the pure joy on their faces. Josie, Hunter, and Isabelle were on one side of the table. Ian, I, Dylan, and Mel, on the other. The parents were at the head of the table. They looked from one side to the other. I could tell Jim was barely holding back laughter.

"Okay, clearly you want to know who won. But I have to say, you all outdid yourselves. Let's call it a tie."

Everyone—me included—groaned. A tie wasn't a win, but we all laughed as we sat down. As it happened, I was sitting next to Dora, who was very chatty. She asked why I loved being a chef.

"Dangerous question. I can talk about the kitchen all day long," I replied and filled her in on some of the basic things I did at the restaurant.

"Ian said you're very talented and hardworking."

Wow, he'd spoken to his mom about me? I just assumed she knew things from passing remarks.

"I try."

In a softer voice for the two of us to hear, she said, "I'm very happy my son met you. You're everything I'd hoped for him."

"Oh." My stomach twisted. Her smile was so happy that I didn't have the heart to tell her that I was only here for six months. She had that dreamy look on her face that Mom sometimes had when she spoke about me giving her grandchildren.

I sighed. My heart was full of happiness for being here tonight, but also a bit of sadness because this wasn't going to last forever. I wasn't ready to let go of Ian yet. The way he looked at me was enough to make my heart skip a beat and to feel like I was the only thing that mattered to him. I already missed him.

"Tell me more about him," I whispered when Ian was too busy giving Dylan shit over the table to pay attention to me.

"Gladly." Then she hesitated, her face full of joy, saying, "You know, no one's asked me this before. I'm not sure where to start."

"Was he different than your other kids growing up?" I wanted to know *everything*.

"Well, each was different in their own way. Ian was always so protective, even of Dylan. Sometimes I think he just went into business with his brother to keep an eye on him. When he was in college, he talked about teaching a couple of times."

"Oh, wow." I loved this tidbit of information and encouraged her to tell me more. We chatted about him until our food was served, but after that, she turned to Mel, and I stopped with the questions. I didn't want to monopolize Dora, even though she was a wealth of information.

"Why are you so silent?" Ian asked later that evening when we entered my apartment. Harper was spending the night at her boyfriend's, so we had the place to ourselves. The bulb in the entryway was burned out, so it was dark.

"I don't know… just enjoying the evening. I loved being around your family. It makes me miss mine."

"Do you have big family gatherings?"

"Not really, and I'd love something like that. The last time I tried to bring everyone together was at my graduation from culinary school a few years ago. It didn't work out, so only Henry and Mom were there. I've kind of stopped trying ever since. I don't want to force anyone to do something they don't want to, you know? I'd love to have what you and your family have. But if I'm lucky, I'll have it with my own family in the future." I sucked in a breath, realizing how talking about a family and a white picket fence must sound to him, and immediately changed the subject. "Your mom is adorable, by the way. She also seemed to think we're a long-term thing. I didn't have the heart to explain everything."

Ian was suspiciously silent. I cocked my head in his direction but couldn't see his expression in the dark. Did I say something wrong? I didn't mean to upset him. I just didn't want him to be surprised if his mom mentioned something.

He took my hand, kissing the back of it, then just feathering his lips against my skin. "I have an idea. What are you doing next weekend?"

I blinked, a bit thrown by the change of subject.

"I don't have plans. Why?" I looked at him expectantly, trailing my fingers up his sexy biceps.

"Do you want us to go somewhere together? A weekend getaway, just the two of us?"

"Oh my God, are you serious?" I asked with a giggle.

"Very serious." He touched my chin with his fingers. I felt the tips and nails along my lower lip. "I want you to be all mine for a whole weekend."

"And what exactly do you plan to do with me?"

"I haven't made up my mind yet. But first, I'm going to make sure you relax. You've been tense these past two weeks."

"You noticed?" Work had become more

intense because a staff member quit, so I was also moonlighting as a pastry chef. I'd offered to help because I had experience, and then I had a lot on my plate. I felt a bit stretched thin, if I was honest. When I offered, I thought they'd find a pastry chef right away. And my sexy guy could tell! Why did that make me swoon?

"Hell, yes. I notice everything about you." He kissed my upper lip, touching the bow briefly with the tip of his tongue. Heat pooled between my legs. Wow. I had no idea how he could turn me on so fast.

"Is this the reward you were talking about? Because you don't—"

He covered my mouth in a sinful kiss. I tugged at his shirt. When we paused to breathe, I realized I'd slipped a hand under his shirt. Wow. This man made me lose my head.

"No. I just got the idea for the getaway tonight. Now, for that reward, I had something much simpler in mind."

He pushed my pelvis against his hips, and I moaned when I felt his hard-on.

"Unless my body is not rewarding enough?" he teased.

"Oh, yes, it is." I laughed, giving him a quick peck on his chin. "Let me find the switch in the living room so we have a bit of light."

As he let me go, I walked along the wall until I reached the living room and turned on the light.

"Do you have lightbulbs?" Ian asked. "I'll change it."

"Yeah. In the kitchen. I'll get you one." It was high up in a cabinet where we only stored stuff we didn't need daily. Ian had already pulled a chair from the dining table to the foyer when I came with the bulb. He climbed on the chair, removing then replacing the old bulb with the new one. I couldn't believe how easily our lives had intertwined.

"Done," Ian exclaimed, climbing down from the chair.

"Thank you, Mr. Handyman," I said playfully.

"Whatever you need. Just tell me, and it's done."

I need you to stay in my life.

"Ellie?" he prompted, looking at me intently. "What's on your mind?"

Oh gosh, did I say that out loud, or was it the look on my face that made him question me?

I took his hand, walking him into the living room, deciding to open up—to the best of my abilities. It wasn't something that came naturally to me. Would I scare him away? My heart lodged in my throat at that thought. It was possible. But I needed to know.

"I just thought that this all feels so easy. You being here, changing my lightbulb."

He put an arm around my waist and unexpectedly tackled me to the couch. We toppled over, Ian first. I landed on top of him without any grace whatsoever.

"What was that for?" I asked, pinching his chest.

"I wanted you closer."

"You mean on top of you."

"Under me. On top of me. Doesn't matter." He cupped my ass, kissing the side of my neck. "I like being here with you, Ellie."

"I've always kept my feelings close to my chest, even in high school. But something about you just makes me want to open up."

"So I'm special."

I narrowed my eyes. "If I agree, will it go to your head?"

"Absolutely."

"Hmm… but you're an excellent guy, so you deserve to know."

"Thanks for the vote of confidence."

I grinned, shimmying on top of him. "Are you staying over for breakfast tomorrow too?"

"If you want me to."

"Hell, yes. But you usually have client calls in the morning."

"I do, but you can bet your sweet ass I'm gonna postpone them."

My grin was even wider now. He was moving the calls for me! I had a feeling Ian would make me lose more than my head. He'd make me lose my heart too. A vision flashed in my mind of Ian and me in a couple of years. Would we live in his apartment? Or rent another place? I could see him replacing bulbs while I cooked us something delicious.

I swallowed hard. Usually, when I thought about the future, I'd think about my restaurant. This was the first time I saw myself with someone. It surprised me. What surprised me even more was the undeniable longing for that version of the future to come true.

Chapter Thirteen
Ian

One week later, on Friday, I picked up Ellie from Soho, where she was shopping with Isabelle in Tess and Skye's store. We were going to Bear Mountain for our weekend getaway.

My phone beeped with an incoming call on the way. I let it go to speaker.

"Hey, Ian!"

It was Henry.

"Henry! I haven't heard from you in a while."

"Sorry, man. Life at a law firm is crazy. What are you up to?"

"I'm—just wrapping up the week." I almost told him I was picking up Ellie.

"Cool! How is Ellie doing?"

"Damn, and I was so proud of you for only asking that question ten times this week instead of twenty as usual."

"Dude! You can't blame me."

"Actually, I can." I always liked riling up Henry, teasing him for being the most overprotective person I know. Because I knew Ellie better now, of course I understood it. The bullying story at school still made me see red. I could sympathize with Henry.

Dialing down the worry wasn't easy. It wasn't a switch you could just flip on and off.

"She's okay, man. I think she's got a lot more work than usual, but she's enjoying it." There, that wasn't a lie. But I didn't like keeping things from my best friend. I wanted to talk about this with Ellie. The last few times we'd been out we never got around to it—but I was going to talk to her about it over the weekend. Initially I'd been completely on board with her suggestion to keep things on the down low, because it didn't make sense to get his hackles up when we weren't sure what was going on between us. But things were different now. I couldn't be the only one noticing the change. I didn't want to keep lying to my best friend.

"That's good. I was thinking about visiting her, but not sure when."

"Did you ask her when it would be a good time?"

"No, not yet. I'll do that."

"Cool. She'll be happy to see you. Want to go out while you're here?"

"Sure."

We spoke a bit about what we could do. I missed my best friend, and that just added to my guilt.

I knew he wasn't going to be pleased, because he wanted the best for his sister, and I was far from that.

But I wasn't the same guy I was in college. And ever since meeting Ellie, I felt different. I'd never felt as free or as happy as when I was with her. Ellie unlocked a side of me I hadn't been aware of.

When I arrived in Soho, I parked and sat in an ice cream shop opposite Soho Lingerie, watching them through the window display. I only saw Ellie's back. She was with Skye in front of a rack of merchandise. I was pleased with how well she fit in with my family and friends. I remembered how much she enjoyed herself at the dinner with my parents. She didn't just exchange pleasantries. I heard her ask Mom about herself and then details of my childhood. She wanted to know stuff about me that no one ever did. I'd never had that in my life. Well to be honest, I never gave any other woman the chance because the interest on my part wasn't there. But with Ellie, it *so* was.

I looked at her intently, and when she finally looked over her shoulder, she smiled instantly when she saw me. Then she took out her phone, and a few seconds later, I got a message.

Ellie: I'm going to wrap this up quickly. I've bought too much stuff.

Ian: I can't wait for you to model everything for me.

Ellie: You wish.

Ian: Oh, I do, and I'll make it happen.

Ellie: Bossy, huh?

Ian: Bossy doesn't even begin to cover it.

***

Ellie

It was love at first sight with Tess and Skye Winchester. There was just no other way to describe it. I was so happy Isabelle called me before going there. The girls were a hoot. I liked their sense of humor and their designs. They had a great sale section.

"I can't believe you have so much stuff on sale," I said. The store was elegant and sensual but not overtly sexy. It was decorated in shades of gold, dark green, and terracotta that matched the neighborhood's vibe nicely. Between the cobblestone streets and the old buildings, Soho made me think of something out of the past.

"Well, we like to offer something for everyone," Tess explained. "Our stuff is a bit pricey, so we know that not everyone can afford to buy it when it comes out, and as soon as it becomes last year's items, we put it on sale. All except for our bestsellers."

"And I love your maternity collection," Isabelle said, rubbing her growing belly.

"Yeah. It took a while to come up with it," Skye said. "I have to be honest, before I had my son, neither of us had experience with the way a body changes and what it needs, and well, once you go through it, you know what you need and what you wish you found in lingerie stores."

"So you and Ian are going to Bear Mountain, huh?" Tess said. "I always knew Ian would change the tune he was singing once he found the right one."

Skye nodded, but Isabelle shook her head. "I wasn't so hopeful, honestly. He's always seemed like an eternal bachelor. He's so different since he met you," she added, nudging me.

My heart was a bit heavy. The way they spoke made me think of dangerous things like if Ian and I could have a future together. I shoved the thoughts to the back of my head in the box titled "Dreams." I was super happy, enjoying what we had now, even though he'd raised the bar so high that I wasn't sure how I'd feel without him. I mean, the man was whisking me away for a weekend, giving me foot rubs, and seemed determined to make me swoon nonstop.

I brought everything I wanted to the table where the cash register was. I couldn't stop touching the set of lacy panties I was buying. I had also purchased a garter belt. I didn't know when I'd wear it, but the opportunity would present itself eventually. I was sure of it.

"Ellie, you're set," Skye said, packing up everything with love in pink paper. "Feel free to drop by at any time."

"Oh, I will," I promised them. "I like you girls."

Tess smiled from ear to ear. "I'm happy to hear that. We were dying to meet you ever since Isabelle told us about you."

I glanced at Isabelle next to me, who seemed very proud to live up to the informant status in the

Gallagher family. "Hey, I like bragging about my siblings."

I was giddy with happiness. I felt a warmth I'd never had with my family. It felt good to have a group of girls to chat with and do stuff like shop together. I was going to miss all this when I went away.

I glanced over my shoulder through the window display while I paid. I had a direct view of Ian in the ice cream shop. To my surprise, he was already waiting in front of Soho Lingerie. After saying goodbye to the girls, I sashayed out of the store with a sway in my hips.

He looked at the bag in my hand and cocked a brow. "That doesn't look like a lot of outfits," he said.

"It's lingerie. It's small."

"Tell me what you bought," he said, putting an arm around my shoulders and walking me down the street. "I didn't park far away."

"Well, I could tell you, but I thought you had a better idea before."

"So I don't even have to convince you to model it?"

"Oh, that's right. I was trying to play hard to get. Damn. I forgot that was my tactic."

He kissed the side of my head, laughing wholeheartedly. "Are you excited?"

"Yes, very. I can't even feel my feet. Or my shoulders." I was still moonlighting as pastry and pantry chef.

"I'll make sure you're relaxed this weekend," he said.

"Funny. I have the same goal, to make sure *you* are relaxing."

I loved thinking about ways to make him happy. Once we were in the car, I began Operation Taking Care Of Ian by giving him chaste kisses on the cheek and the neck.

"Ellie, what are you doing?" he asked.

"I'm starting the weekend and the process of relaxing you." I kissed the point where his jaw met his neck, and he groaned. I pulled back. Okay, so maybe my kisses weren't that chaste. "Okay. I'm just going to stay super still. I don't trust my fingers or my mouth," I said.

He just laughed, shaking his head.

"This car is so fancy," I said, touching the leather seats. I hadn't been inside it since he drove me from the airport.

"I was thinking about selling it and just renting something when I go out of the city but changed my mind after Isabelle moved to Tarrytown. It's useful, though I hate driving in Manhattan."

We dropped by my place first to pick up my bag, and then we went to his. His condo was on the Upper East Side, and he parked the car on the street at the back of his building.

"I'll be right back," he said.

I eyed a food cart a few feet away. "I'm going to buy some provisions for the road."

"The drive is an hour and a half."

"Hey, never stand between me and food."

"Duly noted." He winked before heading to the building. I jogged to the food cart. It sold sandwiches that looked yummy.

"I'll have one with beef and one with chicken. Please put a lot of lettuce in it as well." The lettuce looked freshly chopped, as did the tomatoes, cucumbers, and herbs. It was going to pop in my mouth. I could almost taste all the flavors.

The prep took some time because the guy serving it, Johnny, wasn't moving too fast, but that was okay. Perfection couldn't be rushed.

"Are you done?" Ian asked, surprising me, kissing the side of my neck. I broke out in goose bumps.

"Not yet. He's going to heat the sandwiches too. I'll come to the car afterward."

"Sure." He kissed my neck again.

I nudged him playfully with my elbow. "Hey, we said we'll keep our hands to ourselves."

"No, you said that you had to do that, not me," he whispered against my neck. I didn't just have goose bumps on my arms now. I also had them on my legs and my intimate area.

"Hey, go to the car," I said.

He wiggled his eyebrows but let go of me, wheeling his small suitcase to the car. I turned to look at the food truck.

While I was waiting, another customer showed up, a beautiful blonde who seemed to look funny at me. She ordered a sandwich with beef jerky too.

"Was that Ian?" she asked out of nowhere.

I blinked. "Yes. You know him?"

“I live in the building next door. We met while jogging. Fucked a couple of times too."

Johnny straightened up.

My eyes bulged. "You just broadcast that information to everyone?"

"No, but you two seemed very cozy. I thought you deserved a warning."

"About what, exactly?" I crossed my arms over my chest, looking her straight in the eyes, pulling myself to my full height.

"Ian is just Ian. He's not serious about anything or anyone."

I held up a palm in front of her face. "Stop right there. I'm not interested in any of this."

"Are you sure? By the way you're getting all riled up, I'd say that you're pretty deep into this.” She flailed a hand toward Ian’s car “A word of caution. Don't get involved."

How dare she? Maybe she was trying to warn me, but it was coming across hateful to me. "What I do is none of your business."

"Leah," Ian greeted, coming up behind me. He put an arm around my waist.

"Ian," she said with a nod, still looking at us funny.

"Are the sandwiches ready?" he asked me.

"Yes, they are," Johnny answered, wrapping

them up in a plastic bag and handing them to me, looking between Leah and me with a strained expression. Poor guy. I was betting he didn't hear conversations like this often.

"Okay, so we're done then, right?" Ian said. He seemed oblivious to the fact that Leah was glaring at us. "Bye, Leah," he said just before we walked to the car.

We ate in silence in the car. I was still thinking about Leah.

Ian might not have realized in front of the cart that something was off, but it sure took him less than ten minutes to realize it in the car.

"Ellie, is something not okay? You're too silent," Ian said after we ate.

"You really didn't see it, did you?"

"What?" He honestly looked unaware.

"The way she was looking at us."

"She? Who? Oh, Leah? What do you mean?"

I sighed, shaking my head. "She was sort of warning me off you before you came over."

Ian clasped his hands tight around the wheel. "She what? Why?"

"She also informed me that you slept with her."

"We had some fun a while back, like two years ago, but I was upfront about it. She brought that up?" He looked stunned. "Why would she do that?"

"I'm going to go out on a limb and say that she's still holding a grudge, but it doesn't matter."

"Yes, it does. It's affecting you." And right

there, I knew he wasn't hiding anything. Instead, he cared about me and how I felt. Honesty was a biggie for me, maybe because my family didn't have a lot of it to go around.

"It's not, Ian," I said in a reassuring tone. "It's okay. I was just ambushed, that's all."

"Look, I can explain everything. There's just not much to it."

"You don't have to. I'm not judging you for your past. That would be ridiculous. Let's just enjoy this afternoon and think about all the things we are going to do around Bear Mountain State Park."

"I want to tell you anyway. I don't want any secrets or barriers between us. Before you, I just dated casually. Very casually. I'd call it hookups more than dating, but I was always honest about what I was looking for. I don't make false promises, and I don't lie to anyone."

"Okay. Thanks for sharing that with me."

Even after Ian explained to me his past dating habits, it would be untruthful to say the encounter didn't dampen my mood. Which was so ridiculous. The past didn't matter. It didn't belong to us, just as the future didn't either. What Ian and I had was for now. It was amazing, and I was going to enjoy every second of it.

Be careful, Ellie... you're falling fast.

Chapter Fourteen
Ian

"This place is amazing," Ellie exclaimed when we entered the hotel suite. It was spacious, with a living room, a bedroom, and a balcony that overlooked the thick forest of Bear Mountain State Park.

I kissed the back of her hand.

"I'm glad you like it."

She nodded, looking around. I wanted to make sure she was all right after the run-in with Leah. I hated that my past was thrown in her face like that. Even though I explained my dating MO, I still felt as though something was off. No matter what Ellie said, it affected her, and I wanted to rectify that.

"Ellie, talk to me. You're still thinking about Leah?"

She bit her lip, shaking her head. "No. Look. I'm not paying attention to that. Let's just enjoy the weekend."

"Are you sure we're good?"

She nodded vigorously. "I'm not going to let anyone spoil our weekend. I mean, look at this beautiful room and the forest outside. Do you think I'm going to think about anything except this? Well, maybe you."

I chuckled. "Thanks for including me."

Her smile was the size of Texas now. It filled me with immense pleasure that I'd brought it on. I had this incessant need to see her happy.

Scratch that.

To *make* her happy. Ellie kissed one corner of my mouth before moving to the other one. I pulled her hips flat against me, running my palms down her ass cheeks.

"Hmm… I see someone doesn't even want to leave the hotel room," she said.

"Yes, I do. But only after I have my fill of you."

"It's a good thing we had that snack on the road."

Thank fuck we were already inside the room, because I wanted her so much that I would've made a spectacle of us outside. I touched her cheek, skimming my fingers from her jaw up to her ear, then covering that same trail with my mouth. The kisses were meant to be reassuring, but soon enough, I was craving *her*. I wanted more. I tried to make her mine.

"Ellie," I whispered, "I want you." She clasped my wrist, saying nothing. But by the way her fingers dug in my hand, I knew she wanted me just as badly. Pulling back, she looked around with a curious smile. I hooked an arm around her waist, pulling her flush against me, murmuring in her ear, "Tour later."

My voice was almost a growl. I couldn't even think straight. That's how much I wanted her.

She looked at me sideways, a smile playing on her lips. "Oh, really? Why do I think I'm about to get the tour of the bedroom anyway?"

"Not the bedroom," I said in her ear, "just the bed. You'll be *very* intimately acquainted with the bed. I promise you that." Goose bumps broke out on her skin. Fuck, this woman was going to kill me. How could she be so responsive to what I said?

"I'm going to guess it's in that direction," she said, pointing to the only door leading out of the suite's living room.

She looked at me, flashing me a cheeky smile, then darted to the room. What was she playing at? I followed her, feeling curious. She turned on the light, and first headed to the luggage. The hotel staff put it next to the bed. She took out her toiletry bag, putting it on the nightstand before going all the way to the corner opposite the bed.

"I want to take off my clothes myself. You sit on the bed," she said, "and just watch."

I tilted my head to the right, narrowing my eyes. I sat on the bed saying nothing, just watching her. She swallowed hard, shimmying a little.

"Well?" she asked, sounding a bit uncertain.

"We play by your rules until you're naked, Ellie. Then we'll play by mine, and you'll do everything I tell you, understood?"

Her eyes widened. She nodded, breathless. I sat at the edge of the bed, watching her slide her hands underneath her dress. I didn't realize what she was doing first. Then I saw that she was lowering her tights. And when they reached midthigh, she pulled her dress farther up, turning slightly, so I had a full view of her ass while she pushed her tights down her legs slowly, taking them off. I groaned. Her ass was just perfection in those thongs that only covered her crack and her pussy but left the buttocks completely uncovered.

Then she took off her dress, silently tossing it on the floor. She had a matching black bra and panties made of silk, and I needed to touch her. I craved to feel her skin under my hand and my mouth. I tugged at the sheet. A low groan reverberated from my throat. A satisfied smile played on her lips. Ellie was playing a game, wasn't she? I'd show her just how well I could play it too. She touched the fabric of her panties and her bra, drawing her forefinger up one strap and then the other, clearly meaning to tease me. But I knew just what was going to make her speed up the process. Standing up, I took off my own clothes, and I sure as fuck didn't take my time with it. I got rid of everything in a matter of seconds. Her eyes widened. Her cheeks were red. She didn't say anything. I sat back on the bed, thighs spread wide, gripping my cock.

"Ian," she whispered, eyes even wider, clenching her thighs together.

My tactic was a double-edged sword, because the second I gripped my erection, I knew that I needed her even more badly. I moved my hand up and down slowly, watching her. She looked at me, transfixed. Her hand was shaking slightly when she unclasped her bra. It fell to the floor, revealing her gorgeous breasts.

"Come closer, Ellie," I said, and she didn't disagree. I knew she was ready to play by my rules. She was ready to surrender to me. She walked slowly, hooking her thumb in the elastic of her panties, pushing those down her legs as well. They were almost at her knees. She stood in front of me, and I yanked them down all the way to the floor. I couldn't help myself. I leaned forward, darting my tongue out, licking along her opening. She gasped, bucking forward. Her legs shook.

I cupped both her ass cheeks with my hand, keeping her steady.

"Wait," she said, with a trembling voice, "I have a condom in my toiletry bag." Her legs were shaky as she moved to the nightstand, rummaging in the bag, and came back with a condom. I looked straight at her when she ripped off the foil and then kneeled before me, sliding it on. I took in a deep breath, gritting my teeth. This was the first time she'd touched me since she entered the bedroom, and I was already on edge. She rose to her feet, watching me intently.

"My rules now, Ellie," I said, right before pulling her in my lap. She did as I said, straddling me. She rubbed herself against my cock. The sight was insanely sexy. "Come on, ride me," I said. She took me in, lowering herself on my erection.

She wanted to go fast, but I gripped her hips.

"Slower," I commanded.

"I don't think I can be slow," she murmured.

"You will. My rules, remember?"

Her eyes flared, but she didn't try to move faster than I was allowing her to, sliding down inch by inch.

"Ohhhh." Her voice shook, and so did her body.

"That's it, up and down. Slowly, beautiful, so that I can watch you."

She closed her eyes, bracing her palms on my shoulders as she pushed herself up and down, up and down. I was completely crazy for this woman, for the way we completed each other. She liked to tease me and turn me on, but she wanted to surrender to me too, to give me control in the bedroom. I only lasted a few minutes before I flipped her around so that she was on her back on the bed and I was over her. I was kneeling on the bed, driving inside her.

When she tried to touch her clit, I swatted her hand away, "No, that's mine. You're only allowed to touch yourself when I tell you to." Her eyes flared again. "If I tell you to."

She swallowed hard, moving her hands up to her nipples, circling them. Fuck, she was driving me crazy.

"I want you to touch me everywhere," she said. Leaning over, I took her nipple in my mouth, obliging her. I wanted her to have all the pleasure in the world, but drip by drip, in a crescendo mode that would bring her the most intense orgasm. I moved to the other nipple, sucking it too, driving inside her faster and faster, and I could already feel her coming. She was tightening her inner muscles, but I wasn't going to give her the release so quickly. I wanted to take her a notch higher. Pulling back, I stilled inside her, feeling her tightness around me. When I pulled out, she opened her eyes wide, gasping.

"Turn around," I told her. She did just as I said, no questions asked, no hesitation. She trusted me to do to her everything I wanted, and that turned me on more than anything else. She looked at me over her shoulder as I positioned my cock between her spread thighs and gasped when I slid inside. Somehow in the past few seconds, she'd grown even tighter.

"Ellie, fuck," I whispered. "Just like that."

She spasmed around me as I slid inside until I was all the way in. Her buttocks pressed against my thighs. She panted, barely able to breathe from pleasure. She stretched her arms along the bed, digging her fingers in the pillow. I kissed her upper back and her cheek. Her face was sideways, eyes pinched closed, and she was flushed. Her face was so tight, as if this was too much pleasure to bear. When I knew she really couldn't take anymore, I slid my fingers between her and the mattress.

She came the second I touched her clit. She was so beautiful. I wanted to memorize every detail about this moment—the way her neck arched and her mouth opened wide as she cried out my name. I tried to stave off my orgasm so I could give her a second one, but she clenched so tight that I couldn't hold back any longer. I buried my hand in her hair and my mouth in the crook of her neck as I came, shuddering, and convulsing, and nearly blacking out from the pleasure.

"You're amazing," I whispered in her ear, and she gave me a sated smile.

We stayed in bed for over an hour.

"You'd be a happy man just spending the whole weekend lying down and ordering room service, huh?" she asked.

With Ellie? Yes. But never before her.

"Guilty as charged." I turned toward her, caressing her cheek. "But I know that you need to be more active to relax."

Her eyes widened. "How do you know that?"

"You go out walking the city every morning."

She smiled sheepishly, hiding half her face in the pillow. "Well, I want to make the most of my time in New York, so I'm going to explore it whenever I get a chance."

The reminder of her departure felt like a punch to the gut. I moved closer to her, touching her shoulder, skimming my hand over her waist. The connection I felt to her went deeper than a fling. I knew it in my bones. Could she feel it?

"What do you want to do this weekend?" I asked.

"Enjoy walks around the area, and there are some restaurants we could check out. What do you want to do?"

"You know me. I'm flexible."

She wiggled her eyebrows. "Except when in bed. Bossy man."

I pinched her ass cheek. "You have anything against it?"

"Oh, no. It wasn't a critique. Just an observation. By all means, keep doing it. I love it."

She pressed her pussy against my cock, moving one hand up my shoulder.

I groaned, rocking back and forth. "Let's get out of bed, Ellie. Or we're not going to leave it at all today."

"That's starting to sound more and more appealing."

"Ellie. Shower."

"Bossy again. I like it."

We showered and dressed quickly. Ellie was ready before me. When I joined her in the living room, she was at the window, looking out at the forest. The dress she was wearing… damn. It was short and black, molding to her curves. It dipped in a V down her back, looking so sinful that I wanted to yank it away. I stepped right behind her, trailing my fingers down the exposed skin. She gasped, arching forward.

"Ellie, fuck, what is this?"

"Just a dress," she whispered.

"It's not just a dress." I pushed her hair to one side, touching her earlobe with my mouth. "You're so fucking beautiful that I don't even want to share you with the world."

"Mission accomplished." Her voice was throaty. I put both arms around her waist, keeping her close, resting my chin on the soft skin between her shoulder and neck.

"You like teasing me?" I demanded to know.

"Just a little bit. I like how you look at me when I'm wearing something pretty. Like you can't wait to get me alone."

"Spoiler. I'm always looking forward to being with you."

It was true on a deeper level than I knew how to put in words. It was funny how I could explain complex software algorithms to clients, but when it came to what I felt for Ellie, I was out of my depth.

All I knew was that before she came to the city, I filled my weekends and evenings with stuff to pass the time. None of that had made me happy. But Ellie did. I was looking forward to seeing her during every free moment.

She turned around, tilting her head playfully. "What's going through your mind? You've got a few sexy frown lines."

"Sexy?"

A grin etched on her face. "I can't explain it, but they add to your sex appeal. Not that you need help in that department. It was through the roof before anyway."

"Is that so?"

She skimmed a hand up my arm, squeezing my bicep between her thumb and forefinger. "I noticed these on the first day when you helped me with my luggage."

"Go on."

She moved her other hand down the side of my torso. I thought she'd go for the abs, but instead, she squeezed my butt. "And that right there is the stuff of dreams. As is this." She wiggled against my cock, and it took all my control not to pin her against the window. "But still, a frown is a frown. What gives?"

"I have a lot on my mind."

"Care to elaborate? If I don't know, I can't take your mind off it."

"I talked to Henry today, and it got me thinking. I don't like keeping things from him." I looked at her intently, waiting for her reaction. She bit her lower lip. Did she want us to continue being a secret? I wasn't sure how I'd react if she did. I'd respect her choice, of course, because Henry was her brother, but I wouldn't be happy.

"I don't like it either. And I think that if we explain well, maybe he won't… you know. Be Henry. In the beginning, I thought that this would…" Her voice trailed.

"Would what?" I pressed.

"Don't make me say it." The corners of her mouth inched upward. She was holding back laughter. The tension between my shoulder blades faded.

"Ellie. I'm going to get it out of you, one way or the other."

"I have no doubt. I just thought that we'd have a fling or that you'd get spooked about me being a virgin—"

I cupped her face, looking her straight in the eyes. "Ellie, nothing would scare me away, do you understand? Nothing. And you're not a fling. You're important to me."

She didn't say anything, and I didn't push because I suspected I wasn't the only one who was treading on uncharted territory here.

"I'd love to tell him in person. I am so much better at toning down his brotherly instincts face-to-face."

"He said he wants to visit you."

Her eyes lit up. "Really? He didn't say anything to me. We could tell him when he's in the city."

"Perfect. We'll do it together."

"Uhh… no," she replied in a sarcastic tone, like I couldn't possibly be serious. "We don't want him throttling you. I have to prepare him."

"I know Henry. He's my best friend."

"Yeah… but you haven't banged his sister until now."

I burst out laughing before kissing her deep and wet until she shuddered in my arms. She looked at me with wide eyes, smiling brightly when I pulled back.

"Come on, let's go downstairs to the restaurant. I'm hungry."

"I bet you are, after that sexy *workout* from

earlier."

I laughed, pinching her ass. She yelped, nudging me with her shoulder.

"Maybe Henry will come for my birthday," she said as we left the room.

"When is it?"

"In three weeks."

"Why didn't you tell me?"

She looked over her shoulder, shrugging. "I never make a big deal out of it."

She seemed to love it here, so I could always bring her back. Nah, that was a lousy idea. I wanted to do something new that would make her happy. The good thing was, I had enough time to come up with something.

"Want us to stay out on the balcony for a while before we go to dinner?" she asked.

"Sure."

When I opened the french doors, she leaned against the railing, looking down. I gripped one of her arms tightly with my hand.

She looked at me over her shoulder with a wry smile. "Afraid I'll fall? We're only on the second floor."

I let her go, shrugging. "Sorry. Reflex."

Straightening up, she turned to me. "What do you mean?"

"When Dylan and I were kids, we liked to go rock climbing a lot. Nothing professional, just two kids thinking they're unbreakable. Anyway, one time he slipped from a rock. We were on the edge of a steep mountain. It was the scariest moment of my life. I managed to grab him, but since then I have a healthy fear of heights and going too close to the edges."

Ellie jutted out her lower lip, placing her hands on my shoulders. "Sorry to hear about that. Thank God nothing happened. I promise I won't look down again."

I laughed, kissing her forehead. "You can look all you want, Ellie. I'll rein in my reflexes."

"Please don't, because they're sinfully sexy." She winked at me before turning around. I curved an arm around her waist, and she shimmied against my cock, making me groan. I kissed up and down the side of her neck, enjoying the smoothness of her skin and her floral perfume. I was still thinking about her birthday, slightly annoyed that she hadn't mentioned it. Did she think I didn't care about her birthday? I didn't like this, and I wanted to prove to her that I was different, that I did care.

Ellie was special to me, and she needed to know it.

Chapter Fifteen
Ian

When I had a goal, I didn't stop until I reached it—even better, until I surpassed it. My current goal was to do something for Ellie's birthday that she'd really enjoy.

It was no easy feat, especially given my record with bad gifts. I wanted to surprise her, so my task was doubly hard because I couldn't ask her what she wanted or what she liked. After we came back from Bear Mountain State Park, I thought intently about it for a week, but I wasn't making progress.

I wasn't too proud to admit I needed help. I thought about asking Henry and almost pressed his number but disconnected before it went through. He'd get suspicious if I asked him; dude knew me too well.

Tapping my finger against the armrests of the gaming chair in my office, I debated my next step. There was only one way to do this. I called Isabelle. She knew me well too, but I could use that to my advantage. My sister answered right away.

"Hey, I need a favor," I said.

"Shoot."

"It's about Ellie."

"Ian, be careful with her, okay? You two are spending a lot of time together. Don't hurt her."

I frowned, starting to get pissed. Why did she expect that? Did everyone expect that, including Ellie? I didn't like the thought that she might be waiting for the other shoe to drop.

"I'll pretend you didn't just say that. Her birthday is in a couple of weeks, and I want to do something for her that she'll like."

"Holy shit! I take back everything I said!" my sister exclaimed.

"And apologize," I added.

"I wouldn't take it that far."

"Just find out what she'd like to do, *please.*"

"Why don't you just ask her?"

"Because I want to surprise her."

"Yes, but you can ask her casually. Like, *Oh, what do you usually do on your birthday?* Or *what were your favorite birthdays until now?* Or *is there something you want to do that you've never done before*?"

I leaned back in my chair, considering this. "That could work, but I think the surprise will be bigger if she doesn't know that I know what she likes."

There was a long pause before Isabelle spoke. "Brother, I can't believe you're finally showing signs of being romantic."

"I just want to surprise her," I said.

"You know, when we were kids, I always thought you were adopted," she said out of nowhere.

I burst out laughing. "Isabelle!"

"I mean it. I even asked Mom about it. Couldn't understand why you were so different from Dylan and me."

"You what? Well, I'm sure she told you I'm her favorite."

"You wish. And by the way, you didn't flinch when I called you romantic."

"How do you know? You can't even see me."

"No, but I can hear it in your voice."

"Isabelle, are you going to help me or not?"

"Yes, I'm on it, but first, I want to know some things."

"Sure."

"Where do you see yourself in five years?"

I straightened in my chair. "I'm sorry, is this a job interview and I wasn't aware?"

"I mean it. Just answer me."

"I don't know. Dylan and I will likely double the revenue, and—"

"In your *private* life."

I frowned at my computer, pondering this. I'd never asked myself this question. Was this something people actively thought about? It seemed a bit farfetched, but I didn't want to hurt Isabelle's feelings by telling her that. I just couldn't see the point of this. Some things were out of one's control—even mine.

"You know what, you don't even have to tell me. But think about it."

"Fine, I will. When are you speaking to Ellie?"

"I'll put on my detective hat, and I'll find out

everything you need to know."

I groaned, looking out the window. "Now that you say it, maybe I should have put Josie on this."

"Why?" My sister sounded shocked, so maybe there was something to be said about interpreting the tone of voice.

"Because you have as much tact as I do."

My sister laughed. "I'd get mad if you weren't right. But I have refined my technique over the years, you know?"

"Maybe you can take Josie with you when you go on your detective mission."

"Now you're pushing it, but if it makes you feel better, I will."

"Thanks, Isabelle."

Ellie was important to me, and I didn't want her to have any doubt about it.

I worked two hours purely on coding, and then I did something I hadn't in years. I checked the page of the local high school for teaching jobs. In college, I'd thought seriously about teaching but then changed gears. For the first time, I wondered if I could do both. I didn't think teaching in a school was compatible with running the company, but an idea was shaping up in my mind. I wouldn't need to be there physically to teach. That was one of the reasons I liked coding. I didn't even have to leave the room to do the job. I could set up a platform online that taught coding. I couldn't wait to tell Ellie my idea.

That evening, I got a pleasant surprise when Tess, Ryker, and Skye asked me to have dinner with them at Dumont's—one of the restaurants owned by Skye's husband. The Winchesters were Hunter's cousins, so I saw them at common events, but it had been a while since we'd gone out in an impromptu get-together. All the Winchesters were married or engaged, and some even had kids. That made spontaneous meetings difficult, but the three of them were in Manhattan at one of the Dumont restaurants.

Skye: Can you bring Ellie too?

Ian: She's working late today.

When I got there, Tess, Ryker, and Skye were sitting at a small table in the back, already eating fresh bread with something that looked like cheese spread.

"Hey, Ian. Long time no see," Tess said.

"I was waiting for Ellie in front of your store last week," I said, calling her out on her claim.

"We saw but didn't want to disturb you two," Tess explained.

"How come you guys are having dinner in the city?" I asked.

"Rob asked us to taste some of the new menu items he's added," Skye said.

"So that's why you wanted me to bring Ellie."

Tess winked at me. "That, and so we could spend time with her."

"So, where is the rest of the gang?" I asked.

"Rob is in the kitchen. Cole and Laney are in Rome. Liam is caught in a meeting, though he might join us later. And no other Gallagher had time for us.

In their defense, it was a spur-of-the-moment thing. Rob wanted our opinion before he discussed the menu with his team tomorrow."

"I'm no expert in food, but I like to eat, so I'll give my honest opinion," Ryker said.

"Well, none of us are experts, just foodies," Tess said. She and Skye owned two lingerie shops in the city and had a huge online business, and Ryker worked on Wall Street.

"Why couldn't Ellie come?" Tess asked.

"They're doing some personnel changes, so she's covering for others too. It started a few weeks ago. They're overworking her, and I don't like it."

Tess's eyes bulged. Skye opened her mouth to say something but closed it again. The two sisters eyed each other.

"Is it just me, or does he sound overprotective?" Tess asked. "I've only ever heard him speak like this about Josie and Isabelle."

"It's not just overprotective. He sounds like he cares for her," Skye added thoughtfully.

Ryker cocked a brow. "Why are you talking about him in the third person?"

"I'd like to know too," I said.

Skye and Tess flashed identical grins.

"Sorry, we're just surprised," Skye said. "We heard she was *just* your best friend's younger sister."

"We're behind on the news," Tess said seriously.

"What are you talking about? You met her last week and asked me to bring her here, so you know

I'm dating her."

Tess held up a finger. "Exactly. Dating. But this is more than that. You almost sound… in love."

She was grinning again. I frowned, shaking my head.

"Ellie is on a rotational program. She's got everything mapped out. I can't ask her to change her plans for me."

I didn't sound convincing even to my own ears because I wanted to do just that.

"Okay, enough psychoanalysis for one evening. We're here to eat," Ryker said. Just as I was about to thank him for having my back, he added, "But if Tess and Skye are even remotely right, do yourself a favor and do something about it."

So much for having my back.

Tess narrowed her eyes at Ryker. "When are we only *remotely* right?"

Ryker held up his hands in defense. "Just a figure of speech. But I'm serious. Let's focus on dinner."

To my astonishment, they didn't bring up Ellie for the rest of the evening, but she was on my mind the whole time. When I was with her, I felt such deep happiness that I hadn't even been aware existed. I didn't know if I could go back to the way things were after Ellie left.

We ate the whole menu in forty-five minutes. I liked everything, which I knew wasn't too helpful for Rob. He needed detailed feedback.

"Well, I think that's the best we can do," Skye

said, kissing Rob's cheek. He'd come to the table to interrogate us after we tasted the dessert.

"I'm not a detail-oriented guy, man. Sorry," I added.

"No, this is good. I just wanted an opinion, not a critique." Turning to Skye, he asked, "Want to go home?"

"Yes. Mom said Jonas is sleeping already, but I want to give him a smooch anyway."

"I'll go too," Ryker said. "I don't like leaving Heather alone with the kids in the evening. They have a wild streak before going to bed."

As we finished our drinks, I took out my phone, messaging Ellie.

Ian: Shift over?

Ellie: Yes. Just got home. I can't even feel my feet. And I'm starving. Maria's out of empanadas, and the pizza shop only had the salami option left.

Ian: I'm at Dumont's. I'll bring you something. Want a menu?

Instead of a text reply, Ellie sent me a picture. She was grinning from ear to ear, holding her thumb in an okay sign. It made me laugh.

Ian: Judging by your enthusiasm, that's a yes. I'll be there in half an hour.

Ellie: Harper's sleeping at her boyfriends'. I'll be waiting naked.

Ian: Fucking hell, woman. Why are you tempting me like this? Want me to forget dinner?

Ellie: Oh, no. It was just an incentive so

you get here faster.

I grinned, pocketing my phone before I forgot my head. I ordered food to go as the party split up.

I arrived at her place in twenty-five minutes and knocked at the door. Ellie opened the next moment, wide-eyed, flushed—and still dressed.

I cocked a brow. "What was that about waiting for me naked?"

She blew a strand of hair from her eyes. "You're early."

"Five minutes."

"I didn't even shower."

Wiggling my eyebrows, I stepped inside. "We can do it together."

She was cute as hell all worked up like this. I dangled the bag of food in front of her. She licked her lips and immediately grabbed it, heading to the kitchen. I laughed, following her.

"Already forgot about the shower and everything else, huh?"

She looked at me over her shoulder, smiling sheepishly. "Food trumps everything. Thanks so much for bringing this. Tell me about your day while I eat."

She stood at the kitchen counter, eating directly out of the takeout box while I went through my day.

"I also looked up teaching jobs on a whim. It was something I liked when I was in college. A few times I worked as a teacher's aide helping students after hours, and I enjoyed watching them understand the process."

Ellie looked up in surprise. "Your mom said that she always thought you'd go into teaching."

I jerked my head back. "She did?"

A smile spread on her face. "Did you find anything interesting?"

"Nah, no openings, but then I realized I wouldn't have time for physical teaching, you know, like being in a classroom, but I have a few ideas about how to do it remotely."

"Tell me."

Her curiosity lit *me* up. She was genuinely interested.

"I could design online courses that people with all skill levels could access. I don't have a detailed outline. I only thought about it today."

"It sounds cool."

It felt good to share this with her. I looked forward to talking to Ellie in the evening every day. When we didn't meet, we spoke on the phone. I couldn't keep my hands off her, so while she washed her hands at the sink, I skimmed mine up the sides of her body, pressing my pelvis against her ass. Pushing her hair to one side, I kissed the back of her neck. She sighed softly. Goose bumps popped on her arms. I'd miss these quiet evenings when she left. I'd miss *her*.

Before, I'd never understood why Dylan, Isabelle, and the Winchesters were in a hurry to go home to their partner whenever we were out, but I had learned, and I wasn't ready to give this up.

Chapter Sixteen
Ellie

Going out to brunch on Saturday was practically a rule in New York. Josie and Isabelle asked me if I was in the mood a few days ago, and I'd jumped at the opportunity to hang out with them.

I was smiling from ear to ear as I stepped out of my building. It was a glorious day near the end of October. It was cold, but the sun felt warm on my face. New York looked magical with all the trees in shades of red and yellow and brown. I was meeting them at a restaurant in Riverside Park. On the way, I called my brother. I planned to walk the whole way, even though it would take forty minutes. Maybe I'd Uber back, but for now, I wanted to stretch my legs.

"Hey, sister!" he answered.

"Hey, hope I'm not waking you up?"

"Ah, just a bit. You know how I am on Saturdays."

Oh, I did. I always woke up early, and when I was very young, I'd make a lot of noise on purpose. I was a little devil. As I got older, I prepared breakfast for him. My first attempts were inedible, but he encouraged me to keep experimenting like a good older brother.

By the time my parents divorced, my cooking was already great, so I tried cheering Mom up every Saturday and Sunday with cakes, pies, and omelets. Sadly, I wasn't too successful. She seemed so lost in her grief for a few years, and nothing I did helped.

"Since I moved to New York, I'm quite enjoying the mornings. The city is quieter, and I get so much more done."

"What are you doing today?" he asked.

"I'm meeting Josie and Isabelle for brunch."

"Ian's sisters?"

"Yes, we're getting quite close."

"I was about to say that you always do something with them. What did he do, pawn you off on his sisters?"

"No!" I said defensively. "He checks in regularly." I blushed and was thankful that we weren't using FaceTime for this call, because my brother never missed a facial expression.

"That's good to know. I'll call him and thank him."

"I've heard you want to visit me."

"Yes—wait, Ian told you that?"

I winced. If I wasn't careful, he'd put two and two together. I didn't want to keep things from him anymore, so I hoped he'd come soon.

The only reason I wasn't telling him over the phone was because he'd worry. Face-to-face, I'd have an easier time convincing him that this was good and I was happy. Ian made me happy.

"Yes, we talked about you, and he mentioned

it. Why didn't you?"

It had been over a week since Ian and I went to Bear Mountain State Park. I kept waiting for Henry to bring it up, but he never did.

"Because I wanted to surprise you by coming the weekend after your birthday."

I stopped walking, pressing a palm on my chest. I felt as if my heart was about to burst. My birthday was on a weekday, but it was perfect if he came on the weekend. We could stay up late and catch up on everything.

"Are you serious?"

"Yes!"

"Wow. Thank you. I miss you so, so much."

"I miss you too, Ellie. Listen, I've got to go. Work is calling."

"On a Saturday?"

"Yeah, they don't really have boundaries. Talk later?"

"Sure."

I was so ecstatic that I couldn't stop smiling. I left my headphones on and flipped on a playlist. Sometimes I liked listening to the sounds of the city, but sometimes I just wanted to get lost in the music. I looked around as the city began to wake up. Saturday was the perfect day to sleep in, but years of working in restaurants taught me how valuable the morning hours were and how much one could do in them.

By the time I arrived in front of the restaurant, I was a little sweaty. Okay, so maybe walking for forty minutes wasn't my best idea. Even though it wasn't warm, my armpits were a bit damp, so I headed to the restroom, and I dried them with some paper towels. When I came back to the restaurant, Josie and Isabelle were already sitting at a table. They both looked at me in surprise, so I hurried to the table to sit down.

"When did you arrive?" Josie asked.

"A few minutes ago, but I went to the restroom first."

The place was filling up quickly. It was quite different than the one where I worked. For one, it was much smaller, and it was on the ground floor. We were looking directly out onto the street. Also, the kitchen was open, so you could see the chefs cooking. I understood the appeal of the open kitchen concept. We learned in culinary school that it gave customers a sense of everything being fresh, just because they could see it being prepared. But when I opened my own restaurant, I'd keep the kitchen completely separate. Open kitchens put far too much pressure on staff. I'd worked once in an open setup, and everything was more difficult, from the communication to having to tidy up much more often. It wasn't worth the hassle.

We ordered bagel sandwiches. Mine was with smoked salmon, Josie's with egg, and Isabelle's with pepper spread and caramelized onions. That was an interesting combination, and I asked for a bite.

"Mm, good but not my style," I said. It was tasty, but I found the combination far too strong. I would have used hummus instead of the pepper spread. Josie and Isabelle were sharing their food making all sorts of comments about the ingredients and whose sandwich was better. These two were hilarious. I liked the dynamic they had between them. When Ian had told me about Dylan's near fall, it clicked in my mind what his mom said about him—how he was always protective of his older brother.

"Oh, by the way, Ellie. I'm going to have a party in December. The venue we booked for the wedding wasn't too happy when we canceled, so I promised to throw a random huge party later this year. The wedding was supposed to be in November, but I didn't want to use the same date. Anyway, we're doing a vegan and gluten-free menu for some of the guests, and the chef said she might need help. Do you have any expertise with this kind of cuisine?"

"Yes, a lot. She can reach out at any time. Give her my phone number but tell her to message me first. I don't answer calls from unknown numbers. I get too many spammy calls these days."

"Will do. Thanks." I was so happy that I could help Isabelle out. Both of Ian's sisters had been very kind, so I was thankful I could do something. Isabelle quickly asked, "So, what's your favorite thing about the city?"

"Honestly? Everything. Though right now, I'm in love with this spa I discovered on the Upper West Side. They give amazing neck massages. The neck and shoulders are problematic areas for most chefs."

"Good for you. What else do you plan to do in New York? What haven't you seen? What are you dying to try out?" Isabelle asked.

"I've seen a lot. But since I start work every day at ten, I wake up super early, and museums are practically empty in the morning. And if I don't have to take a cab and get stuck in traffic, I can get a lot done."

"Where have you been?" Josie asked.

"I've visited a couple of museums. I even took the ferry one weekend and went to the Statue of Liberty and Ellis Island. I still haven't been to Coney Island though, primarily because it's far away."

Isabelle scrunched her nose. "You didn't miss out on anything. It's not my favorite place in New York."

"Really? I did read on some blogs that its glory days were over, but I thought maybe they were exaggerating."

Isabelle grinned. "You can always go and make up your own mind, just don't have high expectations."

"What else would you recommend I see?" I asked.

"That depends on what you like. Do you want more museums or Broadway plays? Do you like theme parks? Bars or places to dine?"

"Nah, since I spend my whole day in restaurants, I like doing something different in my free time. I'm not much of a party person. Or a play person, to be honest."

"Hmm… it's hard to give out recommendations if we don't know what you like," Josie said.

"Just give me a list of everything. Ian said he's a good tour guide, but I don't think he is. Lately, we keep getting sidetracked." I blushed, glancing at my coffee. *Why the heck did I say that?* "My God, I don't even have wine to blame this time. What do you think makes me talk so much around you?" I'm sure they suspected, but good God, *way to announce it, Ellie.*

"I just have that kind of face," Isabelle said with a smile. "It makes people want to pour out their heart, which is a good trait for a therapist."

I burst out laughing, even though I was still blushing. "Anyway, let me know all the things I should see. I keep saying I have enough time to see everything, but before I know it, I'll already have started my rotation in New Orleans." My heart sank as I spoke the words. Isabelle was looking at me intently.

"Are you looking forward to that?" Josie asked. I shrugged, taking a swig of coffee to buy myself some time.

"Oh yeah, that's a very interesting part of the program. The Creole cuisine is so rich and combines so many different flavors that it's a privilege to be able to learn it in a local restaurant." Did my voice sound hollow to my own ears? Everything I said was true, but for some reason, my heart wasn't in it.

My heart wanted to stay in New York. With Ian.

***

Ian

Playing tennis on a Saturday morning was my favorite thing to do. It was the best way to casually meet with customers on the weekend and do some schmoozing. A lot of clients liked to play golf or tennis. Golf bored me to tears, so we picked tennis. Dylan despised schmoozing, which was why I usually took the reins. I didn’t mind. It kept our customers happy, and I was a sociable person. Which meant I probably should focus on talking with the customers during each break instead of checking my phone, but I wanted to know what Isabelle had to say so I could start planning.

Dylan cocked a brow at me when I checked my phone for the third time during a five-minute break.

"Anything wrong?" he asked.

"No, I'm just waiting for a message."

"Can you focus on the customers, please?”

"Sure." He was right; I needed to get my head in the game. I looked at them with a bright smile. "Last set, and then brunch is on us."

They both nodded, clearly satisfied. We liked keeping clients happy—they stayed with us longer if we did. And when they want to do additional projects, they come back to us too. It was why we had so many loyal customers. We took good care of them, and they appreciated it. However, that didn't mean I let them win the game on purpose. I had a competitive streak, and so did Dylan, and our customers appreciated that we didn't go easy on them.

The match was very close, but we ended up winning.

"Congratulations!" Andrew said.

"Hey, it was close," I said. "Nice game."

"A win is a win. Doesn't matter by how much. Now come on. I'm starving, and you promised brunch."

"It was a bad idea to play on an empty stomach," Carlos said.

"I agree. Next time we eat breakfast first, and then we play."

Andrew shook his head. "That would mean no champagne for breakfast, and I don't agree with that. Meet you in the restaurant in fifteen minutes." We were all sweating, so we had to shower and change.

"Sure." Once we were alone, I told Dylan, "I'm just going to make a call, and then I'll get ready quickly."

Why wasn't Isabelle calling me? I pressed her number, half expecting her to reject the call. Maybe she was still with Ellie. To my surprise, she answered after the first ring.

"Hey, brother." She didn't sound as enthusiastic as I hoped. "I'm sorry, I don't have any intel for you."

I groaned. So that was why she hadn't sent me

updates. "Why not?"

"She went on and on about the city, and we couldn't insist without her catching on. Ask Josie."

I laughed. "I believe you. Thanks for trying. I'll figure something out."

I was just about to hang up and head to the showers when she said, "I do have some useful info, though."

"Okay."

"We asked if she's excited about her rotation in New Orleans."

"And?" My whole body was on edge, waiting for my sister's answer.

"She said yes because she is looking forward to learning a lot, but I don't think it was true."

"Why not?"

"I can't tell you exactly. It's just a feeling I got based on her body language."

I shook my head but said, "Thanks. Look, I have to go. I need to shower before we take our clients to brunch. I'll talk to her later. Thanks!"

"You're welcome. Sorry I couldn't be more helpful. I think the baby is messing with my detective skills."

"Don't go blaming my future nephew."

"Oh, that's right. Forgot you're already protective of him."

"Clearly, he needs it. Bye, Isabelle."

"Bye."

I didn't share my sister's opinion, but I didn't want to be rude. Isabelle always said that I wasn't a romantic, but I just didn't romanticize anything. I took what people said at face value. I didn't try to read into everything the way she did. In my experience, it was just a way to see what you wanted to see in someone's reaction. I wasn't searching for anything that wasn't there. I was going to make Ellie happy for now. I guessed that was all we had.

Chapter Seventeen
Ellie

On my birthday, I woke up super early, as usual. I was giddy with excitement as I got out of bed, looking at my dresser where I already had my presents from Henry and both sets of parents. They'd arrived yesterday, but I never opened presents before my actual birthday. I dressed up in comfy, warm clothes, brought the gifts to my bed, and shimmied on the mattress as I opened them.

My brother got me a massive travel book from Lonely Planet. My mom and stepdad got me a thick winter coat, making me laugh. This was just like Mom, always thinking I didn't dress warm enough. But I couldn't argue, because it was true. My dad and stepmom sent me a gift card to my favorite online shop that sold handmade candles. Oh, that was so thoughtful of them.

I called everyone right away to thank them. While I spoke to Mom, I heard the doorbell ring. Harper answered it, and a few minutes later, she knocked at mine.

"Mom. I've got to go. I'll talk to you later, okay?" I said.

"Sure, honey."

"What is it, Harper?" I asked, opening the door.

"Something arrived for you."

"More presents!!"

"Happy birthday, Ellie." Harper was holding a giant package of chocolate in her arms.

"Wow. You outdid yourself, roomie."

"Oh no, no. These are not from me. They're from a certain hunk you've been spending time with lately."

"Ian sent me this?" I asked in a strangled voice. Suddenly I was even giddier than before.

"He did. The delivery guy said that there was a card with them, but he got water on it, so it was all wet and illegible."

"I'll take the chocolates, even without the card." I took it from her, putting it on the dresser.

Harper smiled. "You're going to share those, aren't you? I mean, you can't possibly eat them all."

I burst out laughing. "Well, I could, but because I'm generous, I'm going to allow you to have a few."

"Define a few."

"I'm not sure yet. You can start by having one, and we'll go from there."

"Come on. Let's have a celebratory breakfast," Harper said, and I followed her out of the room. "I have to go in twenty minutes, but we have time."

I was surprised to see that she had already set up the table. We usually took turns preparing breakfast, but she insisted that she wanted to do it all.

She put ham and cheese and tomatoes in the oven, which was my trick for getting tomatoes to have taste in the winter months. When we loaded our plates and were ready to sit down, Harper and I clinked our coffee cups. "Cheers. I'd toast with champagne, but it's frowned upon for a teacher to show up at school reeking of alcohol. Happy birthday, Ellie. Since I'm not going to see you tonight, I hope you have a great day."

"Wait. Why aren't you seeing me tonight?"

"Oh shit. You're not supposed to know."

"Know what?"

"I can't tell you anything."

"Harper!"

She pressed her lips together, then mumbled, "My lips are sealed. I have to go."

"No, you don't. You still have a few minutes."

"I am starting early today," she said, making me laugh even more.

"Right. You're just afraid I'm going to question you."

"Obviously." She kissed my cheek and left, but not before heading to my bedroom.

"Oh, so you don't have time, but you can sneak in my bedroom and steal a chocolate?" I called after her.

"I have my priorities," Harper replied before ducking out of the apartment.

I cleaned up quickly after she left, smiling from ear to ear. Ian had sent me chocolate. That was so thoughtful of him, and I loved that he knew just the right kind to get. I went back to my bedroom after the kitchen was clean and looked at the chocolates, then decided to text him. I had some suspicions regarding what Harper said, but I had to be smart to make Ian talk.

Snapping a photo, I added it to my text.

Ellie: Morning. I just got these. Thank you so much. The delivery guy said the card was damaged, care to tell me what was on it?

Ian replied right away.

Ian: I'll tell you when I see you.

Ellie: And when will that be?

He didn't reply. I messaged him again.

Ellie: Harper just told me she wouldn't be seeing me tonight. Do you have anything to do with this?

Ian: Harper's bad with secrets.

Ellie: OMG.

Ian: You think I wouldn't spoil my birthday girl?

Ellie: But it's my birthday. I'm supposed to be the one throwing a party or something.

Ian: You can do that when Henry's visiting on Saturday. This evening you're all mine.

Oh wow.

I had a lot of energy while I showered and dressed. I still had plenty of time until my shift started, but I had too much energy to sit inside the apartment. Dressing warmly in the coat Mom gave me, I hurried outside. November didn't have the best weather for walking. It was pretty cold, but I still loved it. I thought about my family and how much I missed them as I walked leisurely through the city.

My biggest dream was to get everyone in the same place for my birthday once. But it never really worked out. I wasn't sure, but I sometimes I wondered if it was because everyone was actively avoiding each other. I dreamed of celebrating something together as a big extended family. If not my birthday, then maybe Christmas, or just any occasion.

My good mood continued even after my shift started. I'd listened to a catchy tune in the morning, and I played it in my mind even after removing my headphones and starting the salads. I danced to it all day. In the afternoon, when there was a bit of a lull in customers, my boss, the restaurant manager, came to me. "Ellie, it's your birthday today, right?"

"Yes."

"Happy birthday."

"Thank you, Nancy."

"You and I haven't had time to chat, but I've heard lots of good things from everyone in the kitchen."

"Thank you."

"Let's talk some more next week. I'll look at my calendar and let you know when I have time."

I panicked a little but just nodded.

"Okay." It was never a good thing when the boss was extra nice to you and then wanted to talk to you. I'd been fired that way twice when the boss politely invited me to sit down and drink something together, only to tell me that they were cutting staff or whatever. But I pushed it all to the back of my mind. Maybe it would be good news for once, or perhaps I'd have to move to New Orleans sooner than I thought.

My mood dampened a bit after my boss left. I didn't want to think about moving. Before, I always looked forward to a new city and a new challenge. But recently, something had changed inside me, and I knew it was because of Ian. I loved our evenings together and the casual messages we sent during the day, just to catch up with each other. For the first time, I wasn't happy with my nomad life. With Ian, I felt like I belonged right where I was.

My good mood was back once my shift ended. I ran home to change, and Ian was already in front of my building.

"When did you arrive?" I asked him.

"I know your shift ends at six, and you typically only need fifteen minutes to get home, so that's your answer."

"Someone's extremely punctual."

"I was really looking forward to starting our evening together." He was gazing at me with hungry eyes. I pointed a finger at him.

"No, no. Wait with the kissing until we're upstairs."

"Why?"

"Because I don't want the whole street to see us. What will they think?"

"That we're about to have a great night."

"Ian," I warned playfully, walking inside the building. Even though I was tired from work, I chose not to get inside the elevator. After standing on my feet, I needed to move. I took the stairs two at a time, smiling as I heard him behind me. "So, are you going to tell me what we're doing?"

"Yes. You said you don't want to go out because you're tired. So I'm going to cook for you at my place. Pack an overnight bag." That command sounded delicious. It sent shivers all over my body. My heart sighed with happiness. He wanted to spoil me on my birthday. Who was this man? And what was he doing with me?

"Okay," I said, fully aware that my voice was high-pitched. Going into my bedroom, I pulled a backpack from under the bed and filled it with a cute dress I'd change into when I arrived at his place. It was semisexy, but if I didn't wear a bra, it was superhot, and I planned on not wearing a bra. It was black with long sleeves and a deep V-neckline. It only reached midthigh, so it wasn't exactly winter appropriate, but it didn't matter indoors. I also packed a nightgown, and I was contemplating two types of panties. One was black lace. The other was red silk.

"Pack them both." Startled, I looked over my shoulder. Ian was peeking from the doorway.

"How long have you been standing there like

a Peeping Tom?"

"A while. You're cute as fuck."

I blushed.

"Well, get out. You're distracting me. And I don't need two sets of panties."

"Yes, you do."

"Why?"

He stalked closer to me, pinning me with his intense gaze. My breath caught. I licked my lips when he tilted in closer, bringing his mouth to my ear.

"I can use one of them to tie your wrists."

Oh my God. If I felt I was blushing before, it was nothing compared to now. My whole face was on fire—even the roots of my hair felt hot. He captured my mouth the next second in a deep kiss. I moaned as my thighs shook. His mouth was relentless, exploring me deeper and faster. I knew that if we continued like this, we wouldn't leave at all, so I took a step back, turning around.

He put an arm around my waist, kissing the back of my neck as I finished packing my backpack. I felt so special and valued, and my defenses were utterly shattered.

It was strange in a way that I'd been a virgin so many years wondering if I'd ever find someone I cared about, and after meeting Ian, I felt like it all was meant to be. Like I was waiting for this man, for Ian. I couldn't imagine being with anyone else. Ian was my first and only…

"I've never felt like this before," I said. My stomach constricted. *Am I scaring him away?*

"I'm glad I am the first to make you feel new things," he said in my ear. "You're important to me, Ellie. So damn important."

I put a hand over his on my belly. It was on the tip of my tongue to ask just how important, but I didn't get the chance because the doorbell rang.

"Are you expecting someone?" he asked.

"No. It's probably a package delivery. I'm not sure why, but it's never just one person delivering all the packages. They come up at least twice a day. It drives Harper crazy."

"I'll answer. You finish up your packing."

"Thanks." Once he left, I stuffed my panties in my bag of toiletries. That's it. I had everything I needed. I zipped up the backpack just as Ian opened the front door.

"What are you doing here?"

It wasn't a delivery guy. It was Henry.

Chapter Eighteen
Ian

"Hey, come on in," I said, opening the door widely. Ellie burst out of her room the next second. She was still flustered from our kiss before. Her brown hair was wild, her lips red. It would take Henry no time to figure us out. She threw her arms around him, and he lifted her off her feet in a hug.

"What are you doing here? Thought you were coming on Saturday," she said, laughing.

"I wanted to surprise you."

"Oh, you should have told me you're coming today. How long are you staying?"

"Until Sunday. What are you doing tonight?" he asked her. She stepped back from the hug. His eyes zeroed in on her mouth. He turned to look at me. "What's going on?"

Damn. It took him even less time than I predicted.

"I can explain," Ellie said.

"I will." I knew how Henry could get. I felt protective of Ellie. He could be harsh, even though he had her best interest in mind.

"Yes, you will. What the fuck, Ian? I told you to stay away from her."

"I tried, but not very hard," I admitted. "Look, we're together." I couldn't think of the right words to say, and I knew what I just said did not defuse the situation.

"What the—"

"Don't be like this, Henry," Ellie said. "I'm not a kid."

Henry shook his head, looking between the two of us. He was disappointed in me, I could see it in his eyes, and it fucking sucked. I didn't like disappointing anyone.

"Define *you're together,*" he demanded.

Ellie pressed her lips together, looking at me. I stepped next to her, putting an arm around her shoulders. She felt tense. I wondered if it was because her brother had found out or because she was curious about how I was defining our relationship.

"We're dating and spending a lot of time with each other. In fact, I was going to cook for Ellie tonight at my place."

Henry's eyes bulged as Ellie leaned into me. I touched her shoulders, skimming my thumb up to her neck, and felt her relaxing, finally.

I'd given a lot of thought about what to do tonight. Ellie went out in the city a lot, but she seemed happiest when it was the two of us either at her place or mine, so that's what I planned.

"How about we all go out to dinner instead?" she asked. "I'm sure we can get a reservation somewhere."

I looked down at her. "But you don't like going out in the evening. You're too tired. I have enough food for everyone."

"Okay. That sounds like a plan," Ellie said. "I'll just pick up my backpack."

"I'll wait in the living room," Henry said. I went with Ellie, wanting to make sure she was okay. I closed the door to her room, and she looked up at me, pointing her finger at me.

"No, no. *No* kissing."

I frowned at her. "I understood your stance in front of the building, but what's your excuse this time?"

"Henry has X-ray vision, I swear to God. So keep your hands and eyes off me while we're eating. Okay?"

I tilted closer and brought my hand to her neck, skimming and splaying my fingers widely. "I'll behave while he's with us, but once he leaves, you're mine, Ellie. And then I'll devour you." Her eyes widened, and her lips parted as she exhaled a breath. I loved keeping her on edge.

"If you can't behave," she said, totally flustered, "wait for me in the living room with Henry."

I took a step back, holding both hands up. "I'll do that. I can't be in the same room with you and not touch you. Kiss you."

"Or talk dirty."

"That too."

Still holding up my hands, I stepped out of

the room. Henry was pacing the living room.

"Don't be a dick to your sister," I said.

He narrowed his eyes. "This is exactly what I was afraid of. Why didn't you tell me?"

"She wanted to do it face-to-face when you came to the city. Don't ruin her birthday."

"I'm not going to." I hated that my best friend didn't trust me—but all he knew was a version of me from the past, not who I was now, who I was with Ellie.

"Good. Because we're going to have a problem if you do."

"You have some balls to tell me that." He narrowed his eyes but didn't say anything else.

After Ellie joined us in the living room, we Ubered to my place. Henry seemed a bit more relaxed when we arrived. When I opened the door, I barely recognized my apartment.

"What's this?" Ellie asked.

"I asked Isabelle to help me decorate everything to look more festive." My sister had asked if candles were okay, and I said yes, thinking she'd bring one or two, but I saw at least a dozen. Henry jerked his head back, but Ellie looked damn happy.

Whatever. I'd get used to 100 candles if that's what it took to see her like this.

"This is amazing," she whispered. Her eyes were a bit watery. Why was this such a big deal for her?

Henry and Ellie sat down on the barstools at

my kitchen island. I walked to the other side, where the stove was. She glanced at the ingredients with a grin.

"You're making risotto?" she asked.

"It's your favorite," I replied. She'd mentioned that during the weekend at Bear Mountain, and I filed it in my memory. "I also have cake in the fridge."

I poured all of us a glass of white wine before I chopped the onion.

"We're meeting tomorrow, right?" Ellie asked her brother.

"Obviously! I came to visit you," Henry replied.

They both seemed far more relaxed than before. I kept a close eye on Henry while the risotto cooked, ready to intervene if needed. I understood his concerns, but I didn't want him to spoil her birthday.

"Where are you staying?" I asked him.

"I just crashed at an Airbnb downtown."

"Why didn't you tell me? I would have arranged something with Harper so you could stay with us."

"No, you know me, sis. I don't like doing that."

That was true. Henry had never liked crashing with people, even when we were in college. The risotto was done a while later. I put a ton of parmesan on top before we brought the plates to the table.

"So, how long has this been going on?" he asked as we finally started to eat.

"Um, a while," Ellie said nervously. "Almost since I came to the city."

"You've been lying to me all this time?"

"No, Henry. We just knew you'd react like this."

"So no one else knows. She's your dirty little secret?"

"Henry!" My tone was a warning. I was on edge.

"I'm not a secret."

"My family knows we're together," I said calmly.

"So I'm the only one who doesn't know?" Henry replied.

Ellie grinned. "There's no winning with him when he's like this."

"I know. He's my best friend."

"Dude, no offense, but you do realize I had a front seat to all of the shit you did in college. Obviously, I have a problem that you're now going out with my sister."

"I've changed, Henry. I'm not in college anymore. Neither are you; we've both grown up."

He looked at Ellie, who was just smiling widely. "Oh, come on, Henry. It's my birthday. Behave. You're not getting cake and champagne otherwise."

Henry sat back in his chair, finally smiling. "Fine, whatever, you two are adults. I don't have to get in the middle of it. But just so you know, when you hurt her, you and I are going to have a big problem."

I didn't like the use of *when*. It implied it was a sure thing, but I didn't want to be the one to spoil the mood by starting a fight.

"Henry!" Ellie scolded. "Drop it."

"Okay. Okay. I'm not going to bring it up again *tonight*."

We chatted about their parents while we ate the risotto with vegetables. Once we cleared the plates, I brought the cake out of the fridge. I uncorked the champagne, pouring for everyone, and we clinked glasses.

"Cheers," I said. "To Ellie."

"To Ellie," Henry said. We sang a weak *happy birthday to you*. I wasn't much of a singer, so the cat was out of the bag. Brayden heard me once and thought I was sick, the asshole.

Henry stayed with us for another hour before announcing that he was taking off. He kept looking at the candles Isabelle set up around the apartment.

"Okay. You two, I'm going to go back to my Airbnb. Ellie, I'll talk to you tomorrow."

Ellie and I walked him to the door. Once he left, I turned my gaze on Ellie.

"I love all these candles," she said. "I can't believe you asked Isabelle to help you decorate. And that you cooked my favorite meal."

I pulled her to me, pushing a strand of hair behind her ear, touching her temple with my thumb.

"Why are you in disbelief?" I asked.

She shrugged. "I don't know. I guess this is something I'm not used to or something I don't ever expect of anyone."

"What? To make an effort for your birthday?"

"Yes," whispered Ellie.

I put my forehead close to hers. "It makes you happy. I like making you happy." Her eyes clouded; she looked like she wanted to say something. "What's on your mind?"

"It's just that, after the way my parents' marriage ended… I'm not blaming my parents or anything. I know I'm an adult, responsible for what I do."

"Ellie, some things just stay with us over the years. It doesn't mean you're blaming anyone."

"I don't think I let anyone in, you know? I'm not even sure if it was a conscious thing I was doing. But I didn't. I sort of put up a wall around myself, that way I wouldn't be disappointed. No one's gotten in until you." The sheepish look she had touched my heart. "Besides, you *cooked* for me. In my world, that's like a love declaration."

Fuck me. Her words twisted around my chest. I cupped her hands with mine, pinning her against the door, and told her, "It is. I love you, Ellie. I wasn't even sure I was capable of it, but you've got me. What I told Henry was 100 percent true. I've changed since I met you. You've changed me." I cupped her cheek, kissing her mouth descending to her neck.

"I did?" she whispered.

"Yes. And I didn't think it was possible to feel this way." I didn't plan this, but I'm glad it happened. Ellie needed to know I couldn't let her go.

"And I love *you*, Ian."

I straightened up, looking her directly in the eyes. A smile played on her lips, but her eyes were full of emotion. "Thank you for everything you did tonight. And keeping Henry in check."

"I didn't." At least I don't think I did.

"He would've roasted my ass even more if you didn't glare at him every five minutes."

I laughed, caressing the back of her head. "I didn't want anything to spoil the mood for your birthday."

"He didn't. It was honestly the best birthday I've had. Because of you."

I wanted to make all her birthdays unforgettable—every single one of them.

"So I'm going to spoil you tonight too," she went on. "But I have to change first."

"What? Why?"

"I have a sexy outfit in my backpack. Obviously, when I packed it, I had no idea that Henry was joining us."

"It's too inappropriate?" My dick twitched. She laughed, pressing herself against my erection.

"Someone's excited at the thought."

"Very."

"Yeah, it is."

"What if I'd planned a surprise party with

more people?"

She narrowed her eyes. "I know you. You wouldn't do that. You always try to get us to be alone."

"I do. Because you're mine."

"I am," she whispered.

Hearing her surrender like this was chipping away at my self-control. I wanted to claim her mouth and body and all her pleasure.

Chapter Nineteen
Ian

Her smile turned even happier, then was quickly interrupted with a frown. "What are we going to do once my placement is over?"

"I don't know, but I understand that your career is important to you." My gut twisted as I said this, but I went on because I wanted her to know that I had her best interests in mind. What she wanted was important to me too. "I know what it's like to have a goal and focus on it, and I respect that. I want you to have everything you're dreaming of. Let's not think about what happens when your placement's over. We still have months before that."

Her frown intensified. She bit her lower lip.

"What?" I asked.

"I don't know. My boss says she wants to talk to me. That's never been a good sign before."

"Were there any complaints about you?" I asked.

"No."

"And you have been doing one and a half jobs basically since the pastry chef left. That's got to account for something."

"Exactly. I think so too… but…"

"I don't think this is going to go in a bad direction. Just wait and see what happens," I said, "and we'll figure stuff out then."

She nodded. I needed her to know that I was in her corner. I needed to distract her. I didn't want her worrying about anything on her birthday.

"I forgot to give you your gift," I said.

She perked up, looking behind me as if expecting to see her present there. "Then go get it. And can you do it naked?"

"That's a very specific request," I said with a laugh.

"I'm the birthday girl, so you can't say no to me. Even though… Henry's visit did sort of spoil my mood for sexy stuff."

I winked, running a hand through my hair. "You can say that again."

"Sooo… my gift?"

I took the envelope from the TV console, bringing it back to her. She reached for it, snatching it from my hands. She sat upright, taking it from the envelope.

"It's a giftcard for an airplane ticket," she said in surprise.

"For multiple tickets, so you can visit your family whenever you want."

She looked over at me, mouth slightly open. "Ian, this is more than I dreamed of. Thank you so much. This is the perfect gift."

"I thought about it all by myself." I was damn proud of putting that huge smile on her face. "Who do you want to visit first?"

"Well, I just saw Henry, so maybe Mom."

She grinned from ear to ear as she sat on the couch, pondering out loud when she could take time off. I wasn't listening fully, though. I kept thinking about her rotation and what that would mean for us. A few months ago, thoughts about the future weren't even lingering at the back of my mind. But now, they were front and center. It was all I could think about. Ellie had turned everything upside down and shown me a side of life I wasn't aware of before.

I wanted her in my life, but I also didn't want her to give up on her dreams.

I sat next to her on the couch, watching as she browsed for flights.

"I'm not buying anything, I just want to see what I could book," she said, opening browser after browser. We ended up falling asleep on the couch. Sometime during the night, I woke up with a stiff neck. Ellie was curled next to me, with her head dangling in an awkward position. She couldn't spend the night like this, or she'd be sore as hell tomorrow. Careful not to wake her up, I scooped her in my arms, propping her head on my chest. Was that a snore? Fuck, she was so damn cute. She didn't wake at all when I put her on the bed, fully clothed, and I fell right back to sleep too.

Next morning, I woke up to the sound of giggles. Blinking my eyes open, I saw Ellie hovering over me, grinning.

"What time is it?" I asked.

"Six o'clock in the morning."

I groaned. "Why are you awake?"

"Because we fell asleep early. I don't remember coming to bed."

"I brought you in here sometime during the night. You were sleeping in an awkward position. Didn't want you to be sore today."

"Such a gentleman." She smiled brightly, jumping off the bed.

"Time to start the day. And in case anyone is interested, I was thinking we could put last night's plan in action. You know. The one where I put on the sexy dress, you do the super sexy plan with the extra pair of panties. Does it ring a bell?"

My cock twitched. "Fuck, yeah."

"Awesome. While you wake up, I'm going to get rid of morning breath."

She darted out of the room with a wiggle of that sinful ass. I followed her a few minutes later. She was dancing in the bathroom, singing off-key with a toothbrush in her mouth. I rinsed my mouth with the same toothpaste without taking my eyes off her. Ellie was clearly happy. I wanted to keep her this way.

"So, mister," she said once we both finished brushing our teeth, "what do you plan to do to me?"

As a response, I pulled her flush against me.

"You'll have to let me go so I can put on the dress," she whispered.

"Change of plans. I'll just take off your clothes, so you don't need to put on anything else." I kissed down her neck, possessed by the need to have her right here, right now. I needed to keep her. Capturing her mouth, I ran my hands down her neck and shoulders and further down to her waist, tugging at her sweater. Breaking off the kiss, I took her shirt off. "You're so damn sexy," I said.

She groaned in protest. "It's a cotton bra."

"You're fucking sexy," I repeated. "You're the sexiest woman on the planet for me." I took off her bra, touching her breasts, skimming my fingers over her nipples, watching them turn to hard nubs while the skin all over her upper body broke out in goose bumps. Only then did I lower my hand to the button of her jeans, popping it open.

"You want to get me naked before we even get to the bed?" she asked in a teasing voice.

"I want to make you come before we even move from the bathroom." She drew in a sharp breath. I yanked her jeans down, along with her panties. She stepped out of them carefully. Her legs were covered in goose bumps too. I moved up slowly, touching her ankles and her knees. Moving my hands further up, I teased her outer thighs before cupping her ass.

"I'm going to make you come so hard," I promised, kissing her mouth again. I touched her ass with both hands, pulling her against me. I wanted her to feel that I was already hard for her, just from seeing her gorgeous body and how she reacted when I told her what I had planned to do to her.

When we paused to breathe, I pushed her

against the sink. She grinned, parting her legs slightly. I moved my hand from her chest down to her pubic bone, nudging her clit with the tips of my fingers. She dropped her head back, moaning.

"I haven't decided yet if I'm making you come with my mouth or my fingers. Maybe I'll do both," I said.

She shuddered, parting her legs even more. I kissed her shoulder and her neck while I moved my fingers in a slow, circular movement over her clit.

"More," she whispered. "Harder, please."

I was going to explode in my pants. I was going to have her, but not before I made her come. I moved my fingers even slower, enjoying her cry of protest. Kissing her neck and shoulder was one of my favorite things to do. Her skin was very smooth.

"Ian!" she cried. Her voice shook. She grabbed my sweater. Light tremors coursed through her. Fuck, she was already there. Her response to me was intoxicating and addictive. I paused, moving my mouth further down her body until I reached her breasts. Looking up at her, I lavished her left breast with attention before moving to the right one. I wasn't touching her pussy now, and she was having pleasure withdrawals. I could see it in her eyes. She needed my touch badly. I lowered my mouth to her pubic bone, grazing her clit with my chin. She cried out when I reached her pussy with my mouth.

"Ian, please. Ian!"

I covered her clit with my lips, tugging a bit

before pressing the flat of my tongue against it. Her hips bucked forward. I grabbed them, keeping her in place so I could explore her all I wanted. I licked her entrance, avoiding her clit until she tugged at my hair, making me smile against her swollen flesh.

Looking up at her, I memorized every detail about this second: the way her mouth was open in a moan, her eyes closed as if she was bracing herself for the wave of pleasure. Her head was tilted slightly to one side and her shoulders hunched. Her whole body was preparing for the orgasm.

I pulled her clit between my lips again and watched her come apart. She arched forward, bucking, but I held her in place. Her cries of pleasure filled the bathroom. One leg shot out as she propped both hands on my shoulders.

"Ian," she murmured. Her voice was very, very weak.

"I've got you, baby. I've got you. I promise."

She straightened up, but she was still faint. She was putty in my hands. I covered her mouth and kissed her, walking her back to my room. I could have her in my bathroom, but I wanted her in my bed. I wanted her everywhere, in my shower, against every wall.

She smiled against my lips, and her body became stronger when we reached the bedroom. She looked at me with a wide, happy smile. She was sated, but I wasn't. I was still hungry for her. I needed my release. I needed to sink inside her. She took off my sweater right away. I got rid of my jeans on my own. "Those panties I told you to bring, where are they?"

Her eyes widened. "In my backpack." She pointed to a corner of the bedroom where she'd dropped it when we arrived.

"Take them out," I commanded.

She nodded, sucking in a breath and going to the backpack. A few seconds later, she returned with her black lacy pants. "What are you going to do with them?" she asked.

I looked her straight in the eyes. "I told you I'd tie your wrists. Unless you don't want to."

"I do want to. I'm just... It's not something I've done before."

"Then I'll be the first one." I felt an immense amount of satisfaction at that thought. So many firsts with this woman. And the last, if I have anything to say about it. "Hold out your wrists for me." She immediately obliged. I crossed her delicate wrists within my thumb and forefinger and then twisted her panties until they were tight enough for what I had in mind. I tied both her wrists together. "Lie on the bed."

She sat down, moving to the center of the bed.

"Hold your hands above your head."

She did as I said, watching me intently. I'd been her first, and yet, she didn't hesitate to give herself to me. To please me. This woman meant so damn much to me, and I wanted to prove that to her every way there was.

I took a condom from the dresser, putting it on because I sure as hell wasn't going to remember to do it later, not when I was this crazy for her. I wanted to possess her very soul. I settled between her legs, kissing up her inner thighs, up her pussy again, pressing my mouth against the swollen flesh. She was still pulsing from before, the aftershocks of the orgasm. She cried out, a long, drawn-out sound I hadn't heard from her before. My dick twitched. I moved up her body, looking her straight in the eyes. She was pulling at her panties, tugging at them.

"I can't touch you like this," she said.

"I know."

"And I can't grab stuff, like the sheets or anything."

"I know, but internalizing all of this is going to make it even more intense. You'll see."

"I believe you," she whispered. "I'm just not sure if I can take it any more intense."

I leaned over her, biting her lower lip lightly. "Oh, you can, trust me. You so fucking can, Ellie. I will give you so much pleasure, and you're going to take every ounce of it." Leveling my weight on one forearm, I positioned my cock at her entrance, nudging her clit with the tip, sliding in a few inches, in and out, massaging her G-spot.

"Ian, wow. Oh, this is... I'm..."

"I don't understand you." She rolled her hips, taking me all in. I loved seeing her claim what she wanted. I thrust inside her hard and deep, feeling my whole body tighten already. She was close again.

Because she was still sensitive from before, I knew it wouldn't take very long. I pulled out, cupping her left buttock and pushing her on one side and then flat on her belly.

She attempted to push herself on all fours, but I put a hand at the small of her back. "Don't. I want you like this." She was such a sight, legs spread wide, ass up in the air, hands tied in front of her, looking at me over her shoulder.

I slid inside her again. This was going to be more intense for her, because her clit was rubbing against the mattress. She pressed her forehead against the mattress, bringing her tied hands to the back of her head and moaning. I leaned over her, whispering in her ear. "I love you, baby. I love seeing you like this.. Come for me." I slid my fingers between her clit and the mattress, applying even more pressure while I exploded inside her.

"Fuuuuuuuuck." I was gone to the world. Everything in me just exploded. I'd never felt pleasure like this. It was shocking, and when I heard her cry out, tightening around me, I knew it was just as intense for her. I thrust inside her until we both rode out the wave of pleasure, then pushed myself off her, lying d next to her, half straddling her with one thigh. I took away the panties from her wrists, but she didn't move. She just nudged me with her head.

A few minutes later, she finally looked up at me. "This is a new record," she whispered. "Usually I can't move after you have your way with me. Now I can't even speak."

"I like where this is going," I said.

She finally turned on one side, moving her fingers on my chest. "And now I can finally touch you."

I took her hand in mine, kissing her wrist. The panties had left a bit of a red mark, but I knew it would fade quickly. "I love you, Ellie."

She grinned from ear to ear as she pulled two pillows under her head. "I love you, too."

Chapter Twenty
Ellie

Spending the weekend with my brother was just what the doctor ordered. We walked aimlessly around the city, mostly in Columbus Circle and along the Hudson. I could tell he was trying very hard not to give me any big brother talk, and I appreciated it.

"Listen, we need to talk about Ian," he said on Sunday evening.

"Damn, and I was proud of you for not saying anything." We'd just entered Grand Central Station. I'd never been here before, but I made a mental note to come early in the morning one day. It was full of travelers right now, and I wanted to soak in the beauty of this place when it wasn't overrun with commuters, preferably with a cup of steaming coffee.

"Listen, he's my best friend, and I believe people can change. Not all of them, but most. Ian doesn't lie, so if he says he's changed, I believe him."

"I sense a *but* coming."

"You're going to New Orleans and then San Francisco. You've wanted to do this program for a while."

"I know, Henry."

"So where does this leave you two? Doing long-distance?"

"We haven't talked about it. I don't know." I looked down at my hands, sighing. "Every time I want to talk about it, I just get this pit in my stomach."

"Ellie, I don't want to stress you out. Both of you are grown-ups. I just want you to be happy."

"Thanks, Henry."

I walked him to the platform and gave him a huge hug before he boarded the train to DC. His words did stick in my mind, though. I knew he was right. Ian and I should talk about what we'd do after my placement at some point. The last time I tried, he didn't seem keen on discussing it, and I got it. I was still swooning from his love declaration and didn't want to spoil our happiness by bringing up the unknown future.

My boss didn't mention our get-together until a week later when she asked me to come a little earlier before my shift started. I was restless. I had a bad feeling in my stomach. But I'd received a good performance review, so I hoped it wasn't going to be bad. Except for that one day when I went to the hospital after my silly fall, I had been a hard worker taking on all the workload requested of me. She was waiting for me at one of the tables right next to the window when I sat down and joined her.

"Hey, I brought you a coffee too," Nancy

said. *Oh, no.* My bad feeling was getting even worse.

I tried to tell myself to enjoy the view and the conversation and see where things were going instead of getting lost in my head.

"Ellie, I wanted to thank you for jumping in when our pastry chef left."

"My pleasure. I love doing desserts."

"You're very good at it. I received great reviews about your work all-around, at the pastry and the salad stations. There have been no complaints about the salads, and you will not believe how often people complain about the salads. You even take care of the special orders perfectly."

"Thank you," I said, relaxing a bit. Perhaps this wasn't going to go where I thought it might.

"Listen, I know you have three months left here and then the rotation will take you to New Orleans, but I just want to put a permanent job offer on the table."

My jaw dropped.

"Wow. Are you serious?"

"Yes, why do you look so surprised?"

I decided to be honest. "Well, let's just say I've met with previous bosses like this before, and it never went well."

She frowned. "I'm sorry. That can happen. I let go of some people this way as well by asking them to lunch. It's a way to soften the blow. I just thought it was smarter to meet before the shift starts. After a long day, we're both so spent it's hard to even think."

"That's true."

She smiled so genuinely and said, "We need someone like you in our pastry station. As time passes, maybe you will rotate to other positions in the kitchen too. It depends on your interest and also how the personnel shifts. I know that Creole cuisine is a big draw for every aspiring chef. I've been to New Orleans too. So if you do prefer to move on with the rotation, there are no hard feelings. Okay? Just keep in mind that at the end of the program, you're not guaranteed a permanent position, and I cannot promise that I'll have anything free by the time you're finished."

"Thank you, and no worries—I know nothing's guaranteed." I couldn't wrap my mind around this. This was very good news, and I couldn't wait to tell Ian.

"Your salary will, of course, be much larger than it is now. I can talk to HR to make you an offer. So that you have everything in black and white."

"Yes. That would be good," I said. "I need to weigh all the pros and cons."

"Smart. I'd do the same. Just know that we don't offer this to many people. I don't want to oversell us, but it's a once-in-a-lifetime opportunity, or at least once in a very long time opportunity. It took me quite a few years to nab a workplace in New York."

"Oh, I know," I said. "I've been applying for a rotation that includes New York forever and always got a no. I also applied for individual jobs, so I know they don't come easy."

"It's a competitive market." She sipped her coffee, checking her clock. "Okay. I have to head back to my station. You are welcome to stay here and finish your coffee. I'll talk to HR. I think they will have your offer maybe in a week or so."

"And then how much time do I have to think about it?" I asked.

“HR is getting us a temp for the pastry station, so that is going to be covered for a couple of weeks. But do tell me as soon as possible.”

I nodded, a bit lost in thought.

“Do you have any concerns? You can talk that out with me later if something comes up.”

I straightened in the seat, tapping my fingers on the table. “My dream is to open a restaurant one day. So the plan was to do several rotational programs, to learn as much as possible.”

“That’s certainly one way to do it. If you work with several chefs, you learn their techniques but don’t copy their style.”

“Exactly.”

“You can also learn in one kitchen, but it’s up to you. And it’s a different experience. But it doesn’t mean you can’t open your own restaurant later down the road. Let me know what you decide.”

“I will, thanks.”

I couldn't believe it. I'd been offered a job in New York. This was honestly more than I'd ever dreamed of. I wasn't sure how much I would be missing out, though, if I didn't go to New Orleans.

That would look cool on my resume. Still, at the end of my rotation, I could be back at square one looking for a job.

My plan to open my own restaurant was only going to happen, at the earliest, ten years down the road or so. For the next few years, I wanted to learn as much as possible. If I stayed at the pastry station, my learning would be limited, but she did hint that I could change positions in the kitchen and learn the other stations. From experience, though, I knew the chances for that were low. Personnel rotation was uncommon in Michelin-starred restaurants.

Still, she'd opened a world of possibilities with the job offer. It was all I could think about for the rest of the day. I couldn't wait to tell Ian.

I texted him in the evening right after my shift ended. I wanted to text him earlier, but I only had a short bathroom break the whole day.

Ellie: I have news. Can I come by your office after my shift?

Ian: I'm at the gym. It's called Genesis.

Ellie: Bad day?

Ian: No. Just intense. I'm gonna be ready in forty minutes. Want to come here?

Ellie: I just googled the address. I'm on my way.

If Google was correct, I would arrive there at about the same time he finished his workout. I walked with pep in my step, trying to imagine his reaction. On the way, I passed a popcorn cart. They had some with salted caramel, and I immediately bought some for Ian. He loved this stuff.

I wondered if something happened or if he was just tired. He always pampered me, but he rarely let me do the same for him. Well, tonight, he was going to get spoiled whether he wanted to or not.

I waited by the entrance, and he spotted me immediately. My God, this man was gorgeous. He was wearing jeans and a black Henley shirt that showed off his abs. He had a thick jacket over his shoulder.

"What's that?" he asked, pointing to the cone of popcorn.

"A treat for you."

Stepping closer, he looked intently at my mouth. "For me, huh? So why do you have sugar on your lips?"

Grinning, I cleared my throat. "I was doing a quality test. Can't let you have bad popcorn, can I? Would ruin my plan to pamper you."

He stopped in the act of reaching for the popcorn. "Your plan to what?"

"You seemed on edge in your text. I thought I'd do something about it. Want to talk about it?"

"Nah. Just usual stuff at the office. Some days are better than others."

"Let's see if I can turn the day around, then."

I nudged him playfully with my shoulder. Instead of reaching for popcorn again, he pulled me in a half hug. I buried my nose in his neck. He smelled divine, like shower gel and deodorant. His skin was still a bit damp. He'd probably showered after his workout. We walked to the park behind the gym. It was lovely, on the edge of the Hudson River. We sat on a bench overlooking the water. The air felt salty, and the crying seagulls instantly made me think I was on vacation.

I soaked in the moment, loving that I was here with this sexy man. I leaned into him, sheltering from the strong breeze.

"What's your news?" he asked.

"I almost forgot! Remember that my boss wanted to talk to me?"

"Yes."

"She offered me a job! A permanent one."

"That's amazing!" He turned abruptly, looking straight at me with a twinkle in his eyes. "How come?"

"She says I'm doing a great job as a pastry chef."

"What did you tell her?"

"That I'll think about it. She made it clear that she'll understand if I move on as originally planned and continue with the rotation."

"What do you want to do?" His smile dimmed a bit.

"I'll make a pro and con list. But honestly, I want to stay. I love the city. And I love you. I've never wanted to put down roots, but now it's different."

He cupped my face, tracing my lower lip with his thumb. "Baby, this is amazing news. But I just want to make one thing clear. Do what is best for you, okay? If you stay, I want you to be happy and sure that it's what you want. Not just because of me."

"Well, it would be because of you too."

He touched my lower lip again, sending heat spiraling through me. No, no, no. I wanted to have my mind clear.

"I'm an important decision factor." He wiggled his eyebrows. "But ten years down the road, when you open your restaurant, I don't want you to look back on this and think *I should have finished the rotation*."

"Okay." This was sound advice, but I had to admit, I was hoping he'd go balls to the wall in celebratory mood, throw me over his shoulder, and say I'm staying because I'm his. He kissed me hard and deep and so dirty that I was certain I was going to combust. He kissed me like he never wanted to let me go. My body was on fire. I couldn't even breathe or think. All I had in mind was *him*. The way he kissed and touched me was all-consuming.

"Mr. Gallagher, what's with this kiss?" I whispered when we paused to breathe. I traced his clavicle over the Henley shirt. His chest was rising and falling rapidly. His gaze was so intense that I couldn't look away even if I wanted to.

"I'm just so fucking happy."

"Oh, good. So I did turn the day around."

"Definitely."

"Great. And I'm not nearly done pampering you yet."

"You're not?"

"No. I have lots and lots of ideas. And I'll test them all out tonight."

Chapter Twenty-One
Ian

The next day, I went out to lunch with Dylan at Dumont's. We were meeting Ryker and Hunter there. My mind was on Ellie ever since we talked about her job offer. I needed to distract myself. Working hadn't achieved that. Sleeping hadn't either. Lunch with the guys was exactly what I needed.

I meant what I said to Ellie. I wanted her to make the best decision. But I was feeling restless.

Dumont's was packed with the lunch crowd, but we found a table for four. We were going to wait for the other two guys to arrive before ordering.

"I want to talk to you about something," I told Dylan. This was a good time to talk about the coding platform I had in mind. At any rate, it might keep my mind off other things… like Ellie.

"Okay, shoot."

"I've been thinking about this for a while. I liked teaching when I was in college. You know I was the substitute for the SQL teacher for a while."

"Yeah, I remember. It was the butt of all jokes that a party guy was a teaching assistant, then everyone shut up once they heard about how good you were."

I nodded. "Anyway, I was thinking about making a platform where kids can learn how to code."

"You mean online lessons?" Dylan asked.

"Yes. They'd be prerecorded, and maybe I'll also have live Q&As. I've put some ideas together. But it would be a huge undertaking, so I'd wait until after the rollout phase of Project Z is over before starting it."

"I think it's going to be a big endeavor."

"Okay, it will. But this in no way means I will step down from my duties at Gallagher Solutions. I'm proud of the business we built. I might just have to split my focus for a while."

"Ian, we're in a position where we can decide what we want to do with our lives. It would be a pity not to do something you really want to do."

"I know many people warned you off about going into business with me."

"I never gave a fuck. You're my brother. I trust you more than any of those morons. Do your thing and tell me if you need anything."

"Thanks, man," I said. The wheels were already spinning in my mind. I already had the structure and bare bones of the platform.

Just then, Ryker and Hunter arrived. Hunter was Josie's husband, and we'd always been on good terms. I couldn't wait to run my idea by these guys because they were smart, and I'd like to listen to their input. Hunter owned a big real estate company, and

Ryker was a Wall Street guru.

"What's everyone ordering?" Ryker asked.

"I'll just go with the daily special. I always get that for lunch." I never had the brainpower to focus on mundane things like what to order for lunch. We all ended up ordering the daily special—some kind of rice and stir fry dish. While we ate, I told them all about my ideas for the platform. As expected, Ryker pitched in with ballpark numbers about the rate of customer acquisition and the lifetime value of a customer. Hunter was talking about cost structures. It was way too early to discuss details like this, but I committed all of it to memory anyway. I was going to circle back later once I put my mind to this more seriously.

I couldn't wait to tell Ellie about all of this. I knew she was going to be proud of me. And just like that, she was front and center in my mind again. I lost track of the lunch conversation for a while.

"What's wrong with you, man?" Ryker asked. I looked up from my plate to find all of them looking at me.

"What?" I asked.

"You're talking like 50 percent less than usual," Hunter said.

"Right, I was just thinking about Ellie. She got a job offer here in New York."

"That's good, right?" Ryker asked.

"Josie said that she was on a rotational program," Hunter added.

"Yeah, but she's doing a great job here, so

they offered her a job," I explained.

Ryker cocked a brow. "Is that good or bad news?"

"Good."

"Then why do you look like someone pissed in your lunch?"

"Because I don't know if she wants to stay. She has this dream to open a restaurant and plans to work with as many chefs as possible in the meantime. She says it's the best way to learn. If she goes on with the rotation, she'd move to New Orleans in a couple of months."

"So you think she might still want to go to?" Ryker asked.

"It's possible." I swallowed hard.

"What do you mean, possible? What did you tell her when you discussed this?" Hunter asked, gulping down water.

"I told her that I want her to make the best decision for herself."

Dylan grimaced. Hunter shook his head.

Ryker just narrowed his eyes, pointing his finger at me. "I don't think that was a very good response, but I cannot explain why. It's just a gut feeling."

"Yeah, I agree," Dylan said. "Maybe Isabelle can put it in words that make sense."

"I haven't talked to Isabelle yet. Why would this be a bad way to react?" I looked at all three of them, trying to make sense of this.

"As I said," Ryker admitted, "gut feeling."

"I want her to stay here," I said. "Before she got the job offer, I even thought about talking to Rob and, I don't know, figure a way that Ellie could stay in New York and work at one of his restaurants or something."

Hunter clapped a hand on my shoulder. "Buddy, I'm sure this is a vital piece of information, and it will come in handy at some point. Make sure you work that in a conversation with her. I'd do it *ASAP*."

"You guys are insane," I said.

"No, we just have more experience with women," Dylan said.

I cocked a brow. "I seriously doubt that."

Hunter shook his head. "Experience that matters."

I was tired of the guys giving me shit. "You have so much experience that you cannot even put into words why anything is a good or bad idea? Yeah, that's very helpful."

"Hey, we're just giving you our opinions," Dylan said.

"Okay, I'm not too proud to admit that I'm no good at this. I think we just confused him," Ryker said.

"Right now, you're annoying me," I informed them.

"Should we call the girls? Josie could have some insights," Hunter said.

"Or we could have an actual family council and call everyone." Ryker spoke seriously, as if he thought that was an option. I looked around the table incredulously. The last thing I wanted was everyone pitching in with opinions.

"Or we could do none of the above," I said.

Ryker opened his mouth, but I shook my head. "Drop it, seriously."

Shaking his head, he grinned at me. "This one's a bit pigheaded."

"Nah, he'll just call Isabelle when push comes to shove," Dylan said. He was right, as usual.

I knew Henry could give me more insights, but we still weren't on the best of terms after his visit to New York. He didn't seem mad exactly, just waiting for the other shoe to drop, and that pissed me off. I wanted to be part of Ellie's future. I wasn't sure what I'd do if she didn't want the same.

Chapter Twenty-Two
Ellie

Three days later, I was a bit overwhelmed by my pro and con lists. I only had time to think about it in the morning. After my shift, I was too tired for any decision-making. I was sitting at the top of my bed with my hair piled up in a bun, door wide open. Harper had already left.

I couldn't believe that my list just kept getting longer on both sides. I was startled when my phone rang. Usually, no one called me this early. To my surprise, it was Isabelle. I answered right away.

"Morning. I hope it's not too early. Ian said you're always up by seven."

"I'm good. Already had a coffee too."

"Ian told me you were offered a job here."

My face exploded in a smile just like that. "Yes, I was. I'm making pro and con lists to decide if I should take it or move forward with my original plan."

"You're making lists?" she sounded incredulous.

"Yes." I went a bit in defensive mode. "Doesn't everyone do that?"

"I guess, but I thought the whole point of the rotation was to get a permanent position."

"Not exactly. It's also about gaining the most experience I can."

Isabelle cleared her throat. "Okay. What does Ian say about it?"

"That I should decide based on what's best for me." Jumping down from the bed, I walked to the living room and sat on the couch. I waited for Isabelle's reply, but when she didn't say anything, I prompted, "Was this why you called me?"

"Not just this. I'm going back and forth with my party planner about the menu. Remember I told you the cook is having trouble with the vegan and gluten-free dessert?"

"Yes." She'd never brought it up again after mentioning it at first. "My offer to help still stands."

"Are you sure? I know you're still doing two jobs, basically."

"One and a half. But I can do it. Tell her to give me a call. Or better yet, just text me the planner's number, and I'll get in contact."

"I'll send it right away. And I just messaged her to let her know you'll call. Thanks!"

"You're welcome."

She texted me the number right after hanging up. I was going to call on my way to work. I'd spent too much time on the list and had to hurry to make it to work on time.

I quickly dressed and headed out of the apartment fifteen minutes later. I still had time to get to the restaurant on foot. I just had to hurry.

It was a cold morning, so I zipped up my jacket, snapping a selfie and sending it to Mom.

Ellie: Thanks for the jacket. It's saving my ass.

After that, I called the event planner. She answered right away.

"Hey, this is Ellie Cavanaugh. I just received a call from Isabelle Gallagher regarding her party."

"Hi, Ellie. Isabelle told me you're calling. Is this about the dessert?"

"Yes. I'm a chef, and I've worked at the pastry station for a while. Now I'm at On Point."

"Wow, I know it. Good for you."

"Thanks. Anyway, Isabelle said the chef at the location has some trouble with the vegan menu. That there are also gluten intolerant guests, and I can help. I just need the number of the chef."

"Oh, sure. Okay. I'll text it to you. Should I send it to this number? Let me write it down, because I'll be texting you from another phone. Or I probably have it on the guest list anyway. What's your full name again?"

"Ellie Cavanaugh."

"Okay. I don't see you on the list. Do you know which table you'll be at?"

"I'm not sure, maybe somewhere with the siblings. With Ian, Dylan, and Josie."

"No, that can't be the one," she murmured. "It's full. Isabelle and Brayden, Josie and Hunter, Mel with Dylan. Ian doesn't have a plus one."

"Oh?"

She laughed. "Yes. When I made the arrangements, he insisted I give them the smallest table. If his sister tried to place single ladies at the table, I should discourage it." She then quickly added, "Oh, I'm sorry, I didn't mean to offend you."

"You didn't," I replied, feeling utterly confused. Worry gnawed at me. Why wasn't I on the guest list?

"You know what, I'll talk to Isabelle about it," she said. "There's probably just a mix-up. And I just texted you the chef's number."

"Thank you." My voice was shaking a bit. When the call disconnected, I took a deep breath and called the chef right away. Despite everything, I wanted Isabelle's party to be perfect. The phone rang a couple of times, and I was about to press cancel when she picked up.

"Hi, I'm Ellie," I said immediately.

"Hi, Ellie. I'm Sheila. You're the consultant chef, right?"

I laughed. "Yes. I suppose you can call me that."

"Okay, great. I managed the entree and main course, but I'm having trouble finding a recipe for the chocolate souffle that has any taste when I use gluten-free flour."

"I have one. I can do the dessert myself if you want, or we can talk it through, and then I can send over instructions."

"Let's do the following. You send me the

recipe, and I'll make it two or three times just to be sure it's perfect. And if I have any trouble, I'll contact you, okay?"

"Sounds great. I'll send you the recipe this evening. I have to write it down since it's only in my head right now. I used it at the restaurant where I was before, but I don't have it stored anywhere."

"I'll be waiting. Thank you so much."

After the conversation ended, I wasn't sure how to distract myself any longer. I couldn't get the planner's words out of my mind. It didn't make sense. Isabelle always spoke as if it was a given that I'd be there. But she never officially invited me. What if Ian didn't want me there?

It was a ridiculous thought, but it bumped into my mind anyway. He said he loved me. But maybe that didn't mean forever for him? My chest tightened.

I loosened the scarf a little bit and almost walked into a pedestrian. That was how lost in my mind I was. I arrived at the restaurant with five minutes to spare until my shift started. I changed into my chef uniform with lightning speed. Even though I had no time left, I called Henry from the personnel room. I felt like I was going crazy.

"Hey, Ellie. How's it going?"

"I'm not sure, honestly."

"What happened? Are you sick? You sound like you have a cold."

I smiled. "No, my nose is a bit runny, but I don't have a cold. Don't worry."

"So, what's wrong?"

"I'm not sure. I, well, you know that Isabelle postponed the wedding but couldn't cancel the venue, so she is still having a party. I spoke to the event planner about something food-related, and she mentioned that Ian is not bringing a plus one."

"That bastard! I'm going to—"

Oh, Jesus. Why did I think that talking to Henry would help? My hot-headed brother wasn't the best person to talk to in a crisis. He lived by the motto *Shoot first and ask questions later.* But he was my brother, and I loved him to bits.

"You're not going to do anything, Henry. I just... I don't know. I needed to talk about this to someone. Am I overreacting? Wait, don't answer that."

"Why not?"

"I'm sure you'll say I'm not. But you always jump the gun, so you're not exactly a role model when it comes to this."

"Thanks for the compliment."

"I'm sorry. I sounded like a jerk."

"No, you're right. I *am* like that."

I heard someone call my name. "Shoot, I have to go. Sorry for dropping this on you. I'm not sure why I did. I love him, Henry. He made me believe that a real relationship was possible, you know?"

"Ellie, I don't know what to say. I'm still happy with no-strings flings, so yeah…."

"I know. Thanks for listening to me. And don't murder Ian, okay?"

He groaned.

"Promise you won't call him."

"Wait a second. There's a huge difference between not murdering and not calling."

"Henry," I said in a warning tone.

"Fine. I won't call him."

"Thanks. Shit, they're calling me again, I've got to get out there. Talk to you later, okay? Bye."

I slipped my phone in one of my back pockets and headed to my station. As usual, the hustle and bustle of the kitchen kept me busy. I didn't have time to think about anything except juggling the salad and dessert orders.

Midway through the shift, Ian texted me. And just like that, my anxiety kicked back in. My heart lodged in my throat.

Ian: Want to meet after you finish?

Biting my lip, I hovered with my thumbs over the screen, typing back before I could talk myself out of it.

Ellie: Sure. What are we doing? I'm in the mood for Dumont's.

Ian: Done! I'll make a reservation!!

It was a good thing I was seeing him tonight. I was going to bring up the party. Talking about difficult things didn't come easy to me. For as long as I remembered, whenever things got tough, I closed up and sort of waited for it to pass. When Dad left and Mom was heartbroken, I always listened because she needed it, but I was the exact opposite. I rarely said anything back. I felt it would only make her sadder and wouldn't help at all.

But I loved Ian. I was head over heels, and I had a feeling I was just going to fumble my way through this conversation, but I was going to try.

I was bone-tired when I finished my shift. In the changing room, I bumped into Nancy, who was spraying her armpits with deodorant. She was around all the time; I had no idea how she did it.

"Hey, Ellie," she said. "Tired, huh?"

"Exhausted." I took out my jeans and sweater but didn't start to change. I was waiting until she left.

"By the way, I have some news for you," she said.

"Oh?"

"Our New Orleans restaurant is also extending you a job offer."

"Wow. Oh, wow." I was too stunned to say anything else. "How come?"

She winked at me. "I told them we want to keep you here. I might have praised you a bit too much, because they want you now."

"I'm flattered."

"Obviously, you can still do the rotation if you want. Their vacancy is at the pastry station too. They sent me your offer this morning. I was so busy that I didn't even get to forward it to you, but I'll do it ASAP."

I nodded, barely believing my luck. Two incredible restaurants were giving me a job offer.

"Thank you!"

"All right, I'm about as refreshed as I can get. I'll leave you to change."

I was still in a daze as I came out of the building, bundled up in my coat. I tightened my scarf around my neck because it was so windy that the cold seeped into my bones instantly. I loved walking, but even for me, it was too chilly, so I Ubered to Dumont's. My nerves hit me full force on the way, and even more so when I stepped inside the restaurant. Ian waved to me from a table in the center of the room. The place was packed.

Despite my nerves, my face instantly morphed into a smile as I walked toward him. He was wearing a Henley shirt again. It was my favorite outfit because it showed off his physique nicely.

"Sorry about the table. I wanted one in a corner, but not even knowing the boss got me that."

"Dumont's is a popular place," I agreed. He kissed the corner of my mouth, lingering with his lips on my cheek. The touch electrified me. The faint smell of his cologne surrounded me like a cloud. Instinctively, I leaned in, and he chuckled.

"I could kiss you, but we might get cited for public indecency."

Clearing my throat, I pulled back. "Hey, don't joke about that. Not when I'm hungry."

He held his hands up in defense. "Wouldn't dream of it. Come on, let's order."

As we sat down, I got my phone out of my pocket, putting it on the table as we each opened a menu. My pulse sped up as I looked at him, wondering if I should bring Isabelle's event up now. My palms were sweaty already. I wasn't sure how to say this without sounding pushy or like I was accusing him of something. I just wanted to clear the air. But perhaps it was best to wait until after we'd eaten.

Chapter Twenty-Three
Ian

We were both so hungry that we cleared our plates in record time. The place was too crowded, and it wasn't relaxing at all. I could barely hear my own thoughts, let alone carry on a conversation with Ellie.

"Want to go?" I asked her over all the noise.

She nodded eagerly. I helped her put her coat on. Something was off with her. All throughout dinner, she tapped her foot against the floor. She didn't just seem tired but nervous. A few times, I had the distinct impression that she wanted to say something but then stopped abruptly. When we walked out on the street, she started fiddling with her thumbs. I planned to find out exactly what was wrong, but I needed to get her to my apartment first. I did my best work when we were alone. The weather had changed for the worse while we were inside; it was colder, and it had started raining too.

"I'm gonna order an Uber." Taking out my phone, I groaned. "No battery."

"I'll order it from mine."

I looked over her shoulder, wondering how

she even used her phone, it was so tiny. Instead of opening the Uber app, she clicked the email icon by mistake. A headline caught my attention.

Subject: *Your New Orleans job offer.*
Text Preview: *Hey Ellie!*
The NO team is delighted that you're interested. I'm forwarding you all the details…

She looked from the phone up to me. My jaw was clenched so tight that my teeth were hurting. I felt as if someone punched me in the chest and then in the face.

Clearing my throat, I stepped in front of her, asking, "You have a job offer in New Orleans?"

"My boss told the crew in New Orleans that she made me an offer. So they made one too. She didn't have time to send it to me until now."

"Wait, so you already knew about it?" Was this why she was so nervous tonight? Did she want to take the job?

"She only told me today, asked if I wanted to see the offer."

Though Ellie didn't seem overly excited about it, I had to know. "What did you tell her?"

"To send it, of course. It's always good to keep the options open."

I jerked my head back. Was I an option to her? She was everything to me. Couldn't she see that? Was I overreacting? I'd been the one who told her that she should choose what was best for her career.

But right in this moment, I realized that I didn't want her to be anywhere else but here, with me. Was I overreacting to an email? Hell, yes. But the thought of losing her made me irrational. She looked at me questioningly, probably wondering why I was so uptight about an email. I had to calm down, but I just couldn't. "Was this what you were so nervous about tonight?"

Her eyes widened. "Umm… no. It was something else."

"Were you going to tell me about this?"

"Obviously." She cleared her throat, shaking her head. "Let's not talk about this now, okay? I've been on my feet the whole day. I want to have a clear head."

"You want to have a clear head… okay," I said slowly. Maybe it wasn't a bad thing though. I sure as hell needed to calm down. But I wanted us to do it together, not apart.

"I'm gonna take a cab to my apartment," I told her, hoping she'd decide to join me so we could talk this through.

She frowned, fiddling with her thumbs on her phone. "Ian, I…" Her voice trailed, and she nodded. "Okay. If you think that's best."

I didn't think this was best at all. I wanted to take her home and keep her there, but as she got in her cab and I got in mine, she'd apparently decided she wanted to be alone tonight. Obviously, tonight wasn't going according to plan. At all.

***

Instead of going home, I went to the office even though it was late. I needed to *do* something to work off this adrenaline. A few hours of coding would help. To my surprise, Dylan was still there.

"What are you doing here?" he asked, following me into my office.

"I want to work on code for a few hours."

"Good. I want to discuss something."

"Not now."

"Come on. I need an honest opinion."

"Not now!" I said in a measured, low voice, sitting in my chair.

My brother frowned. "Who pissed you off?"

I cocked a brow.

"Hey. You show up at the office at this hour, and you're in a bad mood. You're never in a bad mood. Something's off."

"Don't test me, Dylan. Not right now."

"Fine! I'm leaving before you bite my head off."

"Good strategy," I replied just before he left my office. I swear, three seconds later, my sister Isabelle called. I couldn't stop laughing, despite everything. I was sure Dylan put her up to this.

He was taking a page out of my own book. That's what I always did when I couldn't reach my brother: I asked Isabelle to do it. I could just ignore her call, but I didn't want to. Talking to my sister always put things in perspective, so I answered.

"Hey. How are you?" she asked in a chirpy voice.

"Don't pretend like Dylan didn't put you up to this."

"Man, you catch on fast."

"I invented this technique, remember?"

"Well, no, technically, I invented it. You just used it."

"And Dylan ignored it. Until now."

"He says you're in a pissy mood. That's not like you. And I'm going to go out on a limb and guess it's not work related, or Dylan would know the reason. So, spill it. I can't help if I don't know what's going on."

I told her about the crazy conversation at the restaurant. Isabelle was quiet for a few seconds.

"Okay, that's very weird," she said. "Honestly, it doesn't sound like Ellie. I mean, she's helping me with the menu for the party. I don't think that she plans to move and cut all ties with you. She wouldn't offer to help me if that's what she had in mind."

"I think I overreacted to the email."

"That's... possible." My sister was using a gentle tone that she only employed when she tiptoed around me. "I promise I'll find out what's going on, okay?"

"No, I have to talk to her and figure it out myself."

"I can try anyway. That's what I'm here for. Not just to nag and irritate you. Also to help."

"And I appreciate it."

"You do? Because you always give me so much shit."

"I'm about to give you shit now if you keep teasing me. I want to talk to Ellie myself."

"Okay. But I'm here if you need me."

"Thanks, Isabelle."

After hanging up, I drummed my fingers against the table, deciding to wait until tomorrow to call Ellie. I still hadn't calmed down, and I knew I needed to have my shit together before we talked.

I stayed at the office until past midnight, still feeling uneasy when I went to bed. The next morning, I overslept and woke up at ten. Fuck. Ellie had already started work, and lately she was so busy that she put her phone on airplane mode during her shift. I called her once, but it went straight to voicemail.

There was nothing else to do but go to the office. I'd had a productive coding session in the evening, and I wanted to check for bugs before the clients started calling.

I'd slept like shit, tossing and turning, trying to figure out what had Ellie upset. The more I thought about our conversation last night, I remembered that she was nervous *before* the issue with the email came up. Something was bothering my woman, and I needed to know what it was.

At eleven o'clock, my phone buzzed. I broke off the coding session, sure it had to be Ellie. It was Isabelle.

Isabelle: Meet me in the city in the

afternoon? I have something to do on Fifth at four.

Ian: Sure.

I frowned. This seemed out of the blue.

Ian: Why? Did you speak to Ellie?

Isabelle: No, just thought you might need company. Specifically, MY company. And we could talk things out. You know I'm good at that.

Ian: You're right. Sure, it's a date. Thanks, Isabelle.

At four o'clock, I met Isabelle at the address she texted me. She was waiting for me in front of a building with some sort of business at the ground level. The coat she was wearing was so huge that it swallowed her whole. The only things you could see were the baby bump and the red hair spilling around her.

"You look terrible," she exclaimed.

"Thanks." I kissed my sister's temple, because I knew she meant well.

"You really love her, huh? You wouldn't be all out of sorts like this if you didn't."

"Yes, I fucking do. I just need to get to the bottom of what's bugging her. She was acting weird even before we started talking about the email," I responded, aggravation evident in my tone. I glanced around us before asking, "What were you doing here?"

"Gina's moved her office here." She pointed

with her thumb behind her. Gina was her wedding planner.

"Business must be going well if she's moved on Fifth." Rents here were extravagant. The last time I went with Isabelle to a meeting, the office was on the Upper West Side.

"You're not giving me shit for bringing you to another wedding planning event? In my defense, I just thought you might need a distraction."

"I do. And anyway, this is a party now, right? Not a wedding anymore."

Isabelle grinned. "Potatoes, potahtoes."

"Why are you doing the party again? Especially since it's a month later than the original wedding date."

"Because the venue wasn't happy we postponed the wedding, and I still want to do it there next year, and I want to have a good relationship with them. Besides, you know I like parties."

"This is actually an improvement. I thought you were making me suffer through a shopping spree."

"Awww, I wouldn't do that to you. I know you hate it."

We stepped inside the building, and Gina welcomed us in a small area with leather couches.

"Hey, it's great of you to stop by. Everything is coming together," she said as we sat down.

"Even my vegan menu?" Isabelle replied.

"Yes. I got the green light from our chef that she managed the recipe Ellie proposed." As we sat down, she took out a piece of paper. "I couldn't find Ellie on the guest list. I double-checked. She thought she was at your table for some reason." She glanced at me, smirking. "I told her that you don't have a plus one and that you even told me to keep others from matchmaking by adding 'accidental' plus ones." She made air quotes around the word accidental.

"Fuck!" I exclaimed. Isabelle turned to look at me. Gina's eyes widened. The wheels started spinning in my mind. I knew exactly what was going on with Ellie and exactly what I needed to do—and fast.

My sister smiled at the planner. "Gina, would you give us a minute, please? We need to talk about something."

"Sure. I'll go to the foyer and grab a coffee. Do you want one too?"

"No," Isabelle replied. I just shook my head.

"Okay. Just let me know when I should come back."

"Thank you," Isabelle said.

As soon as Gina left, my sister turned to me.

"I told Gina this months ago," I said. I was certain this was what's been bugging my girl.

"You actually told Gina all those things?"

"Which part? That I didn't have a plus one, or that I told you not to pair me with anyone accidentally?"

"Yes. Was any of that wrong?"

"No. It's just not up-to-date anymore." I groaned.

"Ellie doesn't know that. I never officially

invited her. I just assumed you'd do it. And I totally forgot to tell Gina too. Maybe that's why she's on edge."

"Yep." I had no doubt now, and I needed to fix that ASAP.

"So, you agree with me?"

"Uh-huh." This was why she was so nervous last evening.

"Please tell me your plan to fix this consists of more than one-word answers."

"Yes," I said, just to tease my sister. But my mind was spinning ahead about what to do next.

"Why didn't you invite her?" she asked, rising to her feet, pacing the room, stroking her belly.

"Honestly, I forgot. I never think about this stuff, okay? It's not even on my radar."

Isabelle's shoulders dropped. "She probably thought we don't want her there."

"Why would she think that? We've grown close." Close enough that apparently I lost my cool when she got a job offer in New Orleans. "But I'm still pissed about her wanting to keep her options open. I mean, I am all for her doing what it takes for her career. I told her that—that she should do what's best, and we'll figure it out."

My sister winced, running her hand through her hair. "Ian, you're sending mixed messages. First you tell her that she should do what is best for her, and then you get all up in arms about the email."

She sat next to me, narrowing her eyes. She had her counselor face on. "Some might interpret you telling her to do what is best for her as *you* not wanting to make a commitment."

"What the hell?" Why would Ellie think that?

She held her palms up in defense. "I'm not saying Ellie did. Some people could see it as a good thing. I see it as a good thing, as in… you want to figure out how to work things out. But you're usually so… you know. Decisive when you want something, and there's no gray area. You either do something, or you don't. Your overreaction at her getting an email with a job offer is actually more like you than telling her to do what is best for her."

"I was trying not to be a self-centered bastard and tell her I want her here at all costs. How is this backfiring? Before she got the job, I was very close to asking Rob if he could hire Ellie."

To my astonishment, she grinned.

"Baby brother, welcome to the murky waters that are relationships. Hard as hell to navigate, but trust me, they are worth it. The human brain is wired to jump to hasty conclusions when we're stressed."

I still was struggling with Isabelle's train of thought. Maybe because I was a guy, and we didn't overthink things. I pressed my palms over my eyes, shaking my head. "Do you have a scientific answer to everything?"

"Not everything, but lots of things. So, what are you going to do?"

"I'll show her that she belongs with me."

"Excellent. That's exactly what I was hoping to hear. Oh, and the baby agrees. It's kicking me."

I didn't want to lose Ellie. No way, no how. And if that meant me moving to New Orleans to be with her, then so be it. I'd never realized that until that moment, and I had to tell her.

But first, I needed to know that she was absolutely sure of us—the same way I was.

Chapter Twenty-Four
Ian

After I left Gina's, I headed back to the office. All I could think about was Ellie.

"This was one of the most productive project implementations in the history of my company," Brian said. Dylan and I were with one of our biggest clients in the meeting room. My mind wasn't in the game, but it didn't need to be. It was just about wrapping up a project and schmoozing. Even though it wasn't my brother's favorite activity, he instinctively seemed to realize that I wasn't in the right frame of mind for it, so he took the reins.

"We're very happy that the project rolled out the way you wanted it," Dylan said. "If there's anything else we can do, we'll be happy to collaborate on another project."

"I do have something else in mind," Brian said. "And I would like to do it with Gallagher Solutions."

"Do you have a brief?" Dylan asked.

"Not yet, but I'll send it to you as soon as I do. Well, gentlemen, I think this is all. Thank you for taking your time to go through this wrap-up with me." We all stood up and shook hands.

After he left, Dylan sat back in his leather chair in the meeting room, looking at me. "You're totally off your game."

"My mind is somewhere else. Thanks for noticing and stepping up."

"Does this have anything to do with your meeting with Isabelle?" Dylan asked. I nodded, pacing the meeting room. I brought him up to date. I was curious about what he'd have to say. Dylan didn't miss a beat. As soon as I was done, he straightened in his chair. "Okay, now we have all the facts. I think you need some sort of big gesture."

I cocked a brow. "Some sort? And Isabelle thinks you're romantic."

Dylan ignored me. "Would you rather I suggest a meddling brother getting in between?"

"We can skip that part. And I did it by accident anyway."

Dylan laughed. "You accidentally answered my phone?"

Back when he and Mel had a falling out, I'd butted in a bit *too* much. "Okay, no, but you were down. I thought a prank would cheer you up. I'm great at that. Can we get back on track now?"

Dylan relaxed in his chair, keeping his eyes fixed on me and drumming his fingers on the desk. "Be decisive in what you say. Don't leave any room for interpretation. That can backfire quickly. And for the love of God, whatever you do, act now. If you're planning to waste your evening at the office again, I'll personally kick you out."

"I'd like to see you try. But don't worry. I have other things to do."

I'd been working on a plan ever since I was out with Isabelle earlier. It solidified in my brain during the meeting with Brian. Once in a while, Ellie went to that spa she loved on the Upper West Side. I knew exactly what to do. She had an appointment there, but she was in for a surprise.

Two hours later, I was sitting behind the mahogany reception desk, looking straight at the entrance, waiting for Ellie to step inside. It had taken a considerable amount of persuasion to get the staff to cancel all other appointments tonight and leave early, but I could be very persuasive. And I compensated them generously.

I stood completely still when the front door opened and Ellie stepped inside. For a few seconds, she didn't seem to realize that something was different, but then her eyes widened as she looked around the room. There were dozens of flowers everywhere. Her eyes got even bigger when she saw me, and I couldn't resist. I walked around the reception and straight to her. She lit up when I approached. Up close, I could see that she was paler than usual. She lacked that inner joy I loved so much about her. Fuck, no. I was going to bring it all back.

"Ian," she whispered. "How… what is happening?"

"I wanted to see you. I wanted to surprise you."

She narrowed her eyes. "So, you hijacked my appointment?"

"Exactly."

She looked confused.

"Listen, Isabelle and I met with the event planner today. She told me about your conversation with her."

Her shoulders dropped. "Yeah, and you don't owe me an explanation."

"Yes, I fucking do. Listen to me. I told her that months ago, Ellie, before I met you. Of course I want you at all events right next to me."

She looked up at me with a hint of a smile. "You're serious?"

"Yes, of course I am."

"So you just never thought to update her?"

I groaned. "Isabelle asked about this too. Look, this stuff is not really on my radar, okay? That's not something I actively think of. " I cupped her face with both hands, looking into her beautiful blue eyes. "I need to know what you want, Ellie," I said. "Do you want a future with me?" If she said no, I really didn't know what I would do.

"Yes, yes I do. Of course I do."

Relief swept through me. "Do you want to take the job in New Orleans and move there permanently? I'll move with you."

"Oh, Ian. I can't believe you'd do that. But I don't want the job. It's just that, when my boss asked, I didn't want to say no. And anyway, after the call with the planner, I felt a bit lost, honestly. I should have brought it up before, but I'm just not good with conflict. I tried, but I didn't know how to do it without sounding insecure and weird, like now."

She was blushing, and the color was returning to her skin. "Ellie, I *know* you. I know how you are. You'd rather keep things to yourself, I get that. Just like when you were being bullied at school, you never told your mom, afraid she'd worry. You never talked with her about how hard it was for you to hear about her issues with your dad, but you did listen even though it hurt because you wanted to be there for her. You're strong that way—for yourself and others—and you keep everything inside, but you don't have to do that with me. I want to be there for you through everything. I love you."

Her eyes were a bit watery. "Now what?"

"I've been told by my brother to lay my cards on the table." I slid one hand to the back of her head, burrowing my fingers in her thick hair. "I love you, and I want you in my life. When you told me about the job offer here, I wanted nothing more than to tell you to take it and stay with me."

She grinned. "That was kind of what I hoped you would do. Why didn't you?"

"Because I didn't want to be selfish. And then I saw that email, and all I could think about was that I want you here. With me. I know I overreacted. And that I am selfish." I stroked her lips with two fingers, bringing my other hand to her waist.

"That's not selfish, it's possessive, and I like that about you. You're always decisive when you want something, Ian."

***

Ellie

Ian was looking at me with so much warmth that I felt like I was about to burst. "Well, here is me being balls to the wall. I want you, Ellie. In any way I can have you. You mean so damn much to me."

"And you to me," I whispered. He wanted me here. I was over the moon. I couldn't see anything except him, my gorgeous man who wanted me so much. "I love the flowers," I said, glancing around the spa.

"I'm glad you do. I came here determined to first ask you what you wanted before going balls to the wall, and I thought the flowers might sway the odds in my favor."

My face widened in a grin. "Was that Isabelle's idea?"

"No, it was all on my own. And speaking of siblings, I'm surprised Henry isn't here, trying to throw me out a window."

"Oh, I saved you from that. I asked him not to call you, and he listened."

"My, my, someone has softened."

I skimmed my hands down his torso, pressing myself closer. I loved feeling the heat of his body, his muscles beneath my fingers. His delicious smell was home for me, pines and forests and leather. Ian was my home, and I never wanted anything else. I wanted to make this man happy for the rest of my life, just as happy as he was making me.

"I can't believe you did all of this."

"It's just you, Ellie. I'm a different person since I met you."

"So am I," I whispered. "You know, I never believed I could feel about anyone the way I feel about you."

"Tell me more. I like where this is going."

"Before, I never wanted to settle down anywhere. I never felt the need to, but you changed that." Lacing my arms around his neck, I jumped in his arms. He caught me, laughing, and walked with me back toward the reception area. He hoisted me up onto the counter.

"I'm not in the mood for a massage anymore. I want to be alone with you."

"We are alone," he said, wiggling his eyebrows.

"What?"

"You see anyone around here?"

"No, but I thought maybe you'd just cleared out the reception area."

He tilted his head. "Are you kidding? I didn't want to risk anyone ruining our big moment."

"How did you manage to send everyone away?"

"I can be convincing like that."

Oh, this man, I loved him so much. I cupped his face with my palms, loving the way his five o'clock shadow felt against my skin.

I couldn't believe it. He wanted me here. He wanted a future for us. I bit my lip, and this time his groan was more of a growl.

The next second, he leaned in, capturing my mouth in a deep kiss. It electrified every cell in my body until I rose on my toes, placing one hand on the back of his neck and the other on his chest. He was mine. He was all mine.

I kissed him back desperately, needing more, needing to feel close to him. He brought an arm around my waist and placed the other one on my back, as if feeling that I needed more contact. We both laughed when we pulled apart.

He was looking at me intensely again. There was a fierceness in his eyes I'd never seen before. He touched my face with both hands, tipping my head, so I looked right at him.

"I love you, Ellie. You're so damn important to me. You've changed me. I've told you that. It's a privilege to be with you now and in the future. I love everything about you."

"Let's go home," I whispered.

"Hell, yes."

Chapter Twenty-Five
Ian

I didn't need her to ask me twice. I wanted to be completely alone with her too. I needed it. I wanted to explore her the whole night, the whole damn week. The rest of my life.

The Uber ride to my condo was twenty minutes—way too long. I was so damn hungry for her.

The second we were indoors, I pushed her against the wall, kissing her until she hummed against my mouth. Her body was vibrating. I needed to explore every inch of her.

I started by taking off our coats, dropping them in the foyer. Then I lowered myself on my haunches, taking off her sexy ankle boots. Skimming both hands under her dress, I found the waistband of her tights and yanked them down. We both laughed when we heard the sound of fabric ripping.

"I think those are my tights," she said as she stepped out of them. "How am I going to get out of the apartment?"

"You just won't. This is a perfect excuse," I said.

"Oh, I see. So you did this on purpose."

"No, but it worked out the way I wanted." I trailed my fingers up her bare ankles, slowly moving them on the back of her knees and up her thighs. I inched up her sweater dress, following the trail with my mouth on her right thigh until she shivered.

I moved farther up, bunching the dress around her waist and nudging her legs apart. I skimmed my thumb over her panties, between her thighs, until she was soaking wet and gasping.

I looked up at her. I loved seeing her face crumpled with pleasure like this. Her eyes were shut, and she reached back with her hand to the console to steady herself. I wanted to bring her completely on edge so that all her senses would be alert. I wanted to overwhelm her with pleasure and worship her like the goddess she was.

I continued to skim my thumb over that same patch of fabric, only briefly brushing her clit, splaying my hand on her lower belly. I smiled when she took the dress off herself. She was desperate for me. I kissed up her stomach until I reached her breasts and clamped my mouth around one nipple over the fabric. I lavished the other one with attention, too, skimming my thumb over it. I wanted her so sensitive that she could barely breathe from the pleasure I was about to give her.

I smiled against her breasts when she tugged at my shirt and pulled it over my head. We made eye contact for a few seconds before she leaned in to kiss my chest and Adam's apple. She cupped my erection over my jeans, and I groaned.

"Fuck," I exclaimed. The zipper pressing against my erection was almost painful. She pushed my jeans down, and I lost control. I kissed her hard, doing away with her bra and panties. We were both naked before we even stumbled into the living room, and we only made it as far as the kitchen counter.

I took a condom out of a drawer and put it on, liking the hungry look in her eyes when she saw me touching my cock.

“Keeping condoms everywhere, huh?” she teased.

“I like to be prepared.” I turned her around so her ass was facing me, and she looked at me over her shoulder, eyes wide.

"Hands on the counter. Lean forward," I said.

Licking her lips, she lowered herself with her elbows on the counter, but I pressed her back, so her nipples brushed the cold granite. She gasped as a shock wave went through her. Goose bumps broke on her arms, ass, and thighs. I positioned myself at the entrance, first rubbing her clit with my tip until she gasped and then moaned before sliding in all the way.

I needed to possess her. I needed her now. She tilted her head back, moaning my name. I moved in and out, at first a slowly, but then I bent over her, putting one hand on the counter for balance as I increased my pace. I brought my free hand to her pussy, circling her clit. I moved it in large, soft circles, watching her face to see what brought her the most pleasure. Her orgasm formed slowly while I was fighting to stave off mine. I knew she was close when she pinched her eyes closed and balled her hands into fists. If we'd been on a bed, she would have fisted the sheets.

She exploded beautifully. She parted her legs even wider. Her whole body curved while I held her tight, feeling her clench around me.

As she rode out the wave of pleasure, she was soft and pliable in my arms, and I moved us to the couch. We both needed to lie down. Standing up took far too much energy when I wanted to focus it all on her. I lay down on the couch on my back, and she climbed on top of me. She looked down at my erection, sliding down it at her own pace.

"Fuck," I exclaimed. She was so damn tight. She moved in a slow rhythm, driving me crazy. I pushed myself up enough to explore her chest and her breasts and to kiss her. Her tongue desperately searched mine, and I kissed her just the way she liked it: hot, dirty, wet.

I was already on edge because she was so tight, but when I felt her come apart again only a few minutes later, I couldn't hold back anymore. Everything faded when she cried out my name—everything except the shocking pleasure rolling through me. The orgasm took over my entire body. My chest tightened, my muscles clenched, my vision faded.

"Stay like this," I said and held her on top of me.

"We're sweaty, but I like it."

"I'll keep that in mind." I stroked her back, cupping her ass. She seemed lost in thought.

"What are you thinking about?" I asked.

"Can I have all those flowers brought to the apartment?" Her expression was dreamy. I was so proud for putting it there.

"I'll take care of it."

"Thanks! By the way, I'm going to talk to my boss tomorrow and tell her I'll accept the position here."

"Hell, yes. Best thing I've heard." I pressed my mouth against hers, kissing her long and deep. She was *mine.*

"Someone's happy about that," she murmured.

"Yeah. Ellie, are you sure? If you think the rotation is better for your experience, or even moving to New Orleans for a while… we can pull it off."

She frowned. "You hated the idea before."

"Because I thought it meant you'd leave me. I'm on board with anything. As long as you're mine."

"I'm sure. I still want to open my restaurant down the road. And I think I can learn a lot here. But here is the thing. Since meeting you, I realized that building my dream doesn't mean I have to give up on everything else. Thank you for showing me that."

I touched her cheek, kissing her chin. "I spoke to Dylan about the coding platform."

Her eyes lit up. "What did he say?"

"He was excited for me. I'm going to seriously work on it after the rollout for Project Z is over. I can't wait. You're a good influence on me, Ellie. I'm never letting you go."

"I want to be here with you. I'll work out everything else."

"*We* are working out everything else," I reminded her.

Ellie giggled.

"What?"

"I just can't believe you think you're not romantic. Remember when you took care of me when I came home from the hospital? That was super romantic, the way you said to call you because I'm yours."

"You are, Ellie." I brought a hand to her face, cupping her jaw. "All mine."

She giggled, shifting on top of me. I groaned.

"See? That's what I mean. You're romantic and don't even know it. Can you say it a couple more times?"

I rolled her over the next second so I was on top. I buried my mouth in her neck, kissing up to her ear. "Your wish is my command."

Epilogue

Ellie

One Month Later

The day after I officially started my full-time job at On Point, I was over the moon, and I was throwing a party to celebrate. Ian said I could host it at his place, and I loved the idea.

I was in the bedroom where the catering team had brought all the food, laying it on folding tables with chafing dishes and iced trays. There wasn't enough counter space in the kitchen to bring everything at once.

I surveyed the bed, happy with the order. The chef in charge of Isabelle's party, which was taking place the next week, catered the food. Isabelle had advised me not to do the cooking myself because I would be more stressed about cooking than enjoying the party. It turned out she was right. Someone else was in charge of the culinary side, and I was *still* stressing about it.

We had quite a few people coming in. Dylan, Josie, and Isabelle were coming with their family, of course, but I'd also invited the Winchesters. I really liked them. They were a fun group. I straightened up when I heard the doorbell ring. Okay, that was interesting. The guests weren't supposed to arrive for another hour. Were they already here? I left the bedroom quickly and was stunned when I heard voices in the living room. *Oh my God.* My family was here. I had invited them, but except for Henry, no one RSVP'd. Mom said she'd try to make it, and Dad said he didn't think they could leave.

But they were all there in the living room.

"What are you doing here? Why didn't you tell me you were coming?" I asked. My voice wasn't right. It was a bit high-pitched, but hey, I could be forgiven for it, right? I hadn't seen the family together in a long time. Mom had styled her brown hair in a bob since I last FaceTimed with her. It looked good on her, contrasting with her angular cheekbones. Linc, my stepdad, had a big smile on his face. Stephanie, my stepmom, was wearing a yellow dress and looked lovely.

Dad was clapping Ian's shoulder, winking at me.

What was happening? When did Dad meet Ian? I'd thought about introducing Ian to my parents in person whenever I used the voucher Ian had gifted me, but it seemed that it wasn't necessary anymore.

Henry was closest to me, and he hugged me first. I looked at Mom over his shoulder. She was smiling from ear to ear.

"We're surprising you," Mom said.

"Ian did what I never could manage: get

everyone together," Henry said.

"He's a great guy," Mom added.

"I like what I'm hearing. Everyone's singing my praises," Ian exclaimed, looking proud of himself. He hooked an arm around my waist, kissing my cheek from behind.

"Okay, I need details," I said. "When did all this happen?"

"Recently," Ian replied with an air of mystery. I was so immensely happy. I couldn't believe Ian pulled this off. And he thought he wasn't a romantic? I couldn't imagine anything more romantic than this.

"All right. We have some time until everyone else arrives," Ian said, "but we can pop open a bottle of champagne to celebrate Ellie's new job."

"Yes, let's celebrate," I said. My voice still wasn't right. Ian immediately brought a bottle. He poured drinks in seven glasses, and then we all clinked.

"We're so proud of you, Ellie," Mom said. Oh my God, she was a bit teary-eyed. This was so uncharacteristic for her that my stepdad kissed her temple.

Dad spoke next. "You've come a long way, little one. We're proud that you went after your dream. We might not make it there to celebrate every accomplishment, but we're proud of you, and we love you."

Ian was right next to me, putting an arm around my shoulders as if he knew how important this was for me and that I was emotionally in need of his support.

"Ellie, no one is happier than me that you moved to New York. It's not an exaggeration when I say that you've changed my life for the better." He looked at me, and I was startled at the emotion swimming in his eyes. Something clenched in my chest. "I'm so lucky you moved here and wanted to be my girlfriend. And I need luck on my side again today."

Everyone seemed to draw in their breath. What was going on?

He took a step back and lowered himself down on one knee. My breath caught. I brought a hand to my chest. He took a velvet box out of his pocket, holding it out to me. "I'd be the luckiest man if you wanted to be my wife. Here, before everyone, I wanted to ask you—*will you marry me*?"

I clasped my hand there on the velvet box, taking it in my hands for a closer look.

"I think that's a yes," Mom said.

I started to laugh, and so did Ian as he stood up, putting the ring on my finger. It was gorgeous, with a square-cut diamond, and there were also little stones around the edge.

I hugged him tightly, but my throat wasn't working properly, so I couldn't put in words everything I was feeling.

Mom and Linc hugged me first, and then Dad and Stephanie. I could feel everyone's happiness like a blanket around me. Henry hugged both me and Ian at the same time.

Once everyone returned to nursing their drinks, Ian kept an arm around my waist. "My parents will kill me. Isabelle and Josie too," he said.

"Why?" I asked.

"The plan was to wait for everyone to arrive before proposing."

I couldn't help but laugh. "So you couldn't wait, huh?"

"No, I couldn't."

We chatted a bit about everyone's journey, and Ian opened another bottle of champagne. The rest of the guests arrived earlier than we expected, by a full thirty minutes. Mom's eyes were wide when she saw both the Winchester and the Gallagher gang. She was used to me making friends wherever I moved, but she wasn't used to me letting people in my life the way I'd let in Ian and his family and friends.

Skye, Josie, and Ryker brought their kids, too, so the condo was getting super crowded.

Isabelle took one look at my hand and burst out laughing, nudging Josie, who shook her head, smiling from ear to ear.

"We should have come even earlier. I told you he wouldn't be able to wait," she said.

Ryker gave Ian a thumbs-up. "Great job. Can't believe you went from self-proclaimed bachelor to engaged already! It's a record in this group."

Ian groaned. "Ryker. I worked hard to build my reputation with Ellie's parents. Don't ruin it."

Ryker winced. "Sorry, man."

I leaned into him, kissing his jawline. “Awww, don’t worry about that. They adore you.”

Tess took her nephew from Skye’s arms, and with him on her hip, came to us.

When everyone said their congratulations, I could feel Ian's gaze on me. I looked over my shoulder at him, winking. How could I be this happy?

"Okay, everyone, I'm just going to bring in some appetizers for us to snack on. I'll be right back," I said after a while.

To my surprise, Mom joined me, and we both checked on the canapés: cheese platters and slices of baguette with vegetable spreads. It was mostly food that didn’t need to be refrigerated for that short time. Mom was looking around with a smile. She seemed lost in thought.

"Mom, is everything okay?" I asked.

"Yes.”

“Want to tell me how Dad already knew Ian? Well, all of you?”

Mom couldn’t keep secrets. “Yes, it was honestly the most romantic thing I’ve seen. He spoke to Henry first, who told us he’d be coming to visit us.”

Holy shit, he’d gone there in person? How did I not notice? I mean, we weren’t living together yet, so there were a couple of nights a week we didn’t sleep in the same place, but still.

“I was so stunned when Ian asked for your hand in marriage. He went to both our households, your dad's and mine, and spoke with each of us, and also told us how important it is for you to see us all together. I'm sorry that I didn't pay attention before."

"Mom, it's okay."

"No, it's not, but it will be from now on. I'm so glad you found him and that you're happy. It makes me fulfilled. For a while, I thought you weren't going to give your heart to anyone."

I couldn't correct her because I had thought the same, but Ian changed something inside me.

I hugged Mom tightly, immensely happy that she was here. "Okay. Let's go back," I said once I pulled back. "I'll take a tray. Can you take one too?"

"Sure."

We each managed to grab two small trays, carrying them to the kitchen island. The group was standing and chatting around the room. I loved seeing the gang come together. I tiptoed to Ian, who seemed to hear me approach anyway, and turned around, immediately putting both hands on my waist. My skin ignited. How could a simple touch affect me so much?

"Thank you for asking everyone to come here," I whispered.

"Anything to make you happy, Ellie. Always." He kissed the side of my neck, and then he turned around to the group. "Everyone, this was supposed to be the moment when I proposed," Ian said loudly. Taking my hand, he held it up for everyone to see. "If you can't see from my fiancée's finger, I was too eager. Thank you all for coming here to celebrate this milestone with us. Being surrounded by our family makes us both happy, and we're looking forward to celebrating many more milestones together."

"Hey, don't you even think about eloping," Josie warned, "or accidentally getting married before the guests arrive."

"Yes. I can forgive missing the proposal, but not the wedding," Isabelle added.

"We won't do that. I promise," I said. Everyone toasted. I loved the happiness practically rolling off everyone.

"Did you decide where you want to have the wedding?" Tess asked.

I pressed my lips together, glancing at Ian from the corner of my eye. "No, he just proposed, but I think we have time. I mean, we haven't even set a date."

"Tell me when you do, and I'll do everything I can to help."

"Thanks."

"The earlier you decide on a dress, the better. It can take forever to have it all done, especially if the style isn't one that they usually carry," Isabelle said.

I was already panicking a little as everyone else started pitching in with wedding advice.

"Eloping doesn't sound so bad now, does it?" Ian whispered when I reached for a piece of cheese.

"Nah, we can't do that," I whispered. "Look how much everyone's looking forward to it."

I never thought that meeting Ian would lead to finding love and bringing my family together like this. I smiled, glancing around the crowded room. With our family and friends around us, we'd figure out everything, one day at a time.

Second Epilogue

Ian

Six Years Later

"This gang is never going to run out of excuses to celebrate something, are we?" Dylan asked while the two of us were bringing out a huge wooden table.

"True," I replied. "But in Josie's defense, this is a very good reason to celebrate."

We were all in Tarrytown at Isabelle and Brayden's house. Those two made good on their promise to fill it up. They had a four-year-old daughter, Casey, and newborn twin boys, Arthur and Craig. Mom was on cloud nine, fussing around her brood of grandkids. Dylan and Mel also had one son, David. As for Ellie and me, we got married three years ago and were planning to wait a few more years before having kids.

She was looking to finally open her own restaurant, and I was fully supporting her in following her dreams. I looked around the yard for her and found her talking to Rob, Skye's husband—

no doubt it was about the restaurant business. Of course, the entire Winchester family was also here, kids in tow.

Dylan and I set the table against the wall of the house.

"I'm going to grab chairs," he said.

"Good. I need to check with the rest on how the plan is moving along."

Josie wanted to surprise Hunter before his birthday in a week, so she'd decided to hold a surprise party.

We needed a reason, obviously. Isabelle volunteered to celebrate the twins turning three months. Hunter bought it—but in his defense, Isabelle had gathered the group here in Tarrytown for lesser occasions. We often celebrated events here—Brayden's star power was as strong as ever, as was the paparazzi interest in them, and this was the only place where they had one hundred percent privacy.

Leaving my brother to bring out the chairs, I went over to my wife, startling her when I put an arm around her waist, kissing the side of her neck.

"Hey, beautiful," I said.

"You scared me," Ellie replied with a laugh. "But keep telling me I'm beautiful, and I might forgive you."

"Noted."

Rob grinned at us.

"What are you two talking about?" I asked.

Ellie shimmied her ass against me. This

woman! Did she want to drive me crazy in public? "He was giving me tips on how not to lose my mind when I open my own restaurant. Since he's running a gazillion, I thought he might be the right person to ask."

"It just gets to be routine after a while, but it's hard work for the first few years," Rob said. His Dumont restaurants were booming. Since Skye's business was also growing by leaps and bounds, they were busy nonstop. She and Tess had gone from two shops to two dozen around the US.

A loud sound pierced the air, making all three of us look around for the source. Rob groaned.

“And that's Jonas,” he said, referring to his son, who was running around with a soccer ball after his younger cousin, Gabriel, Tess's son. “Sometimes you think he's the sweetest kid, sometimes your jaw hits the floor when you watch him boss around the other kids.”

Skye burst out laughing, walking with Tess toward us.

“He takes after you, bossy from morning to evening,” she said, nudging him with her elbow. "Plus, he *is* the oldest one. That right there gives him bossiness privilege."

They were currently fighting on who should kick the ball first. I decided to play referee.

"Come on, Jonas," I said, letting go of Ellie, "I'm going to be your partner."

“I'm gonna go check on Isabelle,” Ellie said, leaving as Jonas nodded, handing me the ball. He was trying to be a goalkeeper, and this wasn't his shtick. He kept following everyone around with a ball.

"Gabriel, watch Ian and learn. You don't want to let Jonas win too often," Tess encouraged.

Skye groaned. "Tess, don't egg them on when they're so little."

Tess grinned. "But how else will they learn about sibling and cousin rivalry?"

I kicked the ball right back, but instead of doing so lightly so it would land near Jonas, it flew all the way back to the house. Well, that was one skill I still had to perfect.

Tess winced. "Okay, I take that back. Do not pay attention to what Uncle Ian does."

Jonas didn't even hear her. He was already speeding toward the house to recover his ball. Gabriel was right behind him. Skye and Rob took off after them.

Tess glanced around us, then whispered, "Are you in on the plot?"

"Obviously."

"Ah, that's why you're here. This is a teaching Saturday, right?"

"Yes, but family comes first." The coding platform grew by leaps and bounds over the past few years, and I was even teaching a few evening classes at a high school and also on the occasional weekend. I felt it was an important skill for young people to have. Finding Ellie was like finding my center and my balance. I wasn't restless anymore. After finding her, everything fell into place.

"And speak of the devil, here she comes."

Josie was strutting through the yard with a smile so huge that if she didn't turn it down, her husband would know she was up to something.

"She's going to give it all away," Tess said, sounding a bit panicky.

"I know, right?"

Josie smiled even wider when she stopped in front of us.

"Sis, friendly warning, Hunter is going to know you're up to something if you keep smiling like that."

She tried to tone it down. It didn't work. "Did you bring everything?"

"Of course. I'm not an amateur," I said, offended.

"Sorry, I'm just double-checking every detail."

The rest are also ready, and because we don't do anything half-hearted in this group, we had several subgroups in charge of a different organizational tasks: the cake, the fireworks, the presents, and whatnot.

Just then, Hunter joined us and we all fell silent. He looked around at us, cocking a brow. "What's happening?"

"Nothing," Josie said a bit too quickly. Next to me, Tess laughed.

"Fine, keep your secrets," Hunter said, kissing the side of her head. "I'm still too jet-lagged from the trip to Paris to catch up. But I'll sober up soon."

He and Cole were successfully expanding into

Europe more and more every year. They'd started with their shopping center in Rome years ago, but that had grown to twelve European capitals.

Josie kissed Hunter's cheek, smiling coyly. Yeah, she might have just telegraphed that she really was keeping secrets. I exchanged a glance with Tess, who nodded almost imperceptibly. It was our sign that she was going to defuse Hunter's doubts. If anyone could do it, it was Tess.

"I'm going to talk to Ryker," I said. "I wanted to ask his opinion on something related to the platform." I was bullshitting, but Hunter was too busy being suspicious of Josie to pay me any attention.

The truth was that every part of the plot had to come together smoothly for the surprise to work. I found Ryker with his sister-in-law, Laney.

"Listen, we have a problem," I said. "Hunter is already suspecting something."

Ryker grinned. "Well, of course he is. He's smart, and his birthday is coming up. I'd be more concerned if he wasn't picking up on these sketchy vibes we're all giving off."

"Okay, everyone, gather round," Tess said loudly a few seconds later.

Laney frowned. "But according to the plan, this was supposed to happen in half an hour."

"Yeah, I think Tess decided that if we wait, the risk of Hunter finding out was too high."

Everyone started slowly walking toward them. Isabelle and Brayden came out of the house, with our parents right behind them, carrying the twins.

Ellie was walking a few steps back, holding hands with Casey. I made a beeline for them.

"Hey, gorgeous," I said.

Ellie flashed me a huge smile. "You're full of compliments today."

"What are you talking about? I'm always complimenting you."

"Mmm, true. Maybe I'm more susceptible today."

"Ellie, can you help me make my dress more like a princess?"

"Sure thing, honey." Lowering herself on her haunches, she kissed Casey's forehead, ruffling the pink dress the girl was wearing. Ellie would make a great mother one day, and I couldn't wait. I wanted to explore everything life had to offer with her by my side. Casey took off once she was happy with her dress. Ellie straightened up, pointing to my eyes.

"What's with that look? I want to know what you're thinking."

I curled an arm around her waist, pulling her closer. "You will. Later. When we're alone."

She grinned. "I can't wait. I can't believe everyone's so involved in this. I'm so happy I was too."

"You're part of the family, Ellie. Part of me."

She sighed, kissing my chin. "You always know just what to say to make me swoon."

"I try my best."

We all looked in Hunter's direction when we

heard him laughing.

"You really thought that I wouldn't know you're throwing me a birthday party?" Hunter asked.

Josie pouted. "I really wanted it to be a surprise."

"Well, the cat is definitely out of the bag," Ellie said.

Hunter looked at all of us, then pulled his wife to him and kissed her cheek, murmuring something in her ear.

Pulling back, he kissed her hand. "Thank you to my lovely wife for this surprise. I also have one for her. I was planning to give it to her later, because our ten-year anniversary is coming soon, but since she surprised me, there is no better moment than now." He took his phone out, holding it out for Josie, who grinned and hugged him tightly.

"He got us tickets to the Maldives," she said to no one in particular.

"That was where they went for their honeymoon," I explained to Ellie.

"Oh, that's so romantic. Look how adoringly he looks at her after ten years."

"Hey, we're going strong with six, and I'm still looking like that at you.

"It's not a competition," she said with a soft chuckle, turning around.

"I still want to win it. I'll prove it to you later," I whispered in her ear.

"Challenge accepted."

I opened my mouth but closed it again when I

noticed Mom coming straight toward us. I'd have plenty of time for dirty talk later. The group geared into motion. Cole would start the fireworks soon.

"Everything is a competition to him," Mom said playfully. I congratulated myself for keeping my mouth shut.

"He comes out winning most of the time too. He *was* the last bachelor of the group, after all," Ellie said.

Mom looked knowingly between us. "Only because you didn't move to New York earlier."

"I agree," I replied easily.

"Love is different for everyone," Mom added. "Some are friends since childhood, but it takes a while for them to figure out they are soulmates, like Josie and Hunter. Some only find each other later in life."

Ellie grinned. "And Ian and I are somewhere in the middle, right?"

Mom started laughing. "Something like that. It doesn't matter how it starts out. Only that it's true, and deep. Life is all about taking things in stride: the joy and the sorrows and finding the little things to enjoy every day. Because no matter how difficult things are, I promise you that you can find joy even in trying times. And I am beyond grateful that all my children are have fulfilling lives."

She seemed to want to add something, but Cole made a big show of calling everyone's attention to the fireworks. They were set up at the edge of the property, along the Hudson River.

"Come on. I don't want to miss the fireworks," Mom said.

"Neither do I," Ellie replied. As we went toward the river, she whispered in my ear, "I love your mom's advice."

"And we're going to follow it to a T. That's a promise, Ellie."

As we sat down on the blanket I'd set out earlier, I thought about my life and how I finally found Ellie. Before, life was fun but lacking… I mean I enjoyed every day, but now I *savored* every day. And it would be my honor to spend my life next to Ellie, making sure she got everything she wanted.

Because she was mine.

Other Books by Layla Hagen

Other books by Layla Hagen

The **Very Irresistible Bachelors** series is complete

- **You're The One**
- **Just One Kiss**
- **One Perfect Touch**
- **One Beautiful Promise**
- **My One and Only**

The Bennett series is also complete. They are a fun family, the romances are HOT and SWOONWORTHY. The series is complete, and each book can be read as a standalone.

- Your Irresistible Love
- Your Captivating Love
- Your Forever Love
- Your Inescapable Love
- Your Tempting Love
- Your Alluring Love
- Your Fierce Love
- Your One True Love
- Your Endless Love

The Connor family is also complete.

Book 1: ANYTHING FOR YOU
Book 2: WILD WITH YOU
Book 3: MEANT FOR YOU
Book 4: ONLY WITH YOU

Book 5: FIGHTING FOR YOU
Book 6: ALWAYS WITH YOU

***

Standalone USA TODAY BESTSELLER
Withering Hope

Aimee's wedding is supposed to turn out perfect. Her dress, her fiancé and the location—the idyllic holiday ranch in Brazil—are perfect.

But all Aimee's plans come crashing down when the private jet that's taking her from the U.S. to the ranch—where her fiancé awaits her—defects mid-flight and the pilot is forced to perform an emergency landing in the heart of the Amazon rainforest.

With no way to reach civilization, being rescued is Aimee and Tristan's—the pilot—only hope. A slim one that slowly withers away, desperation taking its place. Because death wanders in the jungle under many forms: starvation, diseases. Beasts.

As Aimee and Tristan fight to find ways to survive, they grow closer. Together they discover that facing old, inner agonies carved by painful pasts takes just as much courage, if not even more, than facing the rainforest.

Despite her devotion to her fiancé, Aimee can't hide her feelings for Tristan—the man for whom she's slowly becoming everything. You can hide many things in the rainforest. But not lies. Or love.

Withering Hope is the story of a man who desperately needs forgiveness and the woman who brings him hope. It is a story in which hope births wings and blooms into a love that is as beautiful and intense as it is forbidden.

AVAILABLE ON ALL RETAILERS.

Published by Layla Hagen

Published: Layla Hagen 2021

Made in the USA
Columbia, SC
04 November 2023